I0551541

THE DAYDREAMER DETECTIVE BRAVES THE WINTER

MISO COZY MYSTERIES
BOOK 2

STEPH GENNARO

ONIGIRI PRESS

THE DAYDREAMER DETECTIVE BRAVES THE WINTER

This book is dedicated to rice. I cannot go a week without rice. It is my lifeblood.

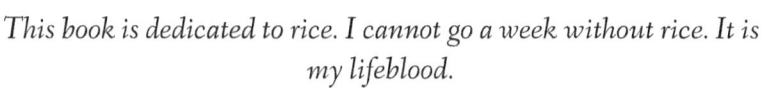

FOREWORD

In Japanese, the most common way of showing respect to another person's social standing is with the use of honorific suffixes that are appended on the end of either first or last names. The most common, -san, means either Mr., Ms., or Mrs.

In earlier versions of this book, and in the whole series, I did use these honorific suffixes. But for 2019 and onward, I have switched to the English way in order to make this series more accessible to English speakers. I hope you enjoy this version!

The town in this novel, Chikata, is completely fictional, though the area I put it in is not. Saitama prefecture is located to the west of Tokyo, and many of the eastern areas are considered to be suburbs of the city. Chikata is located farther out west, nearer to the prefectures of Nagano and Gunma.

CHAPTER
ONE

I wished I could've erased the last two months and lived in that moment forever. Izakaya Jūshi exploded with laughter as a big party behind us ordered another round of drinks and settled into a story about ice fishing. I had no idea ice fishing was so funny, but apparently it was a laugh. December had moved into full swing, and with the temperatures falling below freezing into the coming week, the local lake would be crawling with fishers.

"Do you fish, Mei?" Etsuko lifted her voice from across the table while the men behind us yammered away. Yasahiro, my new boyfriend seated next to me, squeezed my hand under the table.

I sipped my beer. "No. I like to eat fish, but I don't like to catch them. It's not my thing."

"Hisashi and I love to fish during the summer. Sometimes he takes off an extra weekend a month to come with me."

"Sometimes," Hisashi said, waggling his head back and forth. "I'm hoping next year that won't be an issue anymore."

Etsuko turned to beam at Hisashi, her face wide with a broad smile. She swiped her bangs to the side and leaned in to rest her chin on Hisashi's shoulder. "His job has been talking about moving him to this district in the spring. It's a great opportunity. We're planning to buy a house together."

"Really? That's fantastic news," Yasahiro said, lifting his glass so we can toast to Hisashi.

"Yeah. There are a lot of new roads and unmapped areas around here. We have a lot of work to do on bolstering the satellite mapping system."

Hisashi worked for a popular GPS mapping company. Because of Japan's erratic house numbering system, extensive train system, and roadway infrastructure, the mapping companies were always hard at work updating to make everything easier for their subscribers. He worked in the Chiba office, to the east of Tokyo, but had been hoping to move for the last couple of years. When he came to visit Etsuko the first weekend of every month, it took him almost three hours to travel to Chikata. But he came as regular as clockwork because he loved her.

"I'm so happy about this. It's about time. Maybe we can finally get married," Etsuko said, and Hisashi smiled at her before kissing her forehead. I got the feeling this was something they'd both wanted for a long time because neither of them made a fuss about her mentioning marriage.

Etsuko had lived in Chikata all her life. She and Hisashi were high school sweethearts, dated through college, and had been apart for the last three years. Etsuko worked at Izakaya Jūshi Sunday through Thursday with her family but thought about moving to Chiba with him. Her family, though, wanted her here. So the two came up with this arrangement. They talked on the phone every night, he came to visit her the first weekend every month, and she traveled to him the third weekend. The routine worked for them.

I, on the other hand, could only spend a few days without seeing Yasahiro before I got the itch to see him so badly I couldn't sit still. I loved being close to him, talking to him, confiding in him, even though our physical relationship hadn't progressed any further than hand holding and cheek kissing since I was in the hospital. Yasahiro was careful with me, taking baby steps knowing that I felt betrayed and vulnerable when my former boyfriend, Tama, tried to kill me. And these were the only kind of dates we'd had since then, too — double or group dates. We only had alone time at his restaurant, Sawayaka, between lunch and dinner shifts. It wasn't very intimate, but I took what I could get. Yasahiro was busy with work, and I was unemployed, so I did my best to bend to his schedule.

"I'm super happy for the two of you." I raised my glass to Etsuko and Hisashi, and Yasahiro rested his hand on my knee.

"*I'm happy* for you and Yasahiro. I'm always glad to see the two of you when you come in here." Etsuko winked at me, and I stopped a blush by drinking more beer. "It's too bad Hisashi is only here once a month. I wish we could hang out together more."

"I'm sorry I wasn't around the last time you were in town, Hisashi."

He waved me off. "Don't worry about it. Etsuko told me you were in the hospital. I'm glad you're better."

"Me too."

Etsuko reached into her bag and pulled out a phone that lit up and rang with an incoming call. She held her finger up in the air as she glanced at the screen. "Just a moment. I'm going to take this outside." She jumped up from the table and headed out the front door, pressing the pink, owl-embossed phone to her ear. A little owl charm dangled from the case as she walked away. I returned my focus to the table, but Yasahiro and Hisashi were now talking about baseball, one subject I couldn't hack. Baseball bored the heck out of me. I glanced down at my beer, but my attention was drawn to Etsuko's phone sitting on the table. Huh?

Movement outside caught my eye so I stared at Etsuko talking on her phone. She must've had two phones? Her face turned from happy into a frown, her eyebrows pulled together. And although it was only eight degrees outside, she wasn't clutching her arms around herself to keep warm. Making chopping motions with her hand and raising her voice to whomever was on the other side of the conversation, she paced back and forth. I strained my hearing, hoping to catch a word or two, but the men next to us were too loud to hear anything. Etsuko finished off her conversation but didn't re-enter the izakaya right away. She stayed on her phone for a while, typing out something, her fingers and thumbs flying across the touchscreen.

When she turned towards the door, I returned my attention to the table. I didn't want her to think I was spying on her.

She sat down and sighed, sipping on her beer before rubbing her hands together to warm them.

"Everything okay?" I whispered, not wanting to draw attention to her if she didn't want to mention it. The guys were too involved in their baseball conversation to notice, though.

She returned her smile to her face, less bright than it used to be. "Fine. Everything's fine. Are they talking about baseball again?" She rolled her eyes. "Hey, did you watch this week's episode of *I Love Tokyo Legend?* It was so good!"

Etsuko and I had a fondness for detective shows on Asahi TV and this was our new favorite.

The door to the izakaya swung open before I could answer her and in came Kumi and Goro. Kumi and Etsuko had known each other since high school, so they were all a big group of friends that I'd only recently become a member of since I'd moved back home. I waved them over and Kumi sat down next to me and Goro next to Etsuko.

"We were just about to talk about *I Love Tokyo Legend*," Etsuko squealed to Kumi.

Goro rolled his eyes. "Switch places with me Etsuko, so I don't have to talk about these shows." Goro, the police officer, couldn't stand detective shows. He watched them and all he could do was pick out the errors and exclaim, "That's not how it's done!" Kumi had banned him from watching.

"Fine, but don't get Hisashi riled up about the Lions. You know he's a diehard Swallows fan, and *I'm the one* that has to hear about it forever if you continue to bash his team."

"I cannot make any promises," Goro said, switching seats.

I smiled at my new group of friends, placing my hand on Yasahiro's knee under the table and squeezing. He smiled at me before I got sucked into gossiping about TV. I may not have had much in life, but at least I had some girlfriends to gossip with.

Etsuko took another look at her phone as the screen lit up with a message. She frowned before turning it off and dropping it into her purse.

"Let's order another round of drinks first." She raised her hand to catch her brother's eye, and then we descended into a serious discussion of ghosts and local legends and whether we believed them or not.

I totally believed, but that's just the kind of person I was.

CHAPTER
TWO

I f it were up to me, I'd never leave bed during the winter. The house was ice cold when I emerged from my cocoon of blankets and padded out into the main room to switch on the space heater and sit under the kotatsu. I could see my breath fog in the frigid air as I approached the space heater.

December in Japan was not supposed to be this cold.

"Mei, don't turn on the heater!" Mom called from the kitchen, and I groaned in response. I hoped she'd be gone so I could bask in some warmth.

I bypassed the living room and joined Mom in the moderately warmer kitchen. She was making rice and sweet omelets, basically the only food we had left for the next week or so.

"Here," Mom said, handing me a hot cup of coffee. I sipped on the bitter liquid and cringed.

"Are we really out of sugar?" I coughed a few times and slurped some more, hoping I would get used to no milk and no sugar.

"Yes, and I don't get paid for my cooking classes until next week." Mom, dressed from head to toe in hand knit items, looked toasty warm. I should've learned to knit. We had plenty of yarn and not enough sweaters. "I'm also taking on a few shifts at the elementary school and helping set up the deli kitchen at Midori Sankaku. I'm hoping we'll be more solvent by January." She flipped the egg in her rectangular pan, turned the heat off, and set the pan down to cool.

"I wish I could find work that easily." Since getting fired from my job in Tokyo at the beginning of October, I hadn't been able to find a job yet. But I had been applying for part time contract work and sent out several resumes. So far, though, zilch.

Thankfully, my brand-new boyfriend owned his own restaurant, or I'd starve. Mom got meals at her own jobs, but our kitchen at home was pretty bare. We had eaten the stores of leftover sweet potatoes, the ones that didn't burn in the barn fire in November, and we were down to rice and canned goods until the new year.

"Don't worry, Mei. We'll make it through. This is the worst month, but between the free meals and the hot baths at Kutsuro Matsu, we should be fine." Thank goodness we had friends that also owned a bathhouse and I could stay there all day if I wanted. "But..."

Mom bit her lip and turned from me to spoon out rice and add an egg on top.

"But, what?" I steeled myself for the worse and shivered. As soon as I ate breakfast, I was going back to my room to fetch my comforter.

"We need to cut back on expenses. So, no more space heater, mobile phone, or internet."

I nearly dropped my coffee cup.

"Are you serious? It's the middle of winter! And I'm trying to get a job. If they can't reach me via phone or email, then I might as well not exist at all." I set my cup down on the island because my hands shook too much.

I knew we didn't have much in the way of money, but I didn't think it was this bad. Mom had spent a lot of money on hospital bills then the savings were depleted by the end of November. The rest of her money was tied up in investments. I couldn't go without my phone. Sure. Plenty of people didn't use a mobile phone or internet but not when they were actively looking for a new job.

Mom took my hands in hers. "You'll look for a job in the spring, or you can help me here. I hope we'll receive the insurance money for the barn by February, and it should more than cover a new barn, a tractor, and everything else we lost. I wish we could get the money right now, but they have to do an investigation because of the arson, and everything is tied up in the courts now because of Tama."

I take a deep, freezing breath and try to steady my hands enough to pick up my coffee. Damned Tama. *"Your mother loved you so much, always bragging about you to everyone. On and on and on about your talent and how successful you'd be. It made me sick."* I remembered him standing over me with the gas can, and I died a little more inside.

"In the meantime, Yasahiro has free WiFi at Sawayaka, Kumi and Chiyo have it at the bathhouse, and you can go to Akiko's too if you need internet access." Mom grimaced as she mentioned Akiko, and I didn't blame her. I hadn't spoken to Akiko in weeks.

Mom took our bowls of food and headed to the kotatsu in the living area. "We can use the kotatsu while I'm home," she called over her shoulder.

"Be right there." I held my hot cup of coffee between both hands and stared out the window to where the barn once stood.

At the end of October, my life nearly came to an end when my ex-boyfriend, and brother to my best friend, Akiko, burned down the barn with Akiko and me in it. We were lucky to get out alive but everything in the barn was destroyed, including my very limited supply of paints and canvases. I had just gotten back into painting after giving it up for so many years. Now everything was gone. All the sweet potatoes, squash, cabbage, root vegetables, and seeds we stored in the barn that we were supposed to sell or live on, gone. The tractor Mom used every year to prepare the fields for planting was a desiccated and burnt-out hunk of metal sitting in a pile of charred timber.

I squinted my eyes at the corpse of a barn and tried to remember what life had been like two months ago. I was newly unemployed and poor. I couldn't pay my bills, and I had been evicted from my Tokyo apartment. I was living at home with Mom, became a farm girl again, and learned to live on traditional Japanese food, which I did with the help of my new boyfriend, Yasahiro, and his "slow food haute cuisine" restaurant, Sawayaka. My relationship with him was so new that I had only kissed him once before he had to save me from being murdered and then sit by me in the hospital for weeks. We were very good at holding hands so far, and that was about it.

How was I going to tell him Mom and I were too poor to pay my phone bill? Every time something like this happened, I wanted to lie and say nothing was wrong. I didn't want to call attention to how poor we were. But it wasn't even our fault this time around. Instead, our destitution was Tama's fault. He was the one who killed his own father and tried to kill me and his own sister by burning down our only source of income. I wished everyone had listened to me when I suspected he killed his father. Maybe I wouldn't have been stuck in this mess.

I pressed my face to the glass of the door and looked around. Every day I wondered if his yakuza mob pals were going to come back and finish the job. Would they burn down the house? Would they kill me, Mom, Akiko? Or would they just leave us alone because they only blamed Tama for owing them money? He had racked up enough debt with them to kill his own father in an effort to inherit the land, sell it, and steal away with Haruka. Only, I got in the way and stoked his jealousy into a murderous rage. At least Haruka was safe, even if I never liked her much. She was so embarrassed by everything that happened, she flew straight out for California the very next week to live with an aunt and find work in the U.S. I couldn't blame her. Her parents were trying to sell their hair salon. They wanted to retire to Okinawa and be done with the whole mess.

I took another sip of coffee, vowed to ask Yasahiro for sugar packets, and joined Mom in the living room. Slipping my legs under the kotatsu, I sighed in relief. Heat. Finally.

"So tell me more about the deli job at Midori Sankaku," I said, picking up my bowl of egg and rice. Midori Sankaku was the new grocery store in town, and they had bought up abandoned land across the street so they could build a giant greenhouse to supply their stores here and in Tokyo.

"They need an interim supervisor while their current supervisor is on maternity leave. She lives in Aichi prefecture, and they're going to move her here in the spring, which is perfect because I hope to be planting the fields in spring. The deli job will be hard, though." She stopped talking to eat and then massage her fingers. "I'll be in charge of thirty people, and we'll make stewed dishes, sushi, pasta, and several other things to sell in the store. I'll have to leave the house Monday, Wednesday, Friday, and Saturday mornings at three in the morning."

"Mom, that's so early!"

"I know, Mei, but it pays well, and I'll be home every day by 11:00. I can take a nap and then be ready to do work again in the afternoon. Tuesday and Thursday mornings, I don't have to be at the school until seven. In a few weeks, we should be fine again."

I stabbed at the rice in my bowl, even though I knew it was rude to do so. "I wish I had more marketable skills. Why didn't I get your gene for cooking?"

Mom hummed as she set down her bowl and picked up her teacup. "I think, if you hadn't fallen into that fire as a kid, you would have been braver about cooking. But you saw me flambé cheese once and nearly passed out. And then there was the time you set fire to the wooden spoon..." Mom shook her head, and I rearranged myself in my skin, remembering being burned the first time when I was eight and then a month ago in the barn fire. I acquired a new scar on my arm, new burn marks on my back to go with the old ones, and I was told I can't run again until spring due to the smoke I inhaled.

"Anyway, I've had an idea, and I want you to hear me out on it." She cleared her throat, and I shivered in the cold. "I tried to get you a job at Midori Sankaku, but all the positions had been filled months ago. I'm sorry. It was a lucky break the deli manager got pregnant and had to take leave otherwise she would have moved here during the summer. So, I want you to go to Akiko and ask her to help you."

Mom practically growled out Akiko's name, and I couldn't blame her. Ever since Akiko had confessed that she knew Tama was trying to kill their father, and she did nothing about it, I'd avoided her. Mom avoided her. I told Akiko I forgave her while the barn burned around us, but after she got home from the hospital, I kept our communication to a minimum. In my head, I still called her my best friend, but with Kumi in my texts twenty-four hours a day and gossiping with me every time I came to the bathhouse, she was edging Akiko out.

Besides, I still wanted Akiko to be my best friend. I just needed to put some distance between us until everything healed. That and if the town ever found out Tama burned our barn down, she'd be ruined. It was best if I stayed away. The police kept the circumstances of Tama's arrest quiet, and I wanted to honor that.

"What could Akiko possibly help me with? I'm not a nurse."

"Maybe she knows of some work you can pick up? She has an eye on the community that we don't," Mom said with a definitive head nod, then lowered her voice, "and she's damned lucky to have that after all that happened."

I picked up my bowl and finished off breakfast. Going to Akiko was the very last thing I wanted to do. Her brother tried to kill me. I nearly died too because of her actions. But she returned to work with no issues because, in the end, she was a victim just like me. Only Mom and I knew the truth. We never told the police about Akiko's culpability. If anything, Akiko owed me, but it wasn't a debt I was likely to collect on. That was just not the kind of person I was.

I was broke, hungry, and unemployed. Someone came out of this deal in great shape, and it wasn't me. I'd be even worse off if I had to go begging to Akiko to get work because that would be the end of the small amount of pride I had left.

"Maybe," I conceded, but I didn't say anything more. I wanted to save that for the last resort.

"And another thing." She reached over and covered my hand with hers. "Please don't bring Yasahiro here. We can't let him know how bad things are."

"Really?" I deflated in disappointment. "I was hoping he'd help us out if I told him. I trust him, Mom. I don't think he'd gossip about us to anyone." There was a time when I wasn't sure if I could trust him, but now I felt much closer to him and able to open up about things.

"No." Mom was adamant. "Absolutely not. You can tell him our budget is low for food, but that's it."

"That's it? I'm not going to be able to cover up not having phone service."

"Try, Mei." Mom's voice edged on begging, and guilt blanketed me from head to toe. She didn't want to show how desperate we were. I understood, but I was weak and needed things like heat and food. I frowned and covered it up by sipping on my coffee. "Today's my last day off until next Sunday, and it's going to be cold tonight. I was thinking we should heat up the water bottles every night and start sleeping together. It'll keep us warm until this cold snap has passed."

I closed my eyes and held in a sigh. I hadn't slept with my mom since I was a kid. But I also hadn't slept without heat since then either. We'd had a few rough winters and slept together as a family, Mom, my brother, Hirata, and me, all curled up against the frost. This was not how I wanted to live.

"Of course. I'll bring my pillow and blanket to your room."

"Thank you, sweetheart." She patted my hand. "I'm glad you're home."

But I had to wonder if she really was. If I hadn't lost my job and come home, Tama would never have targeted me, burned down the barn, and led us into destitution.

If anything, my being home was a curse.

———

I walked into town and caught the bus to Kutsuro Matsu, Chiyo's bathhouse. I didn't take the bus often, but with Mom using her car to run errands and go to work, this meant I was on my own. Plus, I knew she was trying to save on gas, and it wasn't like I had any money to fill up the tank. Gas was a big expense, so I couldn't drop her off and take the car on my own. I had 2,000 yen on a PASMO card I could use for transportation which I bought before I lost my job and found a month ago when I cleaned my room. I'd almost bought sweets from the convenience store with it. Almost. I was glad I saved it for the bus, though, because the daytime temperature was a balmy two degrees, and I wasn't going to walk to the bathhouse in this weather.

Kumi, Chiyo's daughter-in-law, married to her son, Goro, my local policeman connection, cheered when I walk in the door. She was always so cheerful and eager to hear from me. This was why she'd become my best friend.

"Mei! Oh good. I was hoping you'd come. That was a great night last night, wasn't it? I love that we can all hang out together now. How are you?"

"I'm freezing," I said, and my teeth chattered to illustrate the point. "I haven't been warm since seven. It took all my willpower to get out of bed."

Kumi took my coat and hung it up in the office with hers. "Did you get my text this morning?"

I pulled my phone from my purse and swiped it on. Nothing. No bars. "No. Mom canceled our phones and internet." I sighed and switched to WiFi to find the bathhouse's internal network. It was protected, of course. Not many people at the bathhouse needed internet access. "Can I have access to your WiFi, please?" I steepled my hands in front of my face. "I promise not to stay on too long."

"Of course. And stay on as long as you like. Why did your mom cancel the phones and internet? That sounds like suicide to me." She handed me a slip of paper with a password on it. I typed it in and logged onto the network.

"It's social suicide for sure. I'm glad we switched to texting with Line." Kumi's last message popped up, *"Are you coming today? Mom wants to talk about the new painting."* Another message popped up from Yasahiro, *"I hope to see you at lunch today."* He included a stamp of a puppy squeezing a heart. He'd admitted that he hated using the stamps in conversation, so seeing one so sappy attached to a message made me laugh. He was obviously doing it to make me smile.

I sighed as I slipped my phone back into my bag. "Mom had to cancel the phone and internet because we're broke. I also have to cut back on the heat and eating." I wasn't sure how much less eating I could do, but I'd have to try. Like a car coming to a screeching halt, my brain caught up with my mouth, and I realized I'd just blabbed to Kumi about our situation, even though Mom wanted to keep it quiet. My face paled, all the blood draining from it.

Kumi gasped, placing her hand over her mouth, and I panicked, my heart beating at a swift pace.

"Don't tell anyone," I whispered, waving my hands at her. "I swear, if Mom finds out I told you, she'll be so upset. You know her reputation is at stake."

Kumi's eyes darted to the office door. I turned slowly, dreading whom I'd find there.

"What is this?" Chiyo asked, folding her arms across her chest.

"Nothing." I grabbed my bag. "I'm going to get cleaned up." I tried to brush past both women and make it into the women's room without another word.

"Stop, Mei." Chiyo never raised her voice, but she didn't have to. I halted and kept the tears in my head where they belonged. If I started crying, my blood sugar would drop, and I wouldn't last to lunchtime with Yasahiro. And I had to, *had to,* put on a brave face for him. "Is everything okay with you and your mother?"

"Everything's fine." I glared pointedly at Kumi, and she pressed her lips together. "Mom has a new job, and we're waiting on the insurance money for the barn. Things will be perfect in a few weeks."

More like months, but who was counting?

Chiyo came forward and placed her warm hands on my freezing arms. She was a small woman, short and compact, with glistening black hair and a warm smile. You would never guess she was in her fifties. She barely looked a day over forty.

"How are you handling things since the fire?"

I blinked, momentarily confused. I guessed she didn't hear what I said about us being broke and needing to cut back.

"Oh, *that.*" I huffed a short breath. "That I'm fine with. I still have nightmares about dying in that fire, or Tama coming back to kill me, but that I'm okay with."

"Are you sure?" Her earnest behavior softened me.

"Yes, I'm sure," I said softly, patting her hand to reassure her.

"I wanted to talk about the painting for the men's side of the bathhouse. We had talked about you painting a pine forest?"

My neck slicked with sweat. I flashed back to being in the

barn, tied to the loft's pole, and listening to Tama destroy my paintings and supplies in the space above me. I'd analyzed that moment a million times since. I knew he hated me and my paintings, so why had he destroyed them *before* he set fire to the place? I had one kernel of truth, that maybe he had actually believed I was a good painter and was jealous. But I couldn't believe that. Everyone said my painting style was amateurish and horrible.

"Chiyo, I would love to paint for you. I really would. But everything was destroyed when the barn went up in flames. You know that. I lost thousands of yen worth of art supplies. I would need to buy canvases, new paints, a palette, an easel, brushes..." I waved my hands in the air. "I just don't have the cash to start up again."

She and Kumi exchanged a nod.

"Well, Kumi, Goro, and I want to help you guys out. We've been pooling our money—"

"No," I said, stepping away from her. "I can't take money from you guys. You're already so generous letting us come here for free, and I know you've been treating Mom to dinner."

She closed the distance I put between us. "It would be a loan until you get the money from the insurance company. It would be enough to start painting again."

It was so tempting. A part of me died when Tama destroyed my studio. I didn't realize how excited I was to start painting after having been away from my brushes for so long. And between the prodding of Chiyo and Yasahiro, I had been looking forward to reviving this part of my life.

But it all died in a blaze of condemnation.

A soft mist of depression fell on me. "Where would I even paint? We have no room for it in the house, and it's too cold in there to paint with acrylics. I'd have to switch to oils."

Chiyo narrowed her eyes at me. "What do you mean it's too cold? You can just use space heaters. That's what you did in the barn."

I remembered Tama sidling around the space heater in the loft the day he came to threaten me. He had been planning to kill me days before he actually attempted it. Premeditated. My body chilled a few degrees more.

I looked to Kumi and pleaded for her intervention.

"Mom," she said, and it always surprised me that she called Chiyo "Mom," but I guessed that was what happened when you married. "Let's let Mei relax, okay?" She gestured to me. "There are only two other people in the bath right now. You should be fine in there."

She was referring to my burn scars, which she understood I liked to keep to myself, if possible.

I shrugged my shoulders at Chiyo. "I'll think about it." I bowed to her to cover up my shame. "Thank you for offering."

By putting Chiyo behind me and a wall between us, I hoped to immediately move on from the stress of that conversation. With every moment I spoke, I was dangerously close to revealing the circumstances at home and how rattled I still was from the barn fire. I took a deep breath and crushed myself into the corner of the locker area. *One foot in front of the other, Mei.*

It was hard to bathe myself with other people around. I wanted to hide the scars on my back, and the new one on my shoulder, but that meant showing off my breasts instead, so I bathed on the other side of the station's partition from the ladies that were already lounging in the tubs. They were talking and not paying attention to me anyway, so I was able to slip into the bath without catching their notice. I sat back in the pool and turned my face up to my landscape on the wall. This painting of Mount Fuji took me a few months to paint, and then I hid it away in the barn for years after that. It was one of the last oil paintings I ever did. After that, I wanted my paintings to be edgier, brighter, and crisper, so I switched to acrylics. But I'd never finished anything with acrylics. I had started a million projects that I abandoned not long after.

Following the lines of Mount Fuji, down the slope and into the forest and lake, I remembered how calming it was to paint oil landscapes. Maybe it was a good thing Tama destroyed my studio? Maybe I should switch?

Regardless, I couldn't take Chiyo's money. She had just bought and renovated this bathhouse and taking her money would mean having to admit the situation we were in. I promised Mom I'd keep my mouth shut, and I was going to have to work hard to do that. She was my only lifeline now.

CHAPTER
THREE

managed to leave the bathhouse without running into Chiyo again and took the bus back towards home, stopping at Sawayaka for lunch. By the time I stepped up to the restaurant's door, my stomach was trying to eat itself. I thought cutting back on food would eventually make me less hungry. Instead, my body was in revolt, and my blood sugar was so low at 14:00, I had a piercing headache behind my right eye.

I squinted against the pain, coming into Sawayaka and saying hello to Ana, the hostess.

"It's good to see you," Ana said, giving me a hug and squeezing my shoulders. Her eyes focused on my face for a brief moment before she moved on. She was probably noticing my headache. When I got one, I wore the pain all over my face, between my scrunched eyes, sunken cheeks, and flat mouth. "It's so late! I bet you're hungry?"

"I am, and Yasahiro likes when I come at the end of lunch, so I was biding my time."

"Of course," she said, ushering me to my usual table near the back. "I'll let him know you're here."

I sank into my chair and rested my head in my hands, closing my eyes against the light of midday. I was glad I waited to come in because there was no one here to witness my slow decline. Pressing the heel of my hand into my right eye, I breathed deep into the pain and waited for it to abate. After lunch, I hoped Yasahiro would let me hang out in the main area. I even brought a book. But I had to get through lunch first.

"Headache?" Yasahiro's voice interrupted my brain-calming ritual. I pulled away from the dark of my hands and squinted up at him. "Mei, you've been getting headaches so often lately. I'm getting worried about you."

Concern flattened his features, the tiny scar in his eyebrow straightening as he relaxed his eyes and peered down at me. But I loved it. I loved his concern for me. He'd only known me for a short time, and he could already read me. He genuinely cared.

I totally didn't deserve him.

He set two bowls of noodles down on the table, and halting at first before I knew where his fingers were leading, he laid his warm hand on my forehead.

"Your face is so cold," he said, leaning into the contact. I relished the heat of his fingers on my skin. He'd been in the kitchen for hours and had probably even broken a sweat under the heat of the stove and oven. He was as warm as summer.

He dragged his fingers down my temple to my cheek and stopped to lean down. My breath died in my chest. It'd been weeks since we last kissed and his lips were so close, I wanted to launch off the chair and press mine to his.

"I'm heading out... Oh. Sorry," Ana interrupted, and Yasahiro leaned away from me. My face burst into a blinding blush. I wished the heat would make the headache better, but the rush of blood only made the pain worse. "Sorry!" she called again. I didn't turn around, but instead heard the door open, close, and then her keys in the latch.

Yasahiro sighed, the moment ruined. "Here. Eat. You only look like this when you're hungry."

I glanced down into the bowl and praised all the gods I could think of there was meat amongst the vegetables and noodles. I could use the protein.

After the fire, Yasahiro visited me during the weeks I was in the hospital, and then he spent the following weeks working double shifts at the restaurant to make up for relying on his staff while I was bedridden. Since then, I only saw him when I came here or when we went out on group dates, which was only twice per week if that. No days off to spend together. I was grateful he came to visit me every day in the hospital, but it hadn't done much for our relationship.

"We'll eat and have some coffee?" He sat down across from me, but I shook my head at him. "What? No coffee?"

"No." I laughed. "I mean, yes, coffee. But... come sit next to me. Please?" I picked up my bowl and moved over a seat, and he smiled, his lip twitching before he coughed. He rose from his seat and came to sit next to me. Immediately the space around us shifted, heat radiating off of him. I wished I could attach myself to him like a leech and siphon off his warmth. That was an awful image when I thought about it.

I laid my temple on the edge of his shoulder bone, pressed the edge into my head, and he turned to kiss my forehead. Ah. That was nice.

"Yasahiro, tell me more about your family."

When I was in the hospital, Yasahiro would ask me to talk about my family, usually in an effort to keep me awake and lucid during all the rounds of painkillers I was on. I told him about my older brother, Hirata, and his family. I didn't see them much (maybe once a year) but I did love him despite how persnickety he was. Hirata and his wife were both kind, and their kids were fun and polite. I told Yasahiro about my dad, what little I could remember about him. He died when I was five, dropped dead of a heart attack while out working in the fields. By the time someone found him, he had been dead for several hours. There was no coming back from that. That was also a time when life insurance came through for Mom. It was the only reason she was able to keep the house and farm, though she did sell off some land to make things easier.

"Both my mom and dad are alive and well, and they can't wait to meet you."

I leaned over my noodles and took in a huge mouthful. *Remember to chew, Mei.*

"But you knew that—"

"I didn't know that you had said anything about me."

"Why wouldn't I?"

I kept my mouth shut, only opening it to eat. Why? Because we had just started dating, it was possible the yakuza were trying to kill me, and I was constantly comparing myself to his old girlfriend, the star of stage and screen, Amanda Cheung. It was a blessing we had no internet at the house because the lack of online time would stop me from staring at photos of the two of them together. I wished I could stop myself from searching, block Google Images completely, but I couldn't. I felt the compulsive need to remind myself I'd never be as good or pretty or perfect or wealthy as she was.

"I talk about you all the time. How smart and resourceful you are. How you won me over with your smile."

My face heated to blinding levels, and I cringed against my headache.

"I'm sure you'll be their favorite in no time." Yasahiro jerked his chin at my bowl. "Eat your lunch. I have leftovers for you to take home for dinner."

I sighed, both grateful and ashamed. "Thank you. Um, I was wondering if... Hmmm. Never mind." My hands shook as I lifted the chopsticks to my mouth.

"Did you eat this morning?" he asked, laying his hand between my shoulder blades. I shrugged off his touch, remembering how he could feel the scars on my back through my dress the night of the barn fire. Before everything went to hell.

Yasahiro, being the kind of man he was, didn't remove his hand from my back, but instead dragged the pads of his fingers down the length of the biggest scar before squeezing me across the waist. My skin was so misshapen, he could feel it through a sweater. This was what I loved about him, though. He knew I wanted the love and attention, even when I was uncomfortable with it.

"I did. Mom made egg and rice. But we're out of sugar, and I usually drink my coffee with at least sugar."

He nodded and pulled his phone from his pocket. "I'll send you home with some sugar too. And you should have coffee with cream and sugar before you leave. Isn't your mom supposed to get the insurance check soon? I sent you a text asking, but you didn't respond."

He flashed his phone at me, and I groaned. How was I going to cover this up? I took out my phone and scrolled through my texts. "I didn't get it." I showed my screen to him and his eyes narrowed on the antenna display. I tried to turn off my phone, but it was too late. Stupid move. I was so stupid when my blood sugar was low. It was like I didn't have a brain and my emotions were turned up three hundred percent.

"Why don't you have service?"

Hmmm, if I lied, he would catch me, I knew it. I braced myself. "Mom canceled the mobile phone and internet at home, so I'm only able to receive your texts if I'm on WiFi."

"What?" He grunted in frustration.

My face fell because he sounded angry and annoyed. "I'm sorry. Honestly, there's nothing I can do about it." He had no idea how bad our situation was. We had barely any heat, the fridge was almost empty, and all my clothes were falling off of me because I was losing weight like crazy. Living on 1000 calories a day or less was beginning to take its toll, especially since I was so active walking everywhere.

He quickly took my hand and squeezed. "I know. I know your budget is low. Looking at you now, your eyes look so round and big because your face has slimmed out so much. I hate seeing you like this. The hospital and all those painkillers were no good for you."

"I know." I swallowed hard, guilt coating my feet like mud, pulling me to the ground and slowing me down. I wanted to tell him about the severe lack of food at home, but I couldn't for Mom's sake.

"Well, at least let me send you home with some food I set aside. Your mom said she would be paid this week, so I doubt you need much." I wanted to protest that Mom told me it'd be three weeks at least before she got paid, but I clenched my lips shut. She had lied to him! "And I'll give you a prepaid SIM card too."

A wave of sickness crested in my throat, what little in my stomach threatening to come back up. "No, no. You don't—"

"Stop, Mei. How will I be able to reach you if your phone isn't working? How will I know you're safe and okay? I'm doing this for my own selfish reasons, and you can use the phone for whatever you want. Every time the card runs out of money, you let me know and I'll get you a new one."

I hung my head and let my tears fall onto my baggy jeans.

"Please don't cry," he whispered. "It's not a big deal."

"It is. I'm such a charity case."

"No," he said, standing up and grabbing both of our bowls. "I'm taking care of you because I can. And I know if the situation were reversed, you would do the same. If I had been in the hospital for weeks, you would have been there. If I didn't have food, you would have brought me some. This town owes you and your mom a debt after what you went through. Are still going through." He stopped and tapped my foot with his so that I would look up at him. "Is there anything else I can help you with?"

I was tempted to ask for money, enough to pay for some heat at home, but I shook my head.

"Come into the kitchen with me."

I followed him into the warm, deserted kitchen where stewed dishes bubbled away, rice cooked in the rice cooker, and bowls of bread dough rose next to a warm oven. The air smelled heavenly, and I sucked in a steady, long breath through my nose, relishing every scent. Two months ago, you couldn't pay me to eat traditional Japanese food. I hated it. But I'd learned to love it through Yasahiro's cooking, and when I was starving, literally anything would taste good. I was pretty sure I could eat cardboard most days and it would taste like chocolate.

"Here are more leftovers you can take." Yasahiro opened up one of the fridges. Inside, plastic bowls were stacked up with my name on them. "These here are extra tempura I made last night and leftover rice too. Then this is stewed beef and carrots, raw vegetables, some pickles, and an okonomiyaki with squid." My mouth watered as he pointed to each container. "And then on top is a green tea egg custard I made just for you and your mom. There should be enough here for tonight and tomorrow." He closed the fridge and pointed to a cloth bag next to the bowls of rising dough. "Take them home with this bag."

"Thank you," I said, reflexively bowing. "That's a lot of food. I promise it won't go to waste."

"I'm sure it won't." He squeezed my arm as he slid past me. At the coffee machine, which was a monstrous piece of Italian stainless steel tubes and dials, he made us both Americanos, loading mine with a generous helping of sugar and cream before handing the cup to me. While I sipped on my coffee, he scooped sugar into a container, placed it in the bag, stirred the stewed vegetables, punched down the dough, and hummed into his coffee cup as he made out lists. His employees were all off for another two hours before they returned for the dinner rush, so, in the meantime, he wrote out their tasks for the night, the menu, and a list of any remaining ingredients that needed to be picked up.

I wished I had a job like this, something that was a secure part of my life, something I was made to do like Yasahiro was made for being a chef and a business owner. I needed to find my calling. *I was going to find my calling if it was the last thing I did.* I just had to figure out what that was.

"Can I stay and read until the staff comes back? I don't want to go home yet."

"Sure," he said, setting his coffee cup in the sink. "I have an idea. How about we go out tonight? Just you and me. No one else. We haven't been out together alone in a while."

"Seven weeks," I said, and he stared blankly at me. "Not that I'm counting or anything."

"We haven't been out alone in seven weeks?"

"Nope." I shook my head slowly. "Haven't kissed in even longer."

I gasped and turned away from him, hardly able to believe I said that out loud. It was true, though. The last and only time we'd ever kissed was his reward for winning "the slow food haute cuisine challenge."

"I wasn't sure if you were ready for that yet." His voice lowered, a sexy tone to it curling my toes. I turned back to him and a sly smile, cocked to the side, graced his face. "When the kissing starts, I don't want to stop." He set down his pen and walked slowly to me. Hooking his finger into my belt loop, he tugged me closer to him and my heart raced. "And I usually have no decorum when it comes to public displays of affection either. Blame Paris if you want, but once the physical intimacy starts, I want to hold you..." He placed his hand on my waist, the tips of his fingers inching up against my sweater and seeking out my skin.

"Touch you, kiss you even if the world is swarming around us."

"What if..." I could barely breathe, thoughts of everyone knowing about our relationship because they witness it with their own eyes seized my lungs. "What if I'm okay with that?" I smiled, a broad, lovesick, silly grin that made my head spin.

I'd been denying his interest in me since the very beginning because we'd kept everything behind closed doors, except for his one public confession about dating me during Chiyo's bathhouse opening. Even our group dates had been platonic, all our little touches happening under the table. With him showing affection in the open, there would be no denying our relationship. There'd be no cause for people to question us.

That sounded like a great idea.

He put both hands on my waist, lifted me up and set my butt on the stainless steel island in the kitchen. My blood began to heat, pumping through me so fast I was close to fainting. I was at his eye level, and he locked his gaze with mine, pushing open my legs so he could stand between them. With my headache long gone and blood pooling between my legs, I was so turned on it was a miracle I hadn't jumped him. I took the initiative to run my fingers through the hair at the back of his neck. He smiled as he leaned in and connected his lips to mine. I inhaled deeply through my nose, taking in enough air to sustain a deep kiss.

Waiting this long had made the weeks of slight separation mean even more. He cared about me as a whole person — not someone to sleep with and discard (not that I thought he was like that, but it's what I always fear about men) or play with until he was bored. We pressed our lips together, pausing to hum or smile. His arms pulled me solidly to his chest, and I wrapped my legs around him, trying to abate the ache between my legs. It *ached*, like taking my insides and twisting them into a clump. His lips pulled away for a brief moment, and he groaned before connecting again with mine, his hands directing my head to the side. If he tried any harder, he would pull my soul up straight from my feet.

This time, I didn't end the kiss like I did the first time. He disengaged from me, smiling when I opened my eyes.

"There. Now we're really a couple. Not kissing to reward for a challenge. It's the real thing."

"Like foreplay," I said, bravely, because oh my god, I'd never said anything like that before.

"You better believe it."

I never did get to read before heading home. Kissing until my lips were numb seemed like a better option.

CHAPTER
FOUR

took the evening to go home and calm myself down, eat
dinner with Mom, put her in bed with Mimoji, our fluffy cat,
and send her off to peaceful sleep with some hot water
bottles. She was in bed and out by 20:30, and I wouldn't be home
until midnight. I actually couldn't believe I was going out two
nights in a row! This was unheard of. Even in my solvent days
before I got fired, I would only sometimes go out both Friday and
Saturday nights. I had been more of a homebody back then. Mom
would be up again in the middle of the night to work at Midori
Sankaku, but she'd get a solid six hours of sleep, which was all she
needed at her age. At least, that's what she had told me.

Standing outside at 22:00, I tipped my head up at the night
sky and the wash of winter stars. The air was frigid, below zero
tonight, but I didn't have to wait long because Yasahiro's car was
coming from town. It wasn't as if we had a lot of traffic way out
here in the farmlands, so I was able to see his progress along the
road before he turned into our long driveway. His lights flickered
as he drove through the grove of pine trees and pulled up in the
circular gravel drive.

I jumped in the car and sighed as the warmth of the interior enveloped me.

"Ahhh, I'm so glad you were right on time." I smiled over at Yasahiro, turning down the music on the radio.

"Why didn't you wait inside?"

"I didn't want to disturb Mom and Mimoji. They've been asleep for a while now, and I've been reading at the kotatsu."

He pulled off his gloves and crooked a finger at me, so I leaned over.

"Can I kiss you again?" His breath rushed over my face, and he waited for my response. I answered by kissing him. I should've asked for permission the way he did, but I didn't think he'd deny me. His face and lips were warm, and mine were cold since I had been sitting in a house that was barely ten degrees for the past two hours.

"Mmmm," he said, pulling away and stroking my cheek with his fingers. "I was wondering if I imagined this afternoon and the hour of kissing, but it appears to have been the real thing."

He had no idea how much I cherished these sorts of statements. I saved them, filed them away for later when I didn't believe this was happening — that I was finally dating again. Not only that, but I was dating the hot, successful bachelor who was Chikata's most wanted boyfriend. It *was* hard to believe that I, of all people, was this lucky.

He shifted the car into gear and headed out the driveway. I glanced over at Akiko's house across the street, and her place was lit up and happy, with twinkling Christmas lights along the front porch, the windows warm with light, and smoke curling from the chimney. My house, in comparison, looked vacant — not a light on anywhere, no smoke, and as I was painfully aware of, stone cold inside.

Just thinking about the difference between our two houses made me bitter and angry. Why didn't she offer to help us out? Why did I have to go to her and beg for her help?

I diverted my mind from these thoughts by listening to Yasahiro's music. Whatever it was, it sounded like downtempo French techno.

"How's your French?" I asked him, breaking the companionable silence.

He rattled off a long sentence in French and I blankly stared at him. He laughed. "My French is excellent. I made it a point to not speak Japanese at all while I was living there. It was either French at work and around town or..." His voice faded as he accelerated from a red light that turned green.

"Or English with Amanda? It's okay. You can say her name now. I may only be jealous fifty percent of the time."

"I wish you weren't jealous at all."

"Hey, remember that time you and Amanda went to Ibiza and danced all night in the clubs?" The truth came galloping out of my mouth at breakneck speed. He often forgot his past followed me around on the internet. And seeing them on vacation together was one of my obsessive searches I was glad were at a standstill now with no WiFi at home.

I glanced over at him, his lips pressed together and eyes trained on the roads. He pulled into the parking spot at his apartment, sighed, and shifted the car into park.

"Would *you* like to go to Ibiza? I promise that place is not all it's cracked up to be."

I tossed my hair gently, nothing too dramatic because this could easily devolve. "Please, Yasahiro. I'm sure Ibiza's a blast. *I've* never left Japan, never even been as far as Okinawa. Trust me. If I went to Ibiza, I'd be in the clubs till dawn."

He laughed. "I'd like to see that. And then you'd be sunbathing topless on the beach afterward?"

My nose flared as I inhaled sharply. Amanda had done that (thankfully the images were blurred for me), but...

"No," I whispered. "Never."

His face paled and the humor died a swift death. I opened the door and jumped out of the car.

"Mei, I'm sorry." He jerked forward and grabbed my hand before I could go any further. We were only a few blocks from Izakaya Jūshi and I was sure I could make it there faster than him, but this was supposed to be a date. I let my feet halt. "I forgot." He brushed his lips across my knuckles and inhaled. "That was a stupid thing to say."

"You would never forget, *will never forget*, once you see my back for yourself. Shall we go upstairs now and get it over with? I'll strip and you can witness why I get kicked out of onsens by ignorant people."

Fire had ruined my life so many times, I'd lost count.

"No. Not like this." He pulled me to him and wrapped his arms around me. "Take a deep breath and let it out."

My face was buried in his shoulder so I inhaled deeply into his coat, the scents of cinnamon and sandalwood wrapping around my anger and crushing it to death.

"Come on. Let's go get some drinks and snacks."

He angled me away from his apartment, the apartment I hadn't been to yet, and towards Izakaya Jūshi. I was looking forward to seeing Etsuko, even though this was an "alone" date. I wanted to hear how her day with Hisashi was before he left for Chiba.

Inside, the place was subdued for a Sunday night, a big difference from the packed house and ebullient fishermen of last night. Yasahiro wove through many of the open tables to secure a quiet corner near the back. The air was not too smokey, just a hint of the chicken being grilled at the yakitori bar and no one smoking.

"I'm glad it's not too smokey this time. The doctor warned me that I may have trouble breathing in places with a lot of cigarette smoke." I sat down next to Yasahiro at the table and we placed our coats across from us in the empty chairs.

"Let me know if we need to leave then," he said, taking my

hands and rubbing them absent-mindedly. Once we broke the wall between us earlier today, he couldn't keep his hands off of me. It was comforting. "I almost don't want to buy beer. It's too cold outside."

"It's supposed to be even colder later in the week, in the negatives."

Yasahiro frowned. "It's so strange that it hasn't snowed yet either. I heard this was a Siberian cold front. We should blame the Russians."

"*Da!*" I raised my fist and laughed. "That's literally the only Russian I know."

Hideo, Etsuko's brother, approached the table and clasped hands with Yasahiro. "Yasahiro, Mei. Good to see you. Two nights in a row is unprecedented."

"I wanted Mei all to myself tonight," Yasahiro said, taking my hand and lacing his fingers with mine.

"Ah, young love," Hideo said, laughing. "What can I get you tonight? Etsuko should be here soon." He leaned back to look at the clock on the wall over the grill. "She should have been here thirty minutes ago, but she probably overslept her alarm. She said she was going to nap after Hisashi left."

Yasahiro glanced at me, but I waved to him to order. "You know what's good..."

"It's all good," he said, smiling at me and stroking my hand with his thumb. "I think we'll have some chicken pieces, skin, asparagus..." He leaned forward to look at the menu behind the grill.

"The shrimp is delicious. They're big when the water is this cold," Hideo said, glancing at the menu. "And the grilled scallions."

"Okay. Plus rice and saké."

Hideo left us to our hot towels.

"So back to the subject of languages, you know Japanese and English?" Yasahiro asked, and I thought, wow, he was brave to come back to a subject that nearly killed our date fifteen minutes ago.

"Yes, both. I've never learned anything else. My English is good, though I never get to use it."

Hideo returned to our table and deposited a bottle and two small cups. Yasahiro poured and we drank.

"Do you want to learn French?" he asked, resting his chin in his hand.

"I could, I suppose. I have plenty of time on my hands, being unemployed and all. But I hoped to be spending the time looking for a new job, hopefully some place local."

"You know, I could—"

"Yasahiro," I said, warning in my voice. "I will not work at the restaurant."

He pulled away, mock shock on his face. "How did you know I was going to offer?"

I raised my eyebrows at him.

"Okay. I was going to."

I squeezed his hand. "It's sweet of you to try and help me out so much. I really appreciate every little thing you do. But I can't work at Sawayaka. I'm a disaster in the kitchen, and I'm not going to take hours from any of your servers or Ana. That just wouldn't be right. I'll find work somehow. Maybe I need to find something part time for a while until spring."

"I'll keep my ears open for you. You should consider submitting your resume to those companies that hire out part time people for jobs they're skilled to do."

I nodded as our meal was delivered to the table. "I will. I just need internet access again."

"Hmmm," Yasahiro said, leaning over his food. "Yes, you do. Oh." He reached for his coat and pulled a bag from the inside pocket. "Here. It's a prepaid SIM card. Swap it out for yours and you should be good to go."

I hesitated as he handed it to me but took the bag from him before he started dividing out food.

"Thanks." I didn't know what else to say besides trying to hand it back to him and deny his help, so I slipped the bag into my purse and tried to relax.

We had an easy dinner together, which was nice and normal, just the way I liked it. We talked about his time at school in Paris, and I asked him to speak in French to me. It was juvenile, I knew, but something about hearing the words come out of his mouth made me melt. I told him more about the five jobs I'd had since I graduated college and the two guys I dated since then.

He was quiet and a good listener, but I could tell there were other things going on in his head in our conversational lulls. He may have been thinking about work the next day or how his life differed from mine. For a moment, a wave of jealousy rose up in me and I believed he was thinking of Amanda, but the fear dissipated quickly. He never gave me any indication he ever thought of her unless I brought her up. When I was talking to him, I had his attention at one hundred percent. He said once that Tama used to look straight through people like they didn't exist, which was probably why he went psycho and tried to kill me by kidnapping me, tying me up, and setting the barn on fire around me. But Yasahiro paid attention to all the little things about me. He looked straight in my eyes when I talked, brushed his hand against mine, or straightened out a piece of my loose hair.

At the end of dinner, Hideo came over again, his face plastered with worry.

"Etsuko never made it in tonight, and we're too busy to go find out if she just overslept her alarm or if she's sick or what."

It was late, almost midnight, and the place was pretty busy for a Sunday night. Looked like people came out to have a late night snack and drink before the work week started.

"Want us to go check on her?" Yasahiro asked and nodded to me. "We're done, and I still have to drive Mei home."

Where had the evening gone? We hadn't been on a solo date in so long that the evening flew right by. I wished I could invite myself over to Yasahiro's place and spend more time with him, but we weren't there yet.

"She lives around the corner, right?" I grabbed my coat and scarf, bundling up against the impending cold.

"Yeah. Etsuko lives on the opposite side of the block from me. Her apartment building's back door shares the alley with mine." Yasahiro wrapped his scarf around his neck several times and pulled cash from his wallet.

"If you wouldn't mind, Mom and Dad would appreciate it. They're busy and I'm handling all the tables. Go knock on her door and see if she's asleep. Have her call us if you manage to wake her."

Out on the sidewalk, Yasahiro and I walked shoulder to shoulder against the bitterly cold wind, leaning into the swirls of frost and bits of tree that pelted our outer coats.

"Ugh, it's so cold! I hate winter," I mumbled into my scarf.

"Where's your hat?" He smiled at me from under his black knit cap. "It's December! Time to bundle up."

"I'll remember tomorrow. Hey, does Etsuko do this often? Not show up for work? It doesn't seem like her at all." Except, unless she was having an extra lie-in with Hisashi, which I could see happening. They didn't get to see each other often enough and they both seemed really in love with each other. I couldn't help but think about how amazing Hisashi was to always visit her, once a month like clockwork. And he doted on her too. I hadn't known her that long, less time than I'd known Yasahiro, but I felt it in my bones when they looked at each other. That was love.

"I'm not sure. She has complained about oversleeping or running a lot of errands to me."

"Me too. She was talking about how busy she was last night. Do you know which apartment she lives in?"

"I've been to her apartment once when she was sick and her mom sent me there with a liter of soup." He laughed and rolled his eyes. "Once a chef, always a chef. You can't shrug off the restaurant industry once you're in it. It's like a cult."

We rounded the corner behind Yasahiro's building and came upon a three-story apartment building, well-maintained and joyful looking, with Christmas lights strung along balconies, and a light or two on in other apartments. The whole building would be dead quiet in an hour, so this was a good time.

Yasahiro stopped and looked up at the building. "That's her place," he said, pointing to the dark apartment on the third floor, left of the center stairs.

The vestibule door was open so we let ourselves in and climbed the stairs. Yasahiro warmed up his hands by breathing into them and knocked on the apartment door. "Etsuko!" he called out, though not too loud because other people in the building may have been asleep. "Etsuko! It's Yasahiro!"

Nothing. I tapped my feet and looked around at the other apartment doors. No lights from either of them leaked into the hallway, but there was a weak light from Etsuko's apartment. I crouched down and picked up a sliver of wood from the floor, dread washing down my spine.

"Do you think...?" I showed it to Yasahiro. He took the sliver in his hand and examined it on all sides, looking between it and the door.

I reached past him and tried the doorknob, certain it must be locked, but the knob turned and the door swung inward to the genkan. Shock colored everything a brilliant purple as I registered the deadbolt still out and engaged, but the door on the inside was shredded to pieces, slivers of wood on the floor and shooting from odd angles out of the doorjamb.

"Etsuko?" Yasahiro pushed past me, his hand on my chest, keeping me away from the body on the tatami mat. A small lamp to the right of Etsuko's TV shone down on her body, prone on the floor.

"Call 119," Yasahiro told me, but he wasn't rushing to her because she couldn't be saved. Her lips were white and body stiff, positioned where she was left.

Tears started and I couldn't stop them. "Oh my god," I bumbled out, tears flying from my lips. "Is she dead? She's dead." I'd never seen a dead body before, and I was paralyzed, needing to tell my hands to work, to get the phone from my purse — reach in, grab it, turn it on. I swiped and dropped it as Yasahiro crouched over her body and pressed his fingers to her neck.

"M-m-m-m-my phone? I... I can't."

I had no service. I had completely forgotten. And my hands shook too much to swap out the SIM card.

Yasahiro looked up at me, his face frozen in a frown and eyebrows drawn in. "Right." He straightened up and came to me, turning me away from Etsuko, and pulling his phone from his pocket. "This is why your phone is so important," he whispered into my hair. Circling his arms around me, he dialed and lifted the phone to his face.

CHAPTER
FIVE

"Why am I not surprised to find you here?" Goro asked as he climbed the stairs. The paramedics and another police officer were inside the apartment, taking photos and evidence, while Etsuko lay dead on the floor. Goro straightened the front of his officer uniform and sighed, sadness washing over him. He knew her just as well as Kumi had. They were all life-long friends.

"Trust me. I wish I wasn't here." If it were at all proper, I would've hugged Goro. It was good to see him. He was the one who helped me figure out Tama killed his own father and then pulled me away from the burning barn before it collapsed. I wouldn't want anyone else here to investigate Etsuko's death but him.

"So, tell me what happened," he directed, pulling out his notepad.

"We were having drinks at Izakaya Jūshi when Hideo said she didn't come into work, so he asked us to come by and check on her," Yasahiro reported, squeezing my shoulders. I began to cry again, so he set his head on mine for a moment.

"Are you okay, Mei?" Goro squeezed my shoulder.

"I've never seen a dead person before, outside of a funeral." I glanced at the door, and I was glad I didn't have a direct view of Etsuko. "And I really liked her."

"You were almost dead yourself once. I suppose that's enough for one person." Goro jotted down something in his notepad. "When did you find her?"

"Only a few moments before we called 119. Her brother thought she was home sleeping, and that we would knock on the door and wake her up. I'm sure Hisashi was here not too long before..." My voice trailed off as I realized what I was saying. What if he had done this? I sniffed up and wiped my nose on my glove. "Are you going to call her parents?"

"Kayo went over to the izakaya to break the news."

Goro's partner, Kayo, a young woman I'd only been introduced to once, was his better half, or so he liked to say. I guessed she was in charge of the bad news.

"Did you see anyone around when you came in the building? Anything unusual?"

A harsh clank of metal snapped my attention to the apartment, and Etsuko's body, now on the stretcher, was covered with a sheet. We stepped to the side as they rolled her down the hall and carried her down the stairs.

"No," Yasahiro said, breaking out of a trance, watching the stretcher fade away. "The building was quiet and the front door was unlocked. When we came up the stairs, we knocked on the door, and then Mei saw the splintered wood on the floor. We tried the knob and the door opened, just like it is here now." He waved at the open door. "The lock had been busted, and we stepped into the apartment. Etsuko was right there, and I called 119."

"You called?" He pointed to Yasahiro and he nodded.

"Mei was in shock." He squeezed me again, and I was grateful he didn't say anything about my phone being out of commission, though I figured Kumi would say something to Goro about it. Any news, no matter how trivial, could travel quickly in this town. Chikata was a hub of gossip. It was difficult to keep it hidden how bad off Mom and I were, but I was doing my hardest for Mom's sake. We both wanted to avoid the shame of everyone knowing we're living off leftovers and hanging by a thread.

"What's going to happen, Goro? How did she die?" My voice cracked, and I sucked in a breath to stop my lip from quivering.

"I'm not sure. We'll run the reports and an autopsy, and we'll figure it out. Her family will probably have a funeral sometime this week."

I glanced from him to the apartment, my brain working through all the possibilities. She had been at home and getting ready for work. Maybe she was resting before coming in? Then there was a knock at the door and she didn't let the person in. He or she (I'm guessing he) kicked in the door, they struggled, and he... killed her somehow.

I took half a step towards the apartment, and Goro chuckled sadly.

He jerked his head. "Let's go in. Don't touch anything okay?"

My eyes skipped over the crime scene. "No blood," I said, pointing to the floor.

"Yeah. She wasn't bleeding when we came in," Yasahiro concurred.

"So..." I tapped my chin. "She was hit over the head... or possibly strangled?"

"I'd guess strangled by the looks of the kotatsu and mail on the floor." He pointed to the evidence lying around us — the over-turned kotatsu and a huge collection of bento boxes strewn every-where. "If they fought, she probably tried to defend herself by kicking."

I squatted down and examined the mail. It was a mess of bills, open envelopes, and printed receipts, but I couldn't see them all because Goro told me not to touch anything. The bento boxes were every different style imaginable: Hello Kitty, Rilakkuma,

Miffy, local and foreign mascots. Several of them littered the floor, but there were still stacks of boxes on shelves.

"We'll gather those up and catalog them," Goro said, standing over me. "She'd be upset about what happened to her bento box collection. She loved those." He glanced at the bills. "Maybe she had a debt she had to pay and someone came to collect on it. Stranger things have happened." He raised his eyebrows at me, hinting at Tama. Tama fell in with criminals, the yakuza, and had debts to pay.

"That's not how a shakedown happens, though," I replied, and both guys laughed at me. "What? You both need to read more." I huffed my disapproval and explained. "If you owe money, they don't want to kill you because then they can't collect. They'll scare you or even injure you or your family, but death is the last thing on the list." I turned in the apartment and noticed her futon wasn't out in the main area.

"What about Hisashi? You need to call him. He'd be back in Chiba by now, right?"

Goro pulled his lips in and grimaced. "Yes, but... He's a suspect now. We usually bring in the boyfriend first, if there is one."

"Do you really think...?" My head lightened like a balloon.

"No. I don't. We all know him. Kumi's known him since they were in high school. But..."

"Yeah." We knew Tama and never expected him to kill. Now this.

I hesitated before I continued into her apartment. The kitchen was a basic set-up with a two-burner stove, a sink, and an oven. I pulled on my glove and opened her fridge. She had plenty in there to eat and nothing looked out of place. I opened the oven and it was cold. The bathroom looked fine.

She had a separate bedroom just down the hall. I was tempted to call her lucky because her apartment was twice the size of the apartment I had in Tokyo before I was fired from my job and evicted, but I could never call a murdered sweetheart like Etsuko "lucky." Her futon looked like it was recently slept in.

Hmmm...

"Goro?"

"Yeah, Mei?" He came up next to me and I waved to the futon. "What?"

I pointed to the covers. "Both sides." The covers were peeled back on both sides of the futon. Someone else had been here with her.

"Ah! Good catch. But if she was home, sleeping alone after Hisashi left, she would've pulled up the covers on both sides before getting in. This makes me think he was here."

"Or someone else? I hate to say it, though, because they seemed so in love to me." I shrugged my shoulders, and Goro only nodded in response.

Yasahiro poked his head between us and peered at the bed. "Hmmm, I can't imagine her cheating on him. He was all she talked about."

"Everyone has secrets, I guess." I had a dozen at least, and there were a few I kept from him.

For a moment, Yasahiro seemed bewildered, his head cocked to the side, but he squeezed my hand. "Yeah. Yeah, I guess so."

Either he was too naive to believe people kept secret lovers or he didn't believe Etsuko could've done that or... I didn't want to think about the "or." I had no idea how Yasahiro and Amanda broke up. What if he had cheated on her? What if she had?

I needed to distract myself.

"I want to help." I grabbed Goro's arm, my brain leaping through hundreds of scenarios. I pictured Etsuko in bed with another man, and he was married, but then the wife found out? Or what? I imagined a million different ways this could have gone down. Or, most likely, she slept with Hisashi earlier and was blindsided after he left. Maybe she had never made the bed. Etsuko was fully clothed when we found her.

Goro narrowed his eyes at me. "Fine, but no bets this time. And you call me if you think of anything."

"I called you about Tama and you didn't believe me." I thrust my hands on my hips and glared at him. "Are you going to listen to me this time?"

Yasahiro stepped away. "Oh no. I'll wait outside." He turned and beat a hasty path for the door.

"I know. *I'm sorry.* I don't know how many times I can say I'm sorry, but I am." Goro set his strong hand on my shoulder. "I promise to listen this time. You have good instincts, Mei. I'm glad you're on my side."

I placed my hand over his. "Some days, it's all I have. I may not have a job or money or much of anything, but I can help others when I can. Let me help."

"Okay. Let's look around one more time before we go."

CHAPTER
SIX

never had liked Mondays. What sane person loved returning to work after two whole days off? Now, without an office to go to, my life seemed to drag on every day, one sunrise and sunset blending straight into the next. I barely knew what day of the week it was and wouldn't without Mom getting out of bed and going to work. With Mom gone at 3:00 and only the cat to keep me warm, I shivered in bed until the sun rose and sparkled over a wonderland of frost on the ground and grass. I drank a hot coffee, wrapped up in two blankets, and wondered if we were in danger of the pipes freezing. Mom had left the kitchen faucet dripping on purpose, and it was no surprise to find ice crystals forming on the sides of the sink.

I dressed in layers, walked to the bus stop, and headed to the bathhouse to spend the day with Kumi.

"Etsuko was so sweet," Kumi said, crying into a handkerchief with Chiyo's arm around her shoulder. We all sat on the bench in the front lobby. "How does something like this even happen to her?" She sobbed a few more times and hiccuped. "Goro told me you're going to help find who killed her." She leaned forward and grabbed my sleeve. "Please. Do whatever you can to help. She didn't deserve to die."

"She didn't." I squeezed her hand and she let go. "I liked her a lot too. I was just getting to know her."

"They're picking up Hisashi today. I don't believe he killed her. He loved her so much. They've been dating since high school, and he came to visit her once a month, religiously."

I hugged her and soothed her as best I could. "I want you to remember all the times you've seen her and hung out with her over the past few months. Write down everything you can think of. I'm gathering up as much evidence as I can, and I'll use everything I learn to go out and ask more questions."

"I'll start now," Kumi said, jumping up and heading to the front desk. The brand new Mac there displayed Kumi's own drawings and designs in screensaver mode. She was a talented graphic designer. I envied her and her natural artistic talents. Not only did she run the bathhouse with Chiyo, but she designed the printed materials and the website for Kutsuro Matsu, *and* she ran her own graphic design and branding business on the side. Between Kumi and Goro, they were very comfortable, hoping to have kids within the next few years. They owned a townhouse a few blocks away that they shared with Chiyo, all living happily together.

Kumi wiped her face and eyes, took out a stack of notecards, and sat down, chewing on the tip of a pen. "I'll write some things down while you go warm up in the bath, Mei."

I waved her off. "It's okay. I can stay here and keep you company."

"Nonsense. I need to think." She held her hands parallel to each other and pointed at the cards in front of her with them. "I'm going to focus on all the things I can remember about Etsuko and write them down for you and Goro. We can't let the killer get away."

I frowned, worried about Kumi. What if we didn't find

Etsuko's killer? What if it was Hisashi? Would Kumi be able to accept that? I'd come to accept that Tama tried to kill me, but it was hard to believe at first.

I sat in the hot baths inside the women's area and let the water heat me up from the outside in. The weather was going to be extra cold through the end of the week and I was dreading it. I'd only gone a few nights at home without heat, and it was enough to make me want to pack my bags and fly to someplace tropical. If I even had the money.

Joking around with Yasahiro the other day about going to Ibiza made me daydream for hours about what it would be like to travel with him, and it was easy to slip back into my dreams in the hot bath. I closed my eyes and called up all the images I saw of him with Amanda on vacations, but I erased her and put myself in her place. I gave myself a wide-brimmed white hat and big sunglasses, long, light flowing pants, and a chic, printed shirt. My skin was always perfect in my daydreams, no scars to make people stare at me for all the wrong reasons. Yasahiro gazed at me proudly, the way he always looked at Amanda. I walked the streets of a Caribbean island, arm in arm with him. We ate exotic seafood together. We gambled at the casino and drank cocktails at fancy restaurants.

I opened my eyes and stared up at my painting on the wall. Chiyo was going to offer me money again, and I would have to come up with some polite way to refuse her. It went against everything I held dear to accept charity from my friends. I'd always been independent and so had Mom. I'd always paid my own way with everything, with some small amount of help from Mom or my brother when I needed it. Asking friends for help was out of the question. I would never burden them with my own shortcomings. It was hard enough to take food or help from Yasahiro, but I did it reluctantly because we were dating. I knew it would create a rift between us if I constantly refused his help.

But I needed a job, and I needed one soon. If I didn't start to make some money of my own, I would grow to hate myself. I turned around and rested my chin on my arms, dangling my legs out behind me in the bath as a trio of older women, all of them in their eighties at least, came in to bathe. I didn't know them, so I kept my back from them.

"Did you remember to pick up your prescriptions?" one lady asked another.

"No." She sighed, sitting down on a bench. "I'm hoping my daughter comes by later today before they close."

Another woman shook her head. "You should ask them to deliver them to you."

"They do, sometimes, when they're not too busy."

"The real problem is making it to the grocery store when it opens so I can take advantage of the sales that day. But it takes me a long time to dress and walk to the bus. By the time, I get there, everything is already taken."

The old ladies chattered on about the things they couldn't do anymore now that they were older and less mobile. They appeared to be in pretty good health, despite the good-natured griping. The three helped each other with scrubbing one another's backs, and they laughed and had a great time.

I tried not to stare at them as a new idea formed in my head. What if I could find people that needed help and lent them my own mobility at a price? Was there such a job as professional errand runner? Professional car driver for the elderly? I'd heard of this mobile app called Uber that lets you become an ersatz taxi driver. I wasn't sure if there was a market for that in Chikata, but I figured plenty of elderly people around town could use the help. I didn't even need to drive to help them. I could walk or take the bus.

I sank into the water as the ladies talked about world events. Yes! This was something I could do! I liked to help others (though in a twist of irony, I hated when others helped me), and it was something that always brought me a sense of peace, defining my place in the world. My business degree was all well and fine, and I was capable of writing up proposals or applying for grants or doing basic start-up planning, but helping people was something I actually enjoyed.

Now I had a good reason to go visit Akiko. I didn't need to ask for money or for food or shelter, but I did know what I would ask for. Introductions.

––––––––

Tuesday dawned much like Monday had, cold and frosty. This time, though, Mom was still in bed with me until 6:00 because she didn't have to be at work until 7:00. Even though I wanted nothing more than to roll over in bed and go back to sleep while I could still capture her warmth, I got up. I was slow to exit the bedroom, my joints aching, head foggy and slow, and fingertips frozen. I passed by the indoor thermometer and it displayed four degrees celsius. Four. I wanted to cry.

Mom, though, was doing ten times better than me. She must have found her reserves of energy in storage because she was happy and chipper.

She hummed and smiled while handing me a cup of coffee. I kept myself bundled in the warm blankets while spooning in the sugar Yasahiro provided. I was grateful for any small thing, and sugar was at the top of the list.

Mom opened the fridge and pulled out the *okonomiyaki* egg and squid pancake Yasahiro made us. I peeked into the fridge as she closed it and there wasn't much left in there. I needed to visit him today and gather any leftovers he had for us.

"How did you sleep?" Mom asked as she heated up a pan on the stove. "I slept well. Thanks for sharing the bed with me."

"No problem," I said, my teeth chattering. "It was warm

while we were in there, and yeah, you sleep like the dead. I wish I slept like that." I would drift into sleep, only to be confronted with Etsuko's dead body and flinch awake again. Mom barely moved a muscle.

"I sleep well because of all the hard work I do." Mom flipped over the steaming hot pancake and my mouth watered. Anyone else would have thought Mom's statement was passive aggressive, but I knew better.

"Back when we were harvesting vegetables every day and I was running, I slept like the dead, too. Now that I'm not allowed to run and there's nothing to harvest, I sleep poorly." I glanced out the window at the skeleton of the barn and sipped my coffee, my daily routine. I looked back on the last few months and wondered what the hell happened to my life. I was sure when my boss fired me he thought I'd land on my feet again in no time. Most people would've turned around and found a new job right away. The reality of the situation though was grim. Jobs were hard to come by, and those that had them protected their livelihood with their very souls.

My job was eliminated, my life was downsized, and I lost pretty much everything. Which reminded me...

"When are we going to get the insurance money?"

Mom avoided eye contact with me.

"Sorry." I sighed. "Should I not ask? It's just so cold in here, and I'm trying not to complain, really I am. But I'd like to be able to take a hot bath at home and even cook some eggs and rice." I could do that in the rice cooker, but not if we didn't have eggs nor rice.

Eggs, rice, and a tomato. Mmmm. Plus salt and pepper. It wasn't much of a meal, but it was hot, filling, and easy.

Mom plopped my half of the okonomiyaki on a plate in front of me.

"I heard from the insurance company yesterday. They called me at work. It's not good, Mei. They're saying February now—"

"February?" I nearly spat out my coffee. "We won't survive till February."

"I know," she said, patting my hand. "But we only have to survive until around the end of the year. I'll have my first paycheck in two weeks. I can pay off some outstanding bills and then we just need to get to the thirty-first. Then we'll be able to buy groceries again."

"Mom," I pleaded, setting my coffee down and bringing my hands to prayer position. "Please, let me confide in Yasahiro. He'd be happy to help us. In fact, I'm pretty sure he's going to break up with me when he finds out I've been keeping this from him." I pictured him in my head, boiling mad, telling me to leave his restaurant and never come back. I could practically hear his voice saying he couldn't trust me. This was going to end our relationship, and I... I wanted him. He was the one good thing to come of everything lately.

"Absolutely not. I invested three million yen in his restaurant and my share doesn't pay dividends until next summer. I'm sure it'll be money well spent, and I don't want to pull out now. He'll try to give me back the investment, but I'll need that money for next fall."

"But we need money now."

"Mei, it's not your business."

I clamped my mouth shut. I had no money of my own. What right did I have telling Mom what to do with hers?

Three weeks without buying groceries — my head hurt, a phantom low blood sugar headache pushing through, just thinking about that. I glanced at the pantry and took stock of what we had: cans of beans, wild rice, jars of pickles, flour, and yeast. Plus cat food. Plenty of cat food. At least, Mimoji would be well fed until we were financially stable again.

Maybe I would make bread. I should learn to bake bread. Bread was something I could make without setting the kitchen on fire, right?

"I'll be able to eat at work, and I can take some food home with me if I don't think they'll notice."

I cut into the egg pancake and speared a piece into my mouth. It melted in a puddle of intense flavors. Wow. Every time I ate Yasahiro's cooking, I was reminded how amazing he was.

"Why don't you just ask for the leftovers? I'd hate for them to accuse you of stealing."

Mom's face froze like concrete. "I won't ask for handouts. It's different to eat at work because that's what they provide or to hang out at Chiyo's bathhouse."

"I've been asking for food from Yasahiro!" I stomped my foot but it didn't register under all the blankets.

"That's different, too. He obviously loves you and doesn't want to see you starve."

I wanted to argue with her that he did not love me because he'd never said that, but I shut my mouth. She had a point.

"I'll call him and give him an explanation he'll believe so you won't have to say anything. And I'll, um... I'll have to do some more cuts to expenses in the next few days or we run the risk of not having enough money to pay taxes in February, even with the insurance money, if we get it in time." Mom's brow furrowed as she ate the last of the food in front of her.

"What could you possibly cut now? Haven't we cut pretty much everything already?"

"We'll see," she said, sipping her coffee. "I need to run the numbers. I'll let you know."

A pit grew in my stomach so large it threatened to swallow me whole.

I pulled up my shoulders and threw them back. "I'm going to Akiko later today to ask for help. I have an idea of what I can do to earn money, and we'll see if she can help me."

Mom's face softened with a smile. "Are you going to tell me?"

"No. I don't want to jinx it. Say a prayer for me at the shrine on your way into town."

"Okay. Go back to bed until it's time to go. Akiko usually comes home for lunch." Mom handed a hot water bottle to me, and I shuffled off to find the cat and hopefully doze until my time of reckoning came.

CHAPTER
SEVEN

I dozed, in and out of sleep, until noon when I forced myself to dress and cross the street to Akiko's house. Her car sat in the driveway, and the lights were on in the house, so I approached the front door, confident she was at home. Before my hand even hit the door, though, rough and loud dog barking erupted from inside. I jumped away from the threshold and called out Akiko's name. A dog? She didn't have a dog.

The door opened a crack, and Akiko peeked her head out. "Mei?"

I raised my hand at her. "Hi. I'm sorry to cause a ruckus. I didn't know you had a dog."

"Kirin!" She scolded her dog, a brown and white Shiba Inu she picked up in her arms. "Stop. This is a friend of mine!"

Kirin didn't seem to care and tried to launch out of Akiko's arms at me. I jumped, stumbling over my own feet.

"Maybe I should come back some other time?" I backed away another meter, my feet crunching on the gravel of the driveway.

"No. I'll put her in her crate. Hold on." She closed the door, silence stretching away from me punctuated by lesser dog barks.

It was a bad idea to come here. Akiko had become a complete stranger to me.

I turned to go but she opened the door. "Okay, she's secured. Mei, I'm surprised to see you here!" Akiko bid me to come in, waving her arm at me, and smiling. I couldn't leave after all that fuss, so I stepped inside and took off my shoes.

She leaned in and awkwardly hugged me, looking into my face and frowning. "You don't look so good," she said to me as I took off my coat. "Oh my god, Mei. Are you sick? You've lost so much weight! Your face is so skinny and your clothes are hanging off of you!"

She hung my coat next to hers, grabbed her nurse's bag, and ushered me into her main living room. A huge bowl of ramen with pork and vegetables sat on the kotatsu, the TV was on, and a space heater blasted heat into the room. This place was everything I had dreamed of the last few days, and my body sucked in the warmth greedily.

"When did you get a dog?" I asked, avoiding her other questions.

"Two weeks ago. I've been worried that Tama's yakuza friends will come back and try to kill me in my sleep, so I got the dog, hoping I'd have some advanced warning. I sleep with a knife now, and I've been taking self-defense classes after work."

"I should do that." I licked my lips to moisten them. They were cracked no matter how much lip balm I applied. Funny that Yasahiro didn't mind. "I barely sleep because I'm worried about the same thing. Do you mind if I sit at your kotatsu? I'm freezing."

Her eyes glistened with tears. "You don't need to ask for permission. Please sit. Did you eat lunch? Can I get you anything?"

My mouth watered, considering eating anything she might make for me. I would visit Sawayaka in two hours to acquire more food from Yasahiro, but my head was light, my brain foggy and slow. I swallowed and tried to be strong, but I couldn't even open my mouth to refuse.

"You haven't been eating, have you?" Akiko grabbed my hand, shoved up my sleeves, and looked at my arms. "You've never been this skinny in your life. What's going on?"

"If you have food, I'd love to have some." My voice cracked and my eyes watered, but I was determined not to cry. "We ran out of food and money about a week, maybe ten days, ago, and I had been living on a low-calorie diet before that to try and stretch out our resources. I've been taking leftovers from Yasahiro's restaurant to fill in the gaps."

Akiko's fingers were like fire on my skin. "Your body feels cold to me. Let me get my thermometer."

"No. Please don't fuss over me." I tried to work my mouth but I was suddenly parched. "Can I have a glass of water? That's all I really need."

She ignored me, pulled out a digital thermometer, and took my temperature on my forehead and behind my ear without even asking for permission. "My thermometer is very sensitive," she said, glancing at the read-out when it beeped. "Thirty-five point five degrees. That's low, Mei. A half degree lower, and I'd bring you in for hypothermia."

"It's really cold at home. We haven't turned on the heat in three days."

"Good god, why not? It's below zero most nights."

"No money for heat. No money for gas or food. Which is why I'm here." I sank into a seat at the kotatsu, my body shivering as warmth flowed up my arms and legs. "I need to ask a favor, and I'm horrible at asking for favors so please forgive me if I'm rude or abrupt. I need work. Mom has a job but she won't be paid for at least another week, so I need to bring in some income or I'm going to starve to death in the cold." I groaned, rolling my eyes at myself. "Sorry. I'm sure that's an overstatement and completely dramatic."

Akiko stood up from the table, rubbed her face and looked up at the ceiling for so long I believed she had frozen like that. She hastened to the kitchen and poured a glass of water from a pitcher in the fridge. She then put water on to boil and brought a package of something back to the kotatsu with the water.

"Drink. Did you know that when you're cold, you urinate more? Your body cuts off circulation to your outer extremities and lessens blood by increasing urination. So when you become warm again, your body is thirsty and trying to increase blood to make up for the loss. This is why people lose fingers and toes in the cold."

I gulped down the glass of water, and she unwrapped a block of cheese, cutting off slices, and handing them to me with crackers. "And when you're cold, your body burns off fat first to stay warm. You have no fat left on you to burn. Eat that. Cheese and dairy have a lot of fat, and you need it."

"Once a nurse, always a nurse," I croaked out with a dry laugh.

"This is nothing to laugh about." Her stern face made mine fall. "Why..." She sighed. "Why didn't you come to me weeks ago?"

I shrugged my shoulders and chewed the cheese. She slammed her hand down on the table, and I jumped. I startled pretty easily now.

"I've been sitting here in the warmth every day, eating, watching TV, and you've been suffering right across the street." Her angry voice climbed so high, Kirin barked in the other room. "Kirin, hush!"

"Don't yell at me, please," I whispered. "I've had a rough few days. I lost weight in the hospital and I was never able to put it back on. It just got worse and worse as the weeks went on.

There's nothing I could do and coming here wouldn't have solved anything."

"Look, I know you're mad at me because of what happened with Tama. I'm so sorry. So, so sorry." She grabbed my hand and began to cry, her anger crumbling to sadness so quickly, I was shocked into silence for a moment.

"I need to ask you something..." My voice croaked.

"What? Anything. Please," Akiko begged me, her face wet with tears.

"Why didn't you tell the police about Tama? If you knew... If you suspected he was poisoning your father, you should have said something."

Her face blanched. "I was so afraid. I was afraid of Tama. He was so vindictive. He kept saying it was me who killed Dad." She raked her curled fingers through her hair. "And I could see the police believed him. They believed him over me! And then I was afraid I would be sent to jail because I hadn't turned in Tama when I suspected him... If only I hadn't been a coward and said something, none of that would have happened. I look across the street and see the burnt barn, and I cry."

"You and me both. It had all our winter stores in it. Everything we were going to sell to stay warm and fed this winter."

"Insurance covered it, though, right?"

I shook my head. "This is why I haven't come over. I've been avoiding you to save you from the town gossip. You see, the insurance company won't pay us because the police had to report barn as arson, not an accident. If only it had been my space heater that fell over and did damage, I wouldn't be in this mess. With arson, there needs to be an investigation. We won't be paid for a few more months at least. The police and the insurance company have agreed to keep the cause of the fire quiet, otherwise the investigation would be in the papers naming you and Tama, your family, at fault. That would end you. Mom and I don't want that."

Akiko's face paled, and she covered her mouth with her hand. "No. How dare you make that decision for me?"

I drove my index finger into the table. "It's *not* your decision to make. It's ours. You've lost your father and brother. If this came out, you would lose your job, your house, everything. Mom and I will get by."

"Not if you starve to death!"

"Look, everyone but us and Yasahiro thinks the barn fire was an accident, and Tama turned himself in for the murder of your dad. Just let it be."

I ate another piece of cheese in silence, thinking over my course of action. Arguing about this with Akiko would get me nowhere. I had to steer this back to our original conversation.

"I just need to find some work. I was wondering if you could help me out? I was listening to these older ladies at Kusturo Matsu the other day. They were complaining about how they can't travel places or run errands anymore without assistance." I cleared my throat and drank more water, girding myself for the favor. "I thought maybe you could ask some of your nursing patients if they need help around their houses. I would run errands, pick up prescriptions, go grocery shopping, and then once I can afford gas, I'd be happy to drive them places."

Akiko stared at me, so I rushed on. "I would charge 900 yen per hour with a minimum of one hour, plus expenses. I couldn't front money to buy groceries or anything. They would have to give me money for those in advance, but I would give them their change and a receipt. I promise to be honest and not overcharge. If I could just make enough money for a meal a day, I would be able to make it through to January."

Akiko dropped her head into her hands and ran her fingers through her hair, grabbing at her scalp. I ate more cheese. I felt like my stomach would never be full.

"Does Yasahiro know about this? You two are still dating, right?"

"We are," I said, halting, instantly afraid of her. What if she ran out right now and told him everything? "He knows we're low on food and that's it. He doesn't see me without clothes on." I swallowed, admitting that we hadn't slept together yet. "Nothing else is his business. I've lost weight too slowly for him to notice because he sees me almost every day. I've gotten lucky with that."

"You're crazy," she said, breathing out.

"I am not. No one needs to know how bad things are. In a few months, we'll be on our feet again and there'll be nothing to worry about. I just need something part time to get us through."

"Shhh..." she said, squashing a swear word. "Mei, most of the people I take care of are living off pensions. They have enough money to eat and heat their homes, and that's it."

"Well, they're doing better than me."

She thought about that for a second and nodded. "You're right. I'll see what I can do. Stay for lunch and then come with me on my rounds. I'll introduce you to a few people and explain the situation. You should come with me tomorrow too." She stood up and plucked a tissue from the box next to the kotatsu to dry her eyes. "Stay and have lunch with me. I'll make you ramen."

She left me at the kotatsu, and I breathed out a steady breath, silently praying and thanking the gods I got through that without losing myself. Now I had a chance to make things work.

———

I FOLLOWED AKIKO TO THE HOUSES OF TWO OLD WOMEN AND one old man before I started to feel secure again. One woman wanted me to come by every Tuesday and Thursday morning for an hour to help her visit her physical therapist, and an older man needed me to pick up his prescriptions and escort him to the eye doctor every Friday morning. I left each of them my phone number and texted them so that my number and information was in their address books.

"This is a lot easier than I thought it would be," Akiko said as we drove to her last appointment of the day. The sun had already set since it was after 17:00. This was another thing I hated about winter, all the darkness. Once the sun set, the slight warmth of the day evaporated and then we were left with nothing but cold, frosty air.

We circle the block Yasahiro lived on. "Did you know that's Yasahiro's place right there?" I pointed to his apartment, dark but for a few odd lights on in the window. He was working, and I was sure Sawayaka was crawling with people hoping to be seated for dinner. I texted him earlier to let him know I wouldn't come by, and he was sad he wouldn't see me. I smiled as I remembered his sweet text. I was a lucky girl, living with a string of bad luck.

"Have you been inside yet? I hear it's stunning."

I glanced sideways at her and she laughed.

"I'm serious. He owns the whole building. He was originally going to put his restaurant on the ground floor, but some analysts told him that the main street area would be better for business. It was in the paper." She pulled around to Etsuko's block and stopped the car in front of her apartment building. My neck began to sweat. "So anyway, I heard he hired some famous Tokyo architect to design the inside. It has a bedroom, a huge kitchen, and a spa bathroom." She raised her eyebrows at me. "I'm sure you'll be knocked over by it when you finally see it."

"Probably has central heat and air too," I whispered, thinking about him being in that apartment every day, warm and toasty, eating home cooked meals and drinking fancy French wine while I was freezing and starving at home. I knew that if I told him what I was dealing with, he'd let me stay with him, but then what about Mom? I couldn't leave her in the house alone with no heat. And forcing him to take me in when our relationship was so new did not sound like a good idea. Anyway, I promised Mom I wouldn't say anything, so I wouldn't.

I swallowed in a dry throat while gazing up at Etsuko's building. "Is this where we're going?"

"Yep. She's my last stop for the day. You'll like Mrs. Murata. She's a peach, and I believe she'll take you up on your offer of work too. Her oldest son lives in the United States and her youngest lives in Singapore, so she doesn't have any family to come take care of her. I heard she has a relationship with the young woman who lives across the hall from her, but that's about it."

"A young woman named Etsuko? Do you remember her? She was in school with us, two years behind."

"I thought she looked familiar the last time I met her! Well, good, I'm glad you know her." Akiko tried to exit the car, but I grabbed her arm.

"Wait. Listen. I *knew* Etsuko. Her family is the one that owns Izakaya Jūshi, a few blocks from here."

"Yeah, I know it." Akiko's eyebrows drew inward.

"She died two nights ago. Killed in her apartment. She was a new friend of mine." My voice wavered as I remembered her body on the floor.

"Oh my god," Akiko gasped, her hand flying to her mouth.

"I was there, with Yasahiro. We went to the izakaya on a date, and Etsuko's brother asked us to check on her since we were leaving already. We found her dead in her apartment, and the door was busted." I looked down at my hands clenched together. "I haven't told anyone about it because Goro is investigating. I'm sure the news will leak in a day or two, though. Her boyfriend is the prime suspect. And I really liked him."

I inhaled slowly and exhaled everything from my lungs.

"Mei, you've been through so much lately. I had no idea."

I shook my head, keeping my eyes closed. "Not as much as Etsuko."

"Can you come in with me?" Akiko squeezed my arm, and I opened my eyes.

"Yeah. Yeah, I can. I just wanted to let you know before we step foot in the building."

Inside, the door to Etsuko's apartment was boarded up with caution tape crisscrossed over the frame, and as I suspected, we knocked on the apartment right across the hall.

A little old lady, hunched over and walking with a cane, opened the door and smiled at us both.

"Miss Kano, come in, come in. Who did you bring with you today?" She beckoned us in, and we entered into a disheveled apartment, old magazines were piled against every surface, Imari dishware was stacked on every table, and the TV was blasting at a thousand decibels. Akiko blinked a few times and reached for the TV remote to turn it down.

"This is my good friend, Mei Yamagawa. I think you know her mother, Tsukiko Yamagawa."

Murata's eyes, clouded over as they were, widened in recognition. "I knew your mother when she was just a little girl. My husband and I owned a little tea and cake shop, and she and her friends would come in every Friday to treat themselves after a long week of classes." She grabbed my hand and patted it, looking up into my eyes. "You're a skinny thing. I thought your mother was a famous chef now. Don't you eat?"

Akiko hushed her, while I laughed. I liked this woman. She had the directness of someone who didn't give a damn about polite society anymore. She must have been in her late eighties if she knew my mom when she was younger.

"I love to eat, actually. I'm dating a chef and he loves to feed me," I said, glancing at Akiko who was unloading all her nurse stuff onto the table. I assumed these things were stethoscopes and blood pressure monitors, but I was horrible at remembering technical names of things, especially in medicine. "But it's winter, and food can be hard to come by."

"Mrs. Murata, come sit down. Let's check your vitals and we'll talk." Akiko didn't get up to help Murata make it to the couch. She watched the old lady cross the room and sit down on her own. "Your mobility looks good. Are you making it out to walk?"

"It's difficult to make it up and down the stairs now, but yes, a few times per week."

They talked between them about Murata's heart rate, blood pressure, and blood sugar levels, and Akiko asked Murata's permission if she could discuss her health with me in the room.

"Of course. I don't care," she said, waving her arm at me. "I have some diabetes. It's nothing much."

"Some diabetes?" I asked, with a laugh. "I thought you either had it or you don't."

"Well, if she stays away from sweets and takes good care of herself, she's fine. She barely needs insulin." Akiko draped her stethoscope around her neck. "Mrs. Murata? I brought Mei by here today because she's looking for some part time work. Her job in Tokyo downsized and now she's living at home with her mom."

"What a lucky woman your mom is! To have her daughter at home again." She rubbed her hands together. "My sons left me here with no help. I should have had daughters."

"Mei was wondering if you need some assistance around the house? Or to get to appointments or go for walks?"

"I'm hoping to help a few people per week," I said, picking up the conversation, "in order to assist my mom with the monthly bills. Our barn burned down about a month ago and our budget has been tight since then."

"I heard about this fire! A shame to lose so much over a space heater."

Akiko lowered her eyes and busied herself with her bag.

"It is a shame indeed," I said, agreeing with her. "If you need any help, I'm charging 900 yen per hour, and I can even run to the store for you and pick up groceries. I can do anything you need help with. I was a project manager for five years, and I have a degree in business, so I'm excellent at keeping schedules and delegating tasks if need be."

Murata looked around her apartment, slowly cataloging the contents as her gaze landed on everything within sight.

"I'm not sure how many years I have left on this earth. At ninety-three, I figure another five or so."

Ninety-three! I guessed wrong.

"You don't look a day over forty!" I winked at her. "How can you possibly be twice that age?"

She laughed. "You're hired if you can continue flattering an old woman like me." She sighed, her shoulders hunching over even more. "I want to clean this place up so I can have friends over if I want to, and I go to the doctor often, and I need help getting up and down the stairs. Could you do all that?"

Inside, I melted into a puddle of relief. "I have one other client that needs me a few mornings to help him, but I could come here in the afternoons, if that would work?"

"If you could come Monday through Thursday afternoons that would be good. I'm sure I have enough work for you. I used to have the help of the sweet young woman across the hall, but she died two days ago." Murata shook her head and Akiko touched her knee. "I've been broken up since then. It was a happy thing for you both to be here today."

Monday through Thursday? That would be my best gig yet! I tried not to jump up and down.

"I knew Etsuko. My boyfriend and I were the ones that found her on Sunday." I shook my head to clear the image of her on the floor. "She was a sweet, young woman."

"People that age are not supposed to die before people like me. She was a good person, but I had reason to believe something was going on with her."

This straightened me up and I glanced at Akiko. "Why do you say that?"

"She had a regular boyfriend, but then she had men who

would come and go from her apartment at odd hours. I sleep on a strange shift, never sleeping deeply except for an hour or two here and there every night. So I would be here in the living room and I could hear these men come and go. One came a lot, at least twice per week. I asked Etsuko about him a few times, but she told me he was just a friend. She often said how much she loved her boyfriend, Hisashi, so I didn't think too much about the other men. I took her at her word."

Thoughts churned in my head like a frothy, winter ocean. So, maybe she hadn't been as loyal to Hisashi as I had thought but instead had several lovers. I imagined a fight between Etsuko and a lover, a tall man, dark and handsome. But no, if anything, she would have fought with Hisashi. They had been together forever, and if she had cheated, could he have been angry enough to kill her? Had she cheated on him? I wasn't sure. Wouldn't she have broken up with Hisashi if she wanted to date someone else? He lived far enough away for that to have been a possibility. What had she done to deserve to die? There must have been something big at stake. Something... A debt? A secret? I kept coming back to money in my head. Why was that?

"Mei! Helllllooooooooooo!" Akiko said, waving her hands in front of my face. "You're so spacey sometimes."

"I'm a compulsive daydreamer. I was just thinking about Etsuko and wondering what happened to her. Did the police come by to talk to you?"

Murata stood up and stretched. "No. But they might have come while I was out. I'm not sure."

I stood up to join her as Akiko did. "How about I come by tomorrow afternoon around 14:00? I'll start on cleaning up your stuff here and my friend Goro can come by and ask you questions about Etsuko."

"Goro Hokichi? I knew his mother when she was a kid too. Wasn't she friends with your mom?" Murata hobbled to the door.

I smiled, thinking of my mom and Chiyo, best friends forever.

"Yep. They're still good friends. Goro is a police officer now, and he's looking after Etsuko's case."

"Okay then. I'll see you both tomorrow."

We all bowed to each other at the door, as Murata returned to the TV and turned up the volume.

I had a good lead for Goro! Tomorrow, we'd start gathering evidence.

CHAPTER
EIGHT

I returned home at 18:00 from my day out with Akiko. She had to drop paperwork off at her office, and I tagged along because why would I turn down a free ride home? I wouldn't. Not when it was -1°C outside.

The inside of the house was frigid and dark, and my instincts were on high alert as the door creaked open.

"Mom?" I called out. Mimoji came darting out of the kitchen, and I jumped so high I almost hit my head on the ceiling.

"In the kitchen!"

Once my heart rate returned to normal, I dropped my bag next to the kotatsu and headed into the kitchen. Mom was cooking by candlelight, the smell of seared beef wafting through the cold kitchen, and rice cooking in the rice cooker.

"This is the last of Yasahiro's food, but I brought home leftovers from the school today that we can eat tomorrow." She stirred the beef stew in the pan and added a little water. "Sorry. I know it's not much food, but at least we're eating every day, and we have some rice, too. We'll make it."

I didn't want to complain that my stomach was eating itself most days because I'm sure Mom felt the exact same way. But the shock on Akiko's face said more than the mirror and my baggy clothes did. I was the thinnest I had ever been in my life, and not willingly. Tons of women would diet and exercise like crazy to achieve the results I had, but I knew it wasn't healthy. I *felt* that it wasn't healthy. I couldn't wait for our life to be more stable.

"Are we not turning on the lights now?" I asked, gesturing to the candle.

"No. Only essentials like the fridge and rice cooker. Gas is cheaper." Mom turned off the stove and spooned the beef and rice into bowls for us, and we took them to the kotatsu. "We can use the kotatsu for an hour and then boil water for the water bottles and get in bed. I know it's early, but at least this way we can keep each other warm."

Mom smiled at me, a genuinely happy smile that I was there to keep her warm. Guilt pressed down on me like a tractor on fresh soil. She wouldn't have even been in this mess if I hadn't been there.

"So, I've done the numbers, and we can keep this going and buy groceries next week if we sell the car."

I stopped my spoon halfway from my bowl to my mouth. "You're going to sell the car?"

Oh god, I loved cars. *Loved them.* They were the ultimate luxury in Japan, and I had this sick talent of being able to spot a car's make, model, and year from a hundred meters away. When I lived in Tokyo, I would go to the car show every year and drool over all the new models and the concept cars. I wasn't into racing or anything, but for some reason, cars appealed to me. Mom's Toyota, a ten-year-old Corolla, was in good shape and would fetch her a fair amount of yen, but selling it? That was one of the last things I wanted to see go.

"There's a man I work with at Midori Sankaku who's offered to buy it. I don't need it. Especially now that you're home and I don't have to drive to the city. A bus pass for both of us will be affordable and we don't have to walk far to the bus stop." Mom glanced at me, and I was sure my face was the picture of misery. "Don't be upset, Mei. I know how much you like cars. I was thinking I'd buy a newer used car in the spring. Once—"

"We get the check from the insurance company," I chimed in and sighed. "Why do I feel like it will never come?"

"It will. You should be more positive."

Humph. Me? More positive? Fine.

I ate the rest of the meal and told Mom all about my new clients, and she was so pleased, she laughed and clapped her hands.

"This is a great idea. You should have Kumi design fliers for you and put them up everywhere. I bet you'd snag enough clients in no time."

"I'll have to fit it in amongst all my sleuthing. I'm going to meet up with Goro tomorrow and talk to the woman I met today. She lives across the hall from where Etsuko lived."

Mom raised her eyebrows. "Isn't that funny how that happens?"

"She says she knew you when you were a kid. She owned a cake and tea place on the other side of town?"

"Yomé Murata?" Mom's jaw dropped. "Yes, I know her! Wow. That was a long time ago. I would love to see her. I'll come visit her with you later this week or next."

Though I wasn't warmed by the air, I was encouraged by Mom's enthusiasm and zest for living. Anyone else would be depressed as hell with the situation we were in (I was, that's for sure) but she soldiered on with no worries. She believed everything would come out fine in the end whereas I feared the worst.

When we climbed into our bed with the hot water bottles, I burrowed down under the covers and hoped Mom was right. I had a new job to work at, a murder to solve, and hopefully my nose wouldn't get frostbite in the middle of the night.

Welcome to your new normal, Mei.

CHAPTER
NINE

woke up on Wednesday morning, and the fingers of my right hand and my nose were numb. I couldn't feel them. It was time to start sleeping with gloves on because I couldn't be trusted to keep my hands under the blankets during the night, but I wasn't sure what to do about my face. If only I'd had a ski mask, I could've slept in that. I laughed at this thought. I wasn't a particularly good sleeper to begin with, and all the sleeping restrictions lately — Mom sleeping with me, the clothes, the lack of white noise, and the middle of the night wake-ups — meant I was running on very little rest along with limited calories.

I cupped my hands over my mouth and nose and breathed hot air into them for a few breaths before pulling the covers up over my head and sandwiching my fingers between my legs. It was dark and somewhat warm in my cave of covers. Down at the bottom of the bed, Mimoji was circled into a lump of fur, sleeping away. Trying not to wake him, I wedged my feet up against his butt and sighed.

I wondered what Yasahiro was doing right now. Was he in his warm bed? Or had he already woken up and started making himself breakfast? How had he even owned that whole building?

He came from a family of soy farmers, and I doubted that his family made much more money than we did. How did he afford his fancy schooling in Paris? How had he made enough money to own a whole building and a restaurant? I didn't suspect him of any wrongdoing or anything, but I was really curious about how he made his money, if only so I could learn how to do it myself.

I hadn't seen him since Sunday night when we found Etsuko in her apartment. We'd texted all day every day since then, but no calls or visits. I wanted to visit him, but I also wanted to start working. I couldn't find work if I was hanging out with him doing nothing but sponging off his generosity. I couldn't help my new clients if I was sitting in his restaurant's kitchen making out with him.

Closing my eyes, the kiss came back to me like a punch to the gut. It had been a kiss of passion, a kiss of possession. I'd never been kissed like that before. Tama was a good kisser, as good as any Japanese boy who had a little practice. We were worked so hard as kids to go to school and get good grades that there was no time for dating. Kissing was not the norm in Japan either. It was a new thing within the last two generations, and Yasahiro was probably so good at kissing because he didn't practice it here. He had learned about love abroad. Would I be able to keep up? A rush of heat flowed through me from my toes, up my legs to my belly. Mmmm, that was nice. I was being heated by my own dirty thoughts.

Deep breath.

What was I going to do today?

My new schedule stood as this: mornings on Tuesday and Thursdays with Yamida so I could help her visit her physical therapist; Friday mornings with Shigimo; and Monday through Thursday afternoons with Murata where I would clean and we would go for walks. Assuming I spent at least two hours with every client, I should make around 14,000 yen per week in cash. It wasn't much, but it was better than living on nothing.

So that meant I had this morning free. What were my options? I could go to Kutsuro Matsu, soak in a hot bath, and hang out with Kumi. Then I could visit Yasahiro before I went to Murata's. Hopefully, he'd let me sit in the restaurant and use the WiFi so I could check my email and apply for more part-time jobs. I also hoped he'd give us more food to bring home. I believed we had only one egg left and the custard he made for us. Knowing Mom, she'd saved them for me.

I waited until feeling returned to my fingers, and it was 8:00 before I got out of bed. I wrapped myself in a blanket and headed to the kitchen to heat up water for drip coffee. The sink, though, glistened with a sheen of ice on the inside, and the faucet drips were frozen in a dance of blobs.

"No," I cried, reaching for the tap and turning it. Nothing happened, no water, nothing. That was it! I'd had it. I stepped back and kicked at the sink. I kicked so hard, the reverberation of the metal echoed up my cold, aching legs. I yelled at the sink. I swore at it.

Then the tears came.

This wasn't supposed to happen. At the very least we were supposed to have kept basic necessities — some warmth from the kotatsu, electricity, and water. I couldn't live like this.

I sniffed up and looked around the kitchen, finding a note Mom left on the counter. *"The pipes are frozen in the kitchen, but the bathroom is better insulated and the water is flowing there. Please fill up all the empty water bottles you can find. Keep the sink running in the bathroom. I've fixed the toilet so it'll always run until we're back above freezing again. Love, Mom."*

I closed my eyes and counted to ten, letting the anger, fear, and sadness dissipate. Mom and I would make it through this. I knew we would.

I filled up the empty water bottles in the bathroom, made coffee and ate the custard, dressed, and headed into town, angling my hand-knit-covered head into the frigid wind. Kutsuro Matsu was hopping with people, a van parked outside on the street awaiting its charges who were bathing inside, their voices bouncing around the tiled washroom.

"What's with all the people?" I asked Kumi, working the front desk. She tackled me with a hug, and I stumbled, surprised, before returning the hug, tightening my arms around her.

I glanced up at the loft space above the bathing area, and Chiyo looked down at me. It was her job to sit up there and make sure that both sides of the bathhouse, men on their side and women on theirs, behaved. "You're our new hero, Mei," she said, nodding her head at me.

"Goro said you had such great ideas of how to help find the person who killed Etsuko," Kumi said, pulling away from me. "The police have been going through her mail, email, and phone looking for whomever she was with." She shook her head, slowly, her eyes wide. "I don't believe Hisashi could kill her. He loved her so much." Kumi's voice broke. "You saw it, right?"

"I did." My chest lightened with heartache. "They both loved each other. Anyone could tell."

"What do you think? Who killed her?"

Kumi's face was round and open, interested in hearing what I thought. I took off my coat since the bathhouse was hot. With the extra bodies in the building, the air was rich with steam.

"You're not going to like what I've found out already. I met her neighbor across the hall yesterday, and I plan to talk with her today too. She said men came and went from Etsuko's apartment."

Kumi's eyes filled with tears, and my heart raced in panic.

"Don't be upset. She was such a sweet person. Even if she was sleeping with a dozen men, which I don't think she was, it doesn't mean she deserved to die."

"You know how this town is," Kumi growled under her breath. "You of all people know."

I swallowed, my stomach a cavern hoping for food each time I opened my mouth.

"I do," I whispered. "I've kept everything quiet to protect Mom, protect Akiko." I quickly glanced up at Chiyo, but she didn't hear me. She was engrossed in a magazine. If she knew the situation Mom and I were in at home, she would've lost her mind.

Kumi grabbed my hand and squeezed. She was one of the only people that understood our predicament.

"I hope I can go talk to Hisashi soon. If the police will let me. And I'll do what I can to protect Etsuko and her family, too. I promise. I don't know how much of a role I'll play in this investigation, but I'll do my best."

Kumi nodded and hugged me again. This time, I melted into her warmth for a long moment. I was so rarely hugged, I took what I could.

"Come sit with me and tell me what you've been up to until these people leave. I know you don't want to bathe with too many strangers."

"Great," I said, sighing in relief. "Oh, and I need some help with fliers and business cards. I've started my own business! But I have no money for these things."

She squeezed my waist as she directed me to her computer. "No worries. I can work miracles."

CHAPTER
TEN

Eating lunch in the kitchen at Sawayaka, surrounded by bustling chefs, sizzling pans, and cracking plates, was not what I had planned for today. I sipped on hot noodle soup with fish and pork, trying to eat slowly, so as not to shock my system. The bowl contained at least three meals in one, and my body only had the custard for breakfast. I'd be lucky if I were able to eat all of it. I became full at the slightest provocation nowadays. I used to be able to eat an entire bowl of ramen in one sitting! Not anymore.

I could've browsed on my phone and read articles online or read my book while I ate, but I opted for watching Yasahiro cook and work his way around the kitchen. He had such an ease about him like he was born to run a kitchen. When I thought of the cooking shows I watched on television (when we actually turned on the TV), they were about wives making bento lunches for their husbands. *"I can't wait to get married and have my wife make my lunches every day,"* said one coworker looking longingly at his friend's lunch. I usually turned the channel right then. I always believed men should make their own damned lunches, and women should work right alongside them. Japan could be so backward sometimes. And I was a horrible cook and afraid of setting things on fire for the obvious reason that I was pushed into a fire pit as a kid and now have scars along my back.

Imagine my surprise when Yasahiro asked to date me. Me! Of all people. Me who can't cook. Me who had no job. Me.

The last of the cooked orders were delivered out the door, calming the action in the kitchen, and the staff settled into the last thirty minutes of lunch. Ana, the hostess out in the main area, wouldn't do any more seatings, and everyone would start cleaning and winding down.

Yasahiro came over and stood next to me, leaning his lower back on the island.

"How's lunch?" He checked my bowl, frowning. "Do you not like it?"

"I love it," I said, covering my noodle-filled mouth with my hand. "I'm eating slowly. It's a lot of food."

He ran his fingers down the length of my arm to my free hand. "You've lost more weight," he whispered. "Keep eating."

"It's fine—"

"It's not fine. You're half the size you were when I met you two months ago."

He *had* noticed, and I was stupid enough to think I could hide my skinny body behind baggy clothes. I blushed as I caught one of the dishwashers looking at us. "Please, Yasahiro. Not here."

He cleared his throat. "What do you have planned for this afternoon?"

I sighed, grateful he'd moved on. "I thought I'd stay here and work on my computer for a bit. I was going to submit some resumes and do research on other places to apply for a job. Then I have to go over to Etsuko's old building and meet up with Mrs. Murata."

"She's one of your new clients, right?"

I nodded as I slurped up more noodles and ate a slice of juicy, sweet and savory pork. I closed my eyes and savored every bite. Why did I have to become a starving artist to appreciate good, traditional Japanese cooking? I wished I could slap my past self for being an idiot and eating the junk I ate before meeting Yasahiro.

"Then I have an idea. Not that I don't love spending time with you here, but I have some end of year work to do. Why don't you come back to my place with me and stay there?"

My blood pressure dropped and my vision tunneled. What? Back to his place? I must've turned a sickly shade of white because his face dropped in confusion.

"Do you not want to take this step, Mei?" His voice plummeted to a whisper as he reached into his chef's coat and pulled out a single key on a red cat keychain.

My heart beat so fast I had to press my hand to my chest. I was grateful the kitchen was too noisy for anyone to notice my distress.

"I wanted to give you this key tomorrow on our date, but it's been burning a hole in my pocket all day."

I stared up at him, at his searching eyes, the tiny scar in his eyebrow, his broad chin, then at the key. Wasn't this what I'd wanted for the past few weeks? But it felt like cheating, like cutting in a long line, by being handed the key without ever even having been there.

"Bye, Chef Suga!" The men and women who worked in the kitchen filed out the door, waving and calling goodbye, and walking through the empty restaurant. I caught a glimpse of Ana buttoning her coat to go outside before the door swung closed.

Yasahiro waved to them and turned back to me. He sighed, and brushing his fingers on the side of my face, said, "Here come the clouds."

"What?" I was breathless every time he touched me.

"There's a famous photographer, I've forgotten his name, who took thousands of photos of Mount Fuji throughout his entire life. He used to say he was in love with Mount Fuji, going so far as to call it Fuji-ko, like the mountain was his wife." Yasahiro pulled over another stool to sit next to me, and I turned to face him. "He would say, 'I married such a fickle woman because I can never tell what mood Fuji-ko will be in today.'" Yasahiro's lips quirked. "I saw that painting of Mount Fuji in the bathhouse, and I just knew that you painted that fickle mountain because you identified with it. Cloudy and misty one moment. Clear and bright, shining like a diamond another."

"I don't know what to say."

He took my hand in his. "It's a compliment. I like complex women. I like that you keep me on my toes, that you don't take anything for granted. I never know what to expect with you, at least not yet. I hope to have lots more time to learn all your little quirks." He leaned into me, and I stayed very still, absolutely shocked by his words. I'd never been compared to Mount Fuji, our greatest national treasure, and I didn't feel I deserved that kind of a compliment. He dragged his nose along my cheek to my ear and kissed to my jawline. I scrunched up and smiled, giggling at the contact.

He pulled away and smiled at me. "I want you to have the key. I want you to have access to me, whenever you want it. Access to my space. I have a computer there, food, internet, a comfortable couch, a big screen TV, everything you could want, and it's in the center of town, so it's a good place for you to go during the day between your elderly clients. If you're there, it gives me an excellent excuse to come home more often too."

He slipped the key into my hand, and I rubbed my finger along the cat charm, my mind in a drastic unbelieving state.

Whatever I did, I must be careful to never overstay my welcome or take too much advantage of this. This... This was a gift from the gods. I should pray at a shrine.

"Say something, Mei. I've never seen you so quiet."

I huffed a laugh. "I talk too much sometimes. I'm speechless.

I've never even been to your place, so I can't believe you'd just give me a key like this."

"I know," he said, standing up and grabbing our coats from the hooks by the door. "So we're going to go there now. Grab your bag. I'll give you a tour, and we'll spend the break there, then you can go on to take care of Mrs. Murata."

I was nervous the whole drive to his apartment, though we were in the car for only five minutes. He pulled his hatchback into the tiny parking spot, and my stomach flipped over, realizing I was about to go inside, not just bypass the building to go to Izakaya Jūshi.

"The key unlocks both the outer door and the inner one. If I ever end up renting out the bottom space, I'll change the lock on the outer door." He gestured to me to open it, so I stuck the key in and turned. The door swung open and a light came on. The space inside the door had a cement floor and painted red walls with dark wood stairs that led up. A gray steel door to the right must have led to the retail space.

I climbed the stairs to a large landing where Yasahiro stored a bike hanging from the ceiling and a shovel and snow boots against the wall opposite the door. Snow would come any day. A set of stairs led away and up another level.

"That leads to a deck. It's perfect in the summer. You can see Mount Fuji." He smiled at me, and I looked away.

I slipped the key into the lock and opened the inner door. A light came on inside, and I caught my breath. Akiko was right. His place was stunning.

"Go on," he said, prompting me to step foot inside. The stone floor right inside the door was dark, almost black slate. I took off my boots and my socked feet on the floor were warm.

"Ah! The floor is warm!" I hadn't felt a warm floor in months. My feet were blocks of ice at home.

"Radiant heating. The warm floor in the bathroom is fantastic in the winter." He took my coat, opened a cabinet over a row of cubbies on the wall, and hung up my coat. I felt like an uneducated farm girl gawking at his loft apartment like I'd never seen luxury before.

To the right, windows faced the street and a large couch wrapped around the space in front of a giant flatscreen TV mounted on the wall.

"This here raises and lowers the window screens, if it gets too sunny or you want privacy." He pointed to a flat panel on the wall to the left of the cubbies, a home control system with a touch screen. He navigated to a screen labeled "Window Screens" and lowered them down halfway.

My mouth must've been on the floor because he laughed. "Heat, lights, screens, all of that is in here."

To the left was a massive kitchen with red painted walls a shade darker than the hallway. Pots hung from a contraption over the island around a hood and a giant stove. Cabinets and a sink were on the opposite wall with a dishwasher. A dining table covered the space between the couch and the kitchen island. The perfect place for someone like him to entertain a dozen guests.

He took my hand and dragged me towards the kitchen. "Stove with the built-in grill and microwave are here. Dry foods are in these cabinets," he said, waving his hand over the dark cabinets to the right of the sink. "Plates and glasses are here." He waved to the left of the sink. "This is the pantry." He opened an entire room off the kitchen, and the shelves inside were filled with food. I nearly burst into tears but caught myself with an intake of breath. "Help yourself to whatever you want. The fridge..." was next to the pantry. He opened the door and it was well-stocked, but not too much. He knew how long vegetables and meat kept.

"Now, here's the bathroom." He opened the door to the right of the kitchen and the spa bathroom Akiko boasted about was dark, stainless steel, and masculine. It was clean, too, which was unexpected. The bathroom even had its own closet for linens.

Our bathroom at home was barely the size of a small closet. But this had a deep tub, shower, toilet, double sinks, the works.

"My bedroom is through here." He pointed to the door adjacent to the bathroom. "You can enter it via the bathroom or the other door in the kitchen."

I hesitated for a moment before turning the door handle and stepping into his private space. He had a queen-sized bed with a fluffy duvet, a large closet, another TV mounted on the wall, a dresser, and bedside tables. Over the bed hung framed prints of Paris. I scanned the photos in the room, cities I knew he'd been to: Amsterdam, Singapore, San Francisco, New York, Rio. I was grateful there were no lingering photos of Amanda. Had he thrown them away? Or were they never there to begin with? I wasn't sure, but I believed he had this place renovated after they broke up, so my guess was she had never been here, in photos or otherwise.

"Wow," I whispered.

He nodded, pursing his lips. "Okay, I'll take 'wow.'" He opened the door and walked out to the kitchen, setting his wallet on the island and opening the fridge. But I stayed in his room and sat down on his bed. I wanted to climb in and bury myself under the covers.

He returned with a glass of water for each of us.

"You look stunned."

"I am," I said, sipping and glancing around the room again. "How does the son of a soy farmer afford a place like this? Especially after owning a restaurant."

He sat down next to me. "Investments. Lots of them. Real estate is my other hobby. I'm almost thirty, and I've sunk every yen I've ever had into real estate, buying and selling until I had enough money I didn't know what to do with it. Amanda used to just help herself to whatever she wanted from me." He plucked at the fabric of his pants. "And honestly, I didn't mind. I loved her and I wanted to see her comfortable and happy." Sipping from his glass, he was silent, thinking. "I want the same for you. I've never seen anyone deny my help as much as you do, which only makes me try harder."

"I'm sorry I'm so difficult—"

"Don't apologize."

"Don't interrupt. I wasn't finished." I smacked him on the arm, and he laughed before putting on a mask of mock seriousness.

"I was taught from childhood never to impose, never to show my needs to others. It's a hard habit to break." I stopped and opened my mouth again to tell him about the state of my home, but I couldn't. I couldn't confess without Mom's permission. And once again, I felt like a traitor — to Mom for wanting to blab and to him for not saying something.

"Paris and France taught me a lot, broke me of some bad habits. My parents are always aghast at my actions." He laughed again and shook his head.

"Doesn't that bother you?"

"Not anymore." He nudged my arm with his elbow. "Go. Get a feel for the place. Get comfortable."

I started in his bedroom, ambling through the photos on his dresser, opening the closet doors, and lifting up the sheets on the bed. He watched me as I made my way into the kitchen.

"No tatami anywhere?" I twirled around once, my socks and the shiny hardwood floor making it easy to dance.

"Nope," he said from the bedroom. "I like European modern."

I began to hum and then sing the latest pop song stuck in my head, opening the cabinets in the kitchen, finding the utensils, glasses, and dishware. I took the glass he gave me and refilled it with water from the fridge. I was thirsty again now that I was warm from my head down to my toes. In the bathroom, I grabbed a towel from the linen closet and added it to the towel bar next to his. That one was mine.

"I didn't know you could sing," Yasahiro called from the bedroom. "You have a beautiful voice."

I stammered as I thanked him, and I was glad he couldn't see me from where he was. "I'm a blast at karaoke, but it's been forever since I last went."

In the living room, I stood and looked out the window. He had a view of the street and people out and about. A convenience store was just down the block, a grocer, and a dry cleaner. Plus Izakaya Jūshi was in the opposite direction.

I glanced at the clock and the readout read 14:30. I had thirty more minutes to enjoy the heat and quiet of Yasahiro's apartment, so I needed to pick the best way to do that. I searched around the couch and found a basket of blankets on the far side.

Picking up a soft, heavy blanket and holding the warm fabric in my arms, I stood so he could see me from the bedroom.

"Come join me?"

It was the right idea. His face split into a smile, and he padded across the apartment to meet me. I gestured to the corner of the couch, he sat, and I sat between his legs, pressed my back to his front, and pulled the blanket over us. Reaching back, he fit his fingers between mine, and I cradled his arm to my chest, laying my head into the crook of his shoulder. He was so warm, and the beat of his heart was strong and steady under my ear.

"Mmmm. Good idea, Mei. But it'll be hard to leave this. You know, if you want to stay the night with me, you can, anytime."

I smiled because I was ready to take that leap. I cared for him, and I trusted him to take good care of me.

"Soon. We have thirty minutes. Tell me more about Italy. Do they really drink alcohol all day there?"

He sighed in flashback ecstasy. "They eat and drink all day long if they can." He pulled my arm up and ran his fingers down the length of it, resting my hand on his neck. "Let me tell you about the time I spent in Florence..."

CHAPTER
ELEVEN

Murata's apartment was warm and stuffy as I sorted through the first pile of magazines and newspapers she directed me to. In anticipation of a large amount of recycling, Murata had handed me the recycling guidelines for Chikata as I walked through the door. Of course, I knew them by heart, but it was sweet she thought I needed them.

Trash and recycling in Japan were a serious business. We were an island nation, and we only had so much space to put waste. Everything was either recycled or burned. Thankfully, Murata had many of the required recycling bags, but I'd have to pick up more the next day before coming over. They were sold in the local convenience stores, and she'd cover the cost. I had to bag her old magazines and newspapers and bring them all downstairs to the paper bins for her apartment building.

"I would have done it myself," she said to me as I sorted through her paper collection. "But they were so heavy. I used to drag them down the stairs, but the bags ripped too often. So I gave up and just let them pile up."

"Why don't you stop the deliveries?"

"Crazy girl! I actually *read* them, you know?" She smacked

me playfully on my shoulder. "I don't have a computer so this is the only way I stay up to date on anything."

I knelt down as there was a knock on the door. "Do you want me to get that?" I gestured at the door but she shook her head. "They'll stop distributing paper eventually, though, Mrs. Murata. You can't deny technology forever."

She hobbled to the door. "Hopefully, they'll keep coming until I'm dead."

"Well, isn't that cheerful?" Sheesh. The whole elderly mindset was so final, but I kind of enjoyed the raw reality. There was something comforting about knowing you only had so much time left, so you made the most of it. This was nothing like the terrifying feeling of seeing your life come to an end at the age of twenty-six. I stared into space, the flames in the barn swirling around me. *"You had a second chance, and look what you did with it. Nothing." I'm doing something now, Tama.*

Shaking away the daydream, I counted the papers in the stack in front of me. Murata wanted to clean up her place so she could entertain and see people in her last years, and I admired that. I was happy to help her.

She opened the door, and I heard Goro on the other side introduce himself and ask to enter.

"Look at how big you are now! I remember when you were just a young boy, running and playing in the park with your friends." Murata smiled, doting on Goro as his crooked grin grew. "And now you're a police officer. How do you like your job?"

Goro bowed to her. "I like it very well, Mrs. Murata. Thanks for letting me come by to talk to you." He angled past Murata and nodded to me. "Mei, I see you're busy."

I nodded to him. "I am. She has a lot of recycling to do."

"I'm also baking bread in the kitchen, so please come with me." She waved at Goro to follow her, and he did after unlacing and kicking off his shoes at the door.

I had a good view of the kitchen from my spot, but I kept

busy with sorting and bagging, stacking bags of paper by the door. I wanted to make sure I had enough to take down in a few trips without overloading the bins so other people couldn't use them. When this was done, I'd vacuum and dust.

"You knew Etsuko a long time, isn't that right?" Goro asked, pulling out his notebook. I smiled at the familiar gesture. He was a fastidious note taker.

"She lived across the hall from me for the past five years. Got the place when her parents started employing her full-time at the izakaya. Such a wonderful family." I glanced up to see her shake her head as she lifted a cloth from a bowl. "The funeral is tomorrow. Will you be there?"

"I will indeed." Goro nodded my way. "Will you be there, Mei?"

"I plan to be. I have to help another client get to her physical therapy appointment, but I can come after." Whatever I earned here today would go into an envelope for the funeral tomorrow. Easy come, easy go. "Then I can come back here in the afternoon. Mrs. Murata, please let me know if you need help getting to and from the funeral."

"Sure, Mei." She floured the surface of her counter and dumped the bowl of dough onto it, folding and kneading it.

"So tell me more about Etsuko and anything you may know about her… activities."

"Now I don't want to be a gossip," Murata began, "but she had a lot of people coming and going from her place. Her boyfriend was around one weekend per month. Then there were other men I saw, and she had a book club that met every other week."

Goro smiled. "Yes, my wife was a member. She was good friends with Etsuko."

"Then she must know about the men who came and went from there." Murata shook her head and clucked her tongue. "I don't think she was dating any of them because, when I asked her if she had broken up with her boyfriend, she always said no. But that doesn't explain the men I'd run into on the stairs."

"Is that it? You'd just run into them on the stairs?" Goro's pen was poised in mid-air.

"No," she said, dipping her head. "I would hear them come and go and peek through my peephole." She waved at the door. "Once I heard arguing in the hall. Etsuko said, 'You can't keep coming up to my apartment so often. People will notice.' But that was our landlord, always in his fancy suit. Maybe she was behind on the rent or something. I only ever caught sight of the other men. Once or twice, in passing."

Hmmm, I contemplated this as Murata kneaded the dough on the counter. Punch, slap, turn, punch, slap, turn. Maybe Etsuko didn't pay her rent on time like her bills? I bet Goro would look into it. But what about Hisashi? Was she cheating on him? Did he kill her because she was unfaithful? I tried to imagine the situation in my head, and I couldn't. I could usually daydream up any situation, but this murder scene refused to stick no matter how hard I tried.

"If you can describe any of the other men, I'll have a sketch artist come by and ask you questions. Would that be all right?"

"Sure," she said, pausing and throwing more flour on the dough. "I want to help out. She was such a sweet girl. Whatever she was into, it didn't matter to me."

"What do you mean?"

"Well, maybe she was running a brothel? Or maybe a gambling ring or something?" Murata poked Goro's arm with her floury finger.

He looked over at me when Murata returned to her dough and rolled his eyes. I smiled back as I set another stack of bagged paper by the door.

"It's probably a lot less sinister than that," he assured her.

"Well, she's dead, isn't she?" Murata countered, and both of our smiles fell.

"Yes. That's very true." He cleared his throat. "What else can you remember?"

Murata paused for a moment, turning her eyes to the ceiling before picking up her dough and plopping it into the bowl again.

"There was one other thing. I heard her mention a sleeping fox quite a few times. *Ne kitsune. Ne kitsune.* She said the phrase quite a few times. 'I'm grateful for *ne kitsune.*' She said that to one of the men once. Who's grateful for sleeping foxes? Unless you're superstitious and hope those foxes don't possess you."

She laughed at her own joke and turned the temperature dial on her oven. Goro took notes, nodding but not giving away any thoughts.

"Can you describe any of the men who left her apartment?"

"Yes. Two of them." She dusted off her hands. "They were both young and good looking." She shrugged her shoulders. "You know young men these days. The crazy hair, skinny clothes, and soft spoken ways. They're all the same."

I tried not to laugh. Our generation must have been so confusing to these older folks. I came out of high school relatively moderate, never having gotten into any of the Tokyo fashion trends or body modifications that were so popular now, but plenty of my friends had money to burn on those hobbies. Weekends in Shinjuku, parading around and letting foreigners take their pictures. It was fun but didn't last.

"Hmmm," Goro said, chewing on the end of his pen. "I'll have to search on this one."

Me too. As soon as I got to some WiFi, I was going to start searching for sleeping foxes.

"Notice anything else?" Goro asked as he folded up his notebook and pen. He'd obviously hit the end of his questioning.

"Just the crazy amount of bento boxes that girl loved. I swear she got more every week. I have a box of them addressed to her," she said, waving at a cardboard box in the corner. We both glanced at it, and there was nothing distinctive about it except the stamp on the outside, "Bento Box - 12 ct." I remembered the collection of bento boxes in Etsuko's apartment, lying on the floor around her body and on shelves, undisturbed. She certainly seemed to love them.

"I'll have someone come by and pick that up soon." Goro nodded and stored his notebook in his pocket.

I couldn't delay any longer on my job. "I'm going to take these down to the bins," I said, gesturing at the piles by the door. "I'll be in and out."

I would've loved to stay and hear more of what they had to talk about, but I slipped on my shoes and grabbed a stack of bags, holding the door open with my hip. I glanced over at Etsuko's doorway before I descended the stairs. I imagined her, out on the landing, talking to some hip, young man. Had she been flirting when she said she was thankful for sleeping foxes? What did that have to do with him? And did this have anything to do with her murder?

On the first floor, I found the room for trash and recycling and added Murata's bagged paper to the piles already stacked in the room. The property manager would come and move the bundles out to the curb on the proper days.

When I ascended the stairs and entered the apartment, Goro was finishing up.

"Thanks for lending me your time. I really appreciate it. Here's my card. Call me if you think of anything else? Anything. Even tiny details you may think are insignificant will be helpful." Murata took his card in both of her hands and slipped it into her apron.

"Can I help bring those down for you?" He gestured to the piles by the door.

"Sure. Mrs. Murata, I'll be right back up, and then I can vacuum and dust before helping clean the kitchen."

She waved me on and Goro said good-bye as we grabbed the piles, and I followed him down the stairs. We added the bundles to the stacks in the trash room, and Goro stretched his back before sighing.

"I'm not going to lie, Mei, but this is a strange case. No one has any idea why Etsuko would be killed." He ticked off points on his fingers. "She was a great student in school. She was a loyal family member. She worked hard and never paid her bills late. Kumi thought the world of her, and you know how Kumi is." He rubbed at a shadow of a beard on his cheek. "It looks like a crime of passion and Hisashi swears he had no idea. He's been a wreck since we brought him in on Monday. All of our questions don't break him. He says he was on one of the afternoon trains back to Tokyo. That he left, and she was alive, said goodbye to him at the door. His story checks out, too. There was a train ticket purchased and cameras in Tokyo Station captured him getting off the train."

"Then why don't you let him go?"

"We can't," Goro insisted, exasperated. "He's our only suspect. We've checked everything. As far as we can tell, she had no outstanding debts or connections with organized crime..."

My heart skipped a beat. "You don't suppose... Tama?"

"No." He laid his hand on my shoulder. "I don't. Tama and Etsuko only ever saw each other at the izakaya, and even then, they barely ever talked. The izakaya carried the beer of the distributor that Tama knew, but that's about it. Honestly, we don't expect to ever see Tama again. He'll be locked up for good."

"But I'm here and alive. So is Akiko. That wasn't a part of his plan, and it's possible people could come and collect on his debts."

He shrugged his shoulders. "We don't know what his plan was, and there's been no chatter about it anywhere. The Tokyo and Kobe police departments have wiretaps and surveillance. No one batted an eye at his arrest. Knowing Tama, he *thought* he was a lot more important than he really was."

That could've been the case. Tama blew everything out of

proportion. I mean, who kills their former girlfriend because her mother loved her? Only someone totally out of touch with reality.

"Anyway," Goro continued, "there's literally no reason to kill Etsuko."

"There's no reason *we know of*," I stressed. The image of her talking on the phone, adamant and angry, popped into my head. "There must be something. Have you checked her mobile phone? The night we all went out, on Saturday, she took a call and went outside. I remember watching her and she seemed upset to me."

Goro's mouth twisted. "Well... So here's the thing. I definitely suspect her of something because she regularly deleted the call logs on her phone. When we got it, there was no history. We've contacted the phone company and asked for the records but it'll be another day or two."

My scalp prickled, and I hugged myself against the cold of the recycling room. "She was hiding something, whatever it was."

"Let's keep digging. Call me if you think of anything."

We bowed to each other at the front door, and I re-joined Murata in the apartment.

I felt the need to dig even further into Etsuko's life, but I didn't want Murata to think I was a gossip, so I changed the subject.

"Mrs. Murata, I was wondering something," I said, stepping into her kitchen and lifting the towel on the bowl of dough, already rising again. "Could you teach me to make bread?"

Murata raised her eyebrows at me.

"I'm hopeless in the kitchen, and I want to learn how to make a few things. Bread doesn't look too hard."

She laughed, slapping her hand on the counter.

"Baking is harder than cooking," she said, her voice rising in incredulity.

"Well, I believe there's less chance of me setting fire to something if I bake." I lifted my index finger in the air and smiled.

"Indeed," she said, nodding. "Okay. When you come back tomorrow, I'll teach you some basics."

"Thank you," I said, bowing. "I look forward to learning from a master."

"Flattery will get you everywhere with me, Mei." She laughed again and my insides warmed at the sound. "The vacuum is in the hall closet. Get to work."

CHAPTER
TWELVE

The street was dark when I exited Murata's apartment building. Evening descended swiftly in the winter, the sun setting at a ridiculous 16:30 and earlier every day. A cold wind whipped up the street and blew straight through me, turning me to into a walking block of ice. After spending my day warm at the bathhouse, the restaurant, Yasahiro's place, and Murata's apartment, I dreaded returning to the farmhouse because the evening would be as cold as a brick. Plus, we had no food at home.

I pulled my phone from my pocket as I began to walk home. There was a voicemail I missed while cleaning out Murata's paper piles. *"Mei, I've brought home food from work and am going to turn in early tonight. We can go to the funeral tomorrow after I'm home from working at the school. Don't be too late tonight. It's going to be below zero, and we'll need to sleep together again to keep warm."* The voicemail ended, and I checked the number of the caller. She must have called from the landline at work because her mobile phone was turned off. I was only lucky to have mine because of Yasahiro.

I paused on the sidewalk and turned around. I could see

Yasahiro's apartment from here, only two blocks away. Inside, the kitchen light glowed faintly behind the drawn blinds. I knew it was warm and empty in there, but I should go home to Mom. I turned to keep walking. But we'd have more food at home if I wasn't there to eat it. I stopped walking again. What if I spent the early evening at Yasahiro's? I could help myself to some food, sit in the warmth, and then I'd take the bus home around 20:00.

Reaching into my pocket, I closed my gloved hand around the key he had given me. He told me to come to his apartment whenever I wanted to. He told me to make myself comfortable.

But I had just been there. Wouldn't it have been selfish of me to take advantage of this?

It wasn't selfish if he told me to do it, right?

Two people passed me and stared at me. I jolted out of my head and apologized for standing in the middle of the walkway. I must have looked crazy, staring into space.

Screw it. I was going to Yasahiro's.

I turned and hustled to his street, speeding up my legs and trying to keep them from numbing into oblivion.

Inside his apartment, the light came on, and after taking off my boots and coat, I fiddled with the home controls until I found a lighting solution I was happy with. I set my bag on the large dining room table and pulled my keys out. Wrenching the key ring open, I slipped Yasahiro's key and cat keychain on with all my others. There. Now it was semi-permanent.

I'd been carrying my computer around all day and still not done any work, so I pulled it from my bag and turned it on. While it was booting up, I had time to wander around. I grabbed a block of cheese from the fridge, an orange, and some crackers, put them all on a plate and set them next to my computer. I'd love to open a bottle of wine, but I had no idea what to choose from the giant wine rack in the pantry. I resisted the urge to write Yasahiro a note about the food I took. He told me to help myself.

Taking my glass of water with me, I stepped into his

bedroom, running my hand along the soft duvet before coming to his computer desk on the other side of the room. I shuffled through the pieces of paper on his desk until I found what I was looking for, the WiFi password. I smiled at a photo that must be his whole family. He looked five years younger in the photo, and they were all on a cliff near water.

With WiFi access, I turned on music on my computer, ate cheese and crackers, and got to work. I couldn't help glancing up often to take in my surroundings. This was *my boyfriend's apartment*. He *gave me the key*. I smiled like an idiot as I sent out resumes and applied to part-time positions on various contractor websites. Many of the jobs were in Tokyo, but what could I do? I needed work. The 14,000 yen I'd make a week taking care of elderly clients was not going to work for me long-term, though I already loved it. I wished I could parlay it into a full-time job somehow.

Around 18:00, I started to feel sleepy, yawning and stretching, and unable to keep my eyes open. My choices were to figure out Yasahiro's Italian coffee maker or take a nap, neither of which was a good idea. I forced myself to concentrate on my computer and tried Googling "sleeping foxes *ne kitsune*" but all that appeared were adorable photos of sleeping foxes. I scrolled and scrolled, but I didn't see anything even remotely pertaining to something other than furry forest creatures.

I set my head down on my arms. Maybe I could take a nap. Yeah. Yeah, I'd take a thirty-minute nap, get on the bus, and go home to Mom. It wasn't like I slept well at home any way, so I doubted taking a nap now would hinder me falling asleep later.

I glanced behind me to Yasahiro's bedroom. The bed sang to me, *"Come! Sweet tired person, lay your head upon my fluffy, warm pillows"* in an Italian operatic falsetto. How could I resist?

Slipping under the duvet and pulling up the covers, I breathed out a huge sigh of relief. His bed was warm and soft, and it smelled like him too, orange and sandalwood. I pulled the covers up over my shoulder and said to myself, *"There's no way Tama's yakuza will find me here. I'm behind closed and locked doors in a warm house with food and internet."* I burrowed further down in the warmth, yawned and thought, *"Okay. Thirty minutes. That's all you get."*

Darkness.

Flames climb up my legs, the rich scent of gasoline choking air into my lungs. I can't move. Both my legs and arms are held firmly in place, and no matter how hard I jerk my body, I'm stuck. I try to shake the flames off my pants, but they crawl their way up my belly, searing my skin. I open my mouth to scream, but silence swallows my terror.

"Mei?" A dark figure hovers over me. *"I know you said 'soon' but I didn't expect it to be this quick."*

"No."

Cool fingers glided across my forehead, knocking me awake.

"No!" I yelled, slamming my hands upwards and struggling with covers that wrapped around me like a snake around its prey.

"Ow! Mei!"

My eyelids fluttered, trying to bat away sleep, deep sleep, sleep of the kind I hadn't had in weeks. The lights blazed to life, and I threw my hands over my face to prevent the sudden blindness.

"What? Where?" I croaked out. Where the hell was I?

"Mei. Mei!" I twisted and looked out through my hands. Yasahiro stood next to me, next to his bed, that I was in. I dropped my hands but not before wiping sweat from my forehead. "Are you sick?" he asked, coming towards me. I shrunk away, only getting more tangled in the bedsheets and flailing. "Whoa. It's okay. You were dreaming. I heard you say something about fire and Tama." His face fell, his hands out in front of him, trying to calm me like a wild animal.

I blinked a few times, my dream coming back to me. "Tama was over me, smiling at the fire burning my legs." I shoved the blankets off of me, but I found only my unburnt leggings. They were stuck to me with a fine sheen of sweat, though.

"It was just a nightmare," he said, sitting next to me. He hesitantly reached his arm around me, and I stiffened before softening into his embrace. His hand pushed my sweaty hair back from my face, and he rubbed his thumb along my forehead. "You don't feel feverish."

"I'm not sick. I was... warm in bed. I haven't slept like that in ages. Why are you home so early?" I glanced at the clock. What? "Oh no. It's 22:10?" I looked around for confirmation but didn't see anything else. "Oh god. It's late." I scrambled away from him, off the side of the bed, and put my feet on the floor. The sudden change in position caused my head to swirl in a whirlpool. I snapped my hand out to steady myself.

Yasahiro jumped forward and grabbed my arm. "You're worrying me. What happened?"

"I fell asleep. I just wanted to take a nap." I was still half asleep, in a state I liked to call 'sleep inertia,' and with my defenses down, my mouth opened of its own accord. "I wanted to sleep in a warm room and a warm bed, in a place Tama can't find me."

"Warm... bed?" he asked, his eyebrows pulled together. I pushed past him and headed for the kitchen, slapping my cheek to wake me.

"I need to get home. Now." I threw my computer in my bag.

"Wait," he called, running after me. "Do you not have heat at home?"

I closed my eyes and cursed myself before reaching for my boots. "Of course we have heat at home." It was a lie, a total lie I couldn't pull off. One glance at Yasahiro, and he knew.

"You don't have heat at home. No wonder you've looked so pale and gray these past two weeks. Look, I know it's a point of pride to go without heat during the winter, but it's crazy and you know it."

Anger rose in my chest like a lion running after prey. "It's not like I *want* to live without heat, Yasahiro. Life is tough enough living on one, maybe two, meals a day. But I am *poor*," I said, my voice shaking, "and we have no money for anything." His face tightened, his hands balling into fists. I swore at myself. "Take me home."

"No." His voice was as cold as ice. "No. You're not going back there."

Tears jumped into my eyes, as I grabbed my scarf and coat. "Fine. I'll walk and take the bus."

"Mei." He stepped in front of the door. "Why won't you stay here? Why are you so afraid to stay with me?"

The tears I held inside by gritting my teeth flowed down my cheeks, mixing with the sweat from my sleep. "I'm not afraid of you. I'm..." I swiped at the tears on my face. "I want to stay. I want to eat your food, and drink your wine, and sleep with your body next to mine. This place is like paradise. But I can't leave Mom to brave the cold all on her own. If I don't sleep with her at night, she'll freeze all by herself."

Yasahiro swore in English and grabbed his coat. "Of course. Your mom. Let's go."

We dressed quickly, and he ushered me through the door ahead of him, locking his apartment. Outside, his car was already running, so we got in, and he drove me home, silent for almost the entire drive.

"Are you worried about Tama coming back?" he asked, as he made the turn onto our road.

"No." I sighed. "Yes. Kind of. I know he'll be in jail for a long time, but I keep thinking he'll escape somehow or some error will let him get off or some yakuza will show up and collect on his debts. Akiko got a dog because she's worried they'll come for her. Our farmhouse is old, and we're so far from town. I'm afraid someone will come and set fire to it, and we'll burn in our beds in the middle of the night. I flinch awake at every little sound, and my face and hands are usually numb in the morning."

He pulled the car into the driveway and stopped at the house.

"Thanks for taking me home." I reached for the handle and tried to think of how to end the conversation so he didn't think I was a complete loser, but he turned off the engine and got out of the car. I jumped out and followed him.

"Come on," he demanded, waving to the front door. "Open it."

It was no use arguing with him. He'd just take my bag and open the door, or he'd pound on it until Mom woke up. Yasahiro, as I had come to learn, had a keen sense of justice and what was right and wrong. And he wasn't going to rest until the scales were even.

I unlocked the door, and he marched into the cold, dark house. He pointed to his breath freezing in a fog. "Mei, I can *see my breath* in here." He peered at the digital thermometer mounted on the wall. "It's five degrees in here!"

"Shhh. You'll wake Mom." I waved at him, but he brushed past me into the kitchen. I tried to grab his arm and stop him, but he was too quick for me.

He tapped on the ice flow from the faucet in the sink. "You don't even have water in the kitchen! You can't boil water." He crossed to the fridge, and I stood, motionless and helpless. Inside the fridge were two containers from Mom's workplace and the bottles of condiments and that was it. He closed the door and looked in the pantry. "I thought things were better than this."

"Yasahiro, please." I was ready to beg, to plead, to just be left alone. "Mom and I will get through this. We only need a few more weeks."

"Weeks? You won't make it weeks." He came to me and dropped his voice, the tone changed from enraged to soothing. "Go wake your Mom. Pack your bags. You're both coming to my place."

I shook my head, but he wrapped his arms around me and squeezed. "That's enough. No more hiding. I know how ashamed you must be feeling. We're past that now."

"Mei? Yasahiro? What are you doing here?" Mom stood in the doorway to her bedroom, looking at us both. "Mei, I told you not to bring him here."

I pulled myself from Yasahiro's embrace and went to her. "I'm so sorry. So, so sorry, Mom. I can't hide it anymore."

She sighed, my tears finally registering to her.

"We're going to live at Yasahiro's for a while, until we can afford heat and defrost the pipes." I squeezed her shoulder. "Please. I can't live like this."

It felt weak and unappreciative to say that, but it was the truth and I was tired of lying. I wasn't cut out for a winter of no food, sleep, or heat. I could live in a shoebox, but I couldn't do *this* anymore.

Mom and I cried and packed our bags with enough clothes to last a week. Yasahiro waited in the living room, pacing back and forth to keep warm. "My god, I have no idea how you've been living here. How have you been bathing?" he asked as I handed him my suitcase.

"I go to Kutsuro Matsu and bathe there. Mom goes after work most days."

I took Mom's suitcase as she locked the door.

"And I won't be taking charity from you or anyone else," Mom said to Yasahiro as we walked to the car. "I'm only doing this for Mei's sake."

Yasahiro rolled his eyes and popped his trunk. "Will the two of you get in the car already? You're both stubborn as a mountain. Fuji-ko is right," he mumbled as Mom sat in the front seat and shut the door. "And you're not leaving my place until I say so." He pointed his finger at me. "I don't want you blowing your hard earned money on stupid necessities like food and heat. You deserve to spend your money on stuff like nail polish and getting your hair done."

I blinked at him, his shoulders squared up as he slammed the trunk. "What kind of sexist crap is that?"

"That is not sexist," he insisted. "If you want to spend it on junk food or video games, that's fine too, but you're not going to live like this. I refuse to let that happen. Get in the car."

I scoffed, blowing a huge cloud in front of me. "God, you're so bossy. No wonder you run your own restaurant. I can't imagine anyone ever wanting to be your business partner."

A smile flickered across his lips and his eyes softened. "Do you like bossy?"

An image of him bossing me around in bed hit my brain like a bullet train. What a way to change the subject.

"Ugh!" I balled my hands into fists and stomped my foot before opening the back door and getting in. He was so frustrating!

He got in, started the car, and made eye contact in the mirror, raising his eyebrows at me.

A dam of laughter erupted from my belly to my chest, and I started to giggle, laugh, and finally snort, covering my mouth with my hand. Yasahiro laughed too, hunched over the wheel of the car.

"What is with the two of you? You're both crazy." Mom slapped Yasahiro's arm. "Are we going or what?"

"Yes, ma'am," he replied, starting the car.

Mom and I slept together in his bed, and he spent the night on the couch. It was the best night of sleep I'd had in weeks.

CHAPTER
THIRTEEN

"Mei?" Yasahiro's soft voice filtered into my light sleep, this time causing less alarm and disorientation. I rolled over, cracked open my eyes, and he was standing next to the bed with a cup of coffee. My eyes traveled up from the floor, his bare feet, flannel pajama pants, and black t-shirt, to his messy morning hair and shadow of a beard. Hello.

"Oh good. You're not going to knock me in the face this time," he said, stepping within arm's reach and handing me the mug. I hadn't had a good cup of coffee in two days and just the smell of it was waking me up. I sat up and sipped as he sat on the bed. "You slept on my side."

"You have a side?" I rubbed at my eyes, completely crusted with sleep, probably because I slept so deeply I didn't even remember rolling over during the night. "I thought that only happens when you sleep with someone. I usually take up the whole bed, but not with Mom here."

"Well..." His voice trailed off, and he avoided looking at me while staring into the kitchen.

"How many years did you and Amanda live together?" I sipped at the coffee, trying to cover up my own discomfort. I hated talking about her, but she was a part of his life. Or had been a part of his life. Most days I didn't believe she was in his past.

"Four years. We moved in together after dating for a year. But that was Paris. She had an enormous apartment and I had a tiny one, so I moved in with her."

"Huh. I didn't imagine that."

"You thought it was the other way?" He glanced around at his bedroom.

I sipped more coffee, cradling the hot mug between my hands. "You said you didn't mind that she always helped herself to your things, your money."

"That came later. In the beginning, I was saving, and I lived sparingly. Then I hit it big. I got lucky on a real estate transaction right here in Japan, in Kyoto. I've been good ever since. Amanda floundered between jobs. She always spent her money fast, so I picked up the slack." He shrugged his shoulders. "We were going to marry, so why wouldn't I?"

My chest was tight, hearing the regret in his voice.

"Look, Yasahiro. I can tell that she meant a lot to you." My voice cracked, and I stopped to clear it. "Have you tried to work it out? Maybe your relationship with her is not really over?"

He shook his head, and I gathered all my courage to reach across the space between us and take his hand. He tugged on mine and squeezed, looking me in the eyes.

"It's over. It's beyond over. I could never trust her again."

"What happened?" He'd never said why they broke up, but I got the feeling, whatever it was, it was unforgivable.

"It doesn't matter." He stood up, and taking my hand with him, he urged me from the bed. "I'm making new memories with you now, and she fades more and more every day."

I held my coffee out to the side, but stepped to him and wrapped my free arm around his chest, and he hugged me back. Someday, he'd tell me.

"I'm worried about you. I spoke to your Mom this morning

when she left for work. She promises you both won't return to the house until it gets warmer, and we'll install more security there when that happens. Motion detecting lights and cameras. Maybe even a dog for you?" He pressed his lips against the top of my head. "Until then, you can both live with me."

"Are you sure?" I lifted my face from his warm shirt. "Having my mom around kinda puts a damper on the romance, don't you think?"

"Romance? I didn't say this would change anything. Remember how you said I would need to woo you?"

I had said exactly that. I told him when he first showed interest in me that I wasn't some fast and loose girl. I expected to be wooed.

"Yes. I love wooing."

"First," he said, taking my hand and leading me out of the bedroom, "you're so adorable when you sleep. I've only seen it twice now, and I plan to see it close up soon. Second, there'll be plenty of hours when your Mom is not around, so let's have breakfast together, relax, and then we'll go to Etsuko's funeral."

His face fell from the smile he was wearing.

"I realize that's not the best wooing I've ever done, but I suppose it'll have to do since we can't skip it."

"I'm supposed to help Mrs. Yamida get to her physical therapy appointment this morning."

"I'll drive and we can do that together."

While he finished making an omelet at the stove, I sipped my coffee and sat at the table, rubbing my face and slowly waking up. I lifted my feet from the floor and tucked my knees up, resting my chin on them. I focused my eyes on Yasahiro in the kitchen, as comfortable in his own space as he was in the restaurant. He knew where everything was, grabbing spices in one motion. It reminded me that I'd asked Murata to teach me how to bake bread.

"So, breakfast, Yamida, funeral, and then what? I told Mrs. Murata I'd come by her place today."

He plated our meals and brought them to the table.

"Breakfast, relaxing, Yamida, funeral. Then I need to be here to wait for a delivery, and you can go to Murata's. Then dinner here for both you and your Mom. I'm taking the whole day off." He straightened his shoulders and smiled. "I'm the boss. I can do that."

"Really? The whole day? When was the last time you did that?"

"When you were in the hospital, so, awhile ago." He glanced at the scar on my upper arm, from where a part of the barn fell on me and gave me a second degree burn. Even though it didn't hurt anymore, a red gash slashed across my skin. It was another reminder of how fire and I didn't mix. He still hadn't seen my back.

It'd be the ultimate test. He thought I was pretty and adorable, but seeing my back, scarred and damaged, would probably change that. I'd been preparing my heart, steeling it, in case he ran. I imagined him gasping in surprise, and his face turning white, backing away and leaving me.

"Fuji-ko!" He snapped his fingers between us. "Blow those mists away. Let's have clear skies today. Every time I see you slip away like that, I know where your mind goes, and it's never good. Remember that *I'm here...*" He emphasized this by pointing his index finger at his chest. "Stay with me."

"Okay," I whispered, as I lifted my fork to eat my gourmet breakfast. He had spent weeks at the hospital with me, talking to me, making me talk to him. I would often drift away into my own thoughts, remembering the burning barn, and Tama, my ex-boyfriend, trying to kill me. Keeping me in the present by drawing me back from being stuck in my head always helped. He learned that quickly.

We relaxed for a while, him reading with me on the couch, or on his computer in the bedroom. I checked my email and found no replies to any of my resumes yet. I hated the waiting game. We drove over to Mrs. Yamida's place, picked her up, and took her to her appointment, and she decided to take the bus home.

At 11:30, we arrived at the funeral parlor. Yasahiro was armed with a condolence card, stuffed with money and both of our names on it.

"Thank you," I whispered to him while we waited in line to pay our respects to Etsuko's family.

I glanced around, and Fujita Takahara, the regional manager for Midori Sankaku, the new grocery chain in town that had been buying up land, was two people behind me. I once suspected him of killing Akiko's father, and although he had an ego the size of China, he wasn't the one who did the deed. That was Tama.

I nodded to Takahara, and he smiled, his charm turned to full.

"Mei, it's good to see you. How have you been?"

"Fine. And you?"

He frowned, an unnatural expression on his placid face. "All right. I was sad to hear of Etsuko's death. I often went to the izakaya and got to know her these past few months."

I absorbed this information as everyone else did in line. He should have dropped his voice, but he'd never been any good at caring about anyone other than himself. Hearing him say something nice about someone else was like hearing a dog meow.

"She was a very wonderful and kind person," I replied, nodding my head and moving forward with Yasahiro to pay our respects. I spoke quietly with Etsuko's mother, father, and brother, expressing my deepest condolences and taking Etsuko's mother's hands in my own.

"I heard you're helping Goro and the police to find evidence about Etsuko's death," her mother said, and several people in line behind us murmured between them at this news. My face warmed. "I could never believe Hisashi would hurt her," her mom whispered to me. "It pains me that he won't be here today to say goodbye."

"Mei is always like this." Yasahiro squeezed my shoulders. "I've only known her a few months, but she's always looking out for others, even at her own detriment."

If I could've poked him in the ribs, I would have. He was goading me.

"I'm not sure how I can help, but I will." I bowed to Etsuko's mother before following Yasahiro to pray before Etsuko's body and then into the next room where we'd eat lunch and drink saké until it was time to leave.

I draped my coat over the back of a chair, dropped my purse on the table, and sat beside Yasahiro. People around the room stared at us, but I tried to ignore them. Yasahiro, though, waved in their direction and the people averted their eyes and talked amongst themselves.

"It's like we're animals in the zoo some days," he whispered to me.

"It's my fault—" I began to say and then Goro dropped into the seat next to me.

"Look at you two. Still dating, I see?" Goro grabbed saké cups from the middle of the table and set them in front of us, opening a bottle with a crack of the metal cap.

"I give you Exhibit A," I said, waving to Goro. This is why people were staring at us. Because no one could believe Yasahiro would date someone like me.

"Yes, we're still dating." Yasahiro took my hand under the table. "In fact, Mei is going to live with me through the winter. A little trial to see if she can stand me for more than an hour or two at a time."

I huffed a laugh at the ridiculous lie. I was there because otherwise I would freeze to death. But I took a moment to stare at Yasahiro, and I believed he actually felt that way. I narrowed my eyes at him and he shrugged his shoulders.

"It's the truth."

Perhaps he was as nervous about our relationship as I was. I squeezed his hand as happiness lightened my chest.

"No. Really?" Goro asked, filling our cups.

"Yep. You can find me at his place for the next few months," I said, confidence ringing in my voice. Just then, Takahara passed right behind me, walking to an empty table on the other side of the room. He glanced at us but kept going.

"Then drinks are in order." Goro lifted his cup to us. We clicked cups, said "Kampai," and drank. Kumi sat down a moment later, her face streaked with tears, and Goro turned to hug her and calm her down.

"It feels so surreal. We talked about growing old together. I never thought she'd die so young." Kumi cried into a handkerchief and blotted her eyes.

Yasahiro and I drank, since that was the only thing we could do.

Akiko arrived and I introduced her to Yasahiro again. They had met once in the hospital but that was a long time ago. While those two were making small talk, I got up and walked around, stretching my legs and allowing the alcohol to loosen me up. I didn't think Etsuko's murderer would come to her funeral, but I betted I could pick up some gossip about her if I listened hard enough. I pretended to look at email on my phone while standing behind a group of people eating and drinking at a table far from mine, but they talked about the cold weather and lack of snow, avoiding gossiping about the dead.

At the buffet table, I lingered next to a group of women talking about how Etsuko was too young to die, and how if they died, they didn't want a Buddhist reception. They wanted to be cremated and put into the family grave. "No one should have to look at my dead body," one woman said, shuddering. She glanced at me, and I returned to filling my plate with food. They headed off for a table to continue talking about death in a completely detached fashion, and I was left to stand next to Takahara. Damn. I had been hoping to avoid him.

"So, Mei, I haven't seen you around town."

"Uh, nope. I've been at the house or at Kutsuro Matsu, Chiyo Hokichi's bathhouse. Do you know it?"

"Yes, yes. I've sent many visiting coworkers there. They love it."

I took a long look at him, his fancy suit, expensive watch, perfect hair, and straight smile. There were lots of women in town that found him handsome, but ever since I had my run-in with him over the Midori Sankaku greenhouse, I found him unsettling. No one that slick had any business in Chikata as far as I was concerned. I didn't care how much business he brought to the town.

I speared some ham and popped it into my mouth, wondering how long I'd have to make small talk before I could excuse myself.

"Great. I'm sure they're happy for the business." I nodded my head a few times, unsure what to do with my body or gestures.

"I think they're planning to add in a massage service in the spring."

"I've heard this as well. I'm looking forward to it." This was painful small talk. *Kill me now.*

"I can't believe this is the second funeral I've been to here." He shook his head, but I couldn't tell if his sorrow was genuine or not. I didn't have a high opinion of him, so I wasn't the best judge. "My own father is in the hospital near death. This may not be my last funeral for the year." He stared off into the distance, avoiding the looks of other people in the room.

"I'm sorry to hear that," I whispered, gently placing my hand on his arm. "I hope he makes a miraculous recovery."

"Thank you, Mei." He patted my hand, but his cold skin on mine made me shudder so I returned my hand to my side. "I was wondering if you had time to go out, get dinner? A few drinks?" he asked me, and my heart stopped. Not this again. "I'd love to talk with you about the town and Midori Sankaku's plans here for the future."

I narrowed my eyes at him. "Are you asking me out on a date?"

He nodded with a quirk of his lips, and a shiver ran down the back of my legs. This was the second time he had hit on me in Yasahiro's presence. Why?

"Of course. I think we'd make an excellent team, you and me."

"An excellent team of what?" I stepped away from him, but he closed the distance again.

"You can't really be dating Yasahiro," he said, his voice dropping to a whisper. "I know you're set to inherit your land from your mother when she passes. You and I, we'd make a powerful couple. You're a trusted member of this community, and I'm running all the new business into town."

I had to think hard to shut my open mouth. "You can't be serious." I was dumbstruck. Who did this? At a funeral?

"I am. Come on. How about tomorrow night?" A vision of the two of us together flashed through my head, and bile climbed up to my mouth. Gross.

"How about never." I turned away from him and stalked to my seat. The nerve of that guy.

He smiled at me as he returned to his table.

"You all right?" Yasahiro asked, turning away from his conversation with Akiko.

"I'm fine." But as Takahara made eye contact with me across the room, I felt far from fine.

Something was just not right, and I couldn't put my finger on what.

CHAPTER
FOURTEEN

"Turn, fold, push."

Murata worked dough on her counter space, pushing the dough forward with the heels of her hands, turning the lump ninety degrees, folding it in half, and pushing it with the heels of her hands again.

"See? Now, you try."

I tried to mimic her hand motions, but I failed and the dough barely moved.

"No, no. Push harder. Put your back into it." She smacked me between the shoulders, and I laughed as I pushed the dough. "That's better. You know bakers have good muscles. Didn't you say you were dating a baker?"

"A chef." I turned the dough, folded and kneaded again. "He owns Sawayaka."

"Eh? Yasahiro Suga? *You're* dating *him*?"

"Yep." I pushed, turned, and folded. "We've been dating since the beginning of October."

"How can that be? I've heard he's the most eligible bachelor in town. He lives right behind me, you know?"

"I do," I said, stifling a laugh. "I'm living with him for a little while until our pipes unfreeze at home again."

"I don't believe it," she mumbled, and I shrugged my shoulders at her. This didn't surprise me one bit.

"How long do I knead this? And why do I knead it anyway?"

She picked up the dough and slowly pulled the molded ball of wheat, water, and yeast apart into two chunks. "See how the dough is becoming elastic and sticking together? Kneading develops the gluten into long strings. Without it, bread would be a rock. Kneading and resting the dough over and over makes it rise and become light and airy."

She took over for me, kneading the dough a few more times, rolling it into a huge ball, and holding it in her hands for a moment. "See how it holds its shape now. If it falls into a lump, it's not ready." Plopping the dough into a metal bowl, she covered it and put it in the warm oven. "I heat the oven a little and then turn the light on. That's usually enough to be warm for dough to rise."

There was no way I could do this at home — it was too cold — but I could try making dough at Yasahiro's. I wondered if he would mind.

"So you let it rise until it doubles in size. Then you punch it down, knead it again for a short time, and then bake it. This is my super easy recipe. A child can make this. It's not the best bread but tastes great with butter and jam or cheese."

Murata hobbled to the kitchen table and placed her hand on a stack of paper. "I copied these for you. It's my favorite bread recipes, and your money for today is right next to it. Don't forget it, okay?"

"Okay." I washed off my hands and grabbed the sponge. "I'll clean up here and take out the recycling."

She filled up a glass of water and sat down at the kitchen table.

"You're really dating Mr. Suga? You're not joking around with me?"

I laughed and nodded my head. I should have been annoyed by these people who didn't believe we were dating, but how could I when I barely believed it myself? I sprayed down her counter and scrubbed with the sponge, being sure to lift everything and clean underneath.

"Yes, I'm really dating him, and yes, I'm living with him right now. He's a good man. I'm very fortunate."

"I would think he's fortunate to have you, dear. You seem very sweet and compassionate. Not many people want to help an old lady like me. You reach a certain age, and suddenly, you don't exist anymore."

"Well, I do like hanging out with older people because I love hearing the stories you have to tell. I always got along better with people older than me growing up. I was a terrible babysitter because I didn't like kids." I rinsed out her sponge and got started on the dishes. "But I'm happy to help now, and I'm glad I can make a little money too. At least until I get a full-time job." I hummed as I soaped up and rinsed out a glass. Looking over my shoulder at Murata, she was studying me with her eyes narrowed. "What?"

"Have you ever considered doing this full time?"

"This? Taking care of the elderly? I'm not a nurse."

"No. Not as a nurse. You know, the community center used to have more activities for the elderly, but they cut back when the recession hit. Attendance was low because the center is on the edge of town. It's hard to get to."

I knew the community center was hard to get to as that was where Mom held her cooking classes.

I finished up washing dishes and turned to face her, drying off my hands with a towel. "Would something closer to the center of town be better?" An idea formed in my head of a place where people could gather and do activities all day for a small fee.

She waved her hand and dismissed the idea. "Maybe, but who has the time for something like that? Have you heard anything more about Etsuko?"

My mind, having gone all the way down the first path she mentioned, imagining a little tea shop or home with people gathered, playing card games, talking and eating, throwing birthday parties, came to an abrupt halt. Who had time for that? Maybe me?

I was beginning to believe I'd been going in the wrong direction my whole life. I loved to paint and help other people out and those things had nothing to do with my business degree and Tokyo office life as a project manager or saleswoman. I was at the fork in the road, reading both signs. One read, "Back to Tokyo — to your unfulfilling corporate cycle of dead-end jobs." The other read, "Stay in Chikata. Start something new!" Yasahiro held out his hand to me on the Chikata path, but my feet were planted to the ground like concrete.

I returned to putting the bread ingredients away. "Etsuko was a model daughter and wonderful person," I said, returning to the conversation. "She showed up to work on time. She seemed to have a passion for bento boxes and collecting DVDs. She had a loving boyfriend who's devastated she's dead, but he's the only suspect because she had no run-ins with the law, paid her bills on time, went to work, and visited her family. Goro said they have no information about who could have possibly killed her but Hisashi, which I don't believe. I saw his love for her with my own eyes."

"She always seemed lonely to me, though. Said she missed him while he was gone. Whenever I talked to her, she would complain about how empty her apartment felt. How there wasn't anyone to come home to, like her brother has with his wife and kids." Murata drummed her fingers on the table. "She paid her bills on time with that waitress job she had? What about all the trips she went on? I can't imagine she had much spending money."

"Trips? What trips?" This was news to me.

"About once every other month, she would leave with a rolling bag and catch a cab outside. She even said she was jet lagged once or twice, and I saw duty-free bags. I figured she was traveling with Hisashi, but she never spoke of her trips at length. Perhaps she was meeting someone else?"

That was a good guess. I filed away this new information to give to Goro as soon as I talked to him next. I placed the flour in her cabinet and the yeast in the fridge. "Did she ever date anyone else?"

"She and Hisashi went through a rough patch two years ago and she dated a guy briefly, but he moved away. Got a job in Hokkaido. She talked about the guys she tried to date online." Murata shook her head. "Young people these days. I don't understand you. In my day, you got an *omiai* if you needed to get married." I smiled and resumed tidying up. Omiai were traditional Japanese matchmakers, and Murata would've been scandalized if I told her there were websites that do that now too. "She said most of the people on dating sites are women anyway. Young men just want to work and don't care about having a family. Then she and Hisashi made up and became even more devoted to each other."

I finished up by cleaning her sink and wiping up the floor too.

"Do you think she dated anyone from these sites recently? Maybe she was seeing someone on the side?" My stomach churned with the idea, but I supposed a secret lover wasn't out of the question. Lots of people (people that were not me) cheated or hedged their bets. Perhaps she'd thought Hisashi would never come around and move to Chikata.

"I'm not sure," Murata said, yawning. "She tried group dates and speed dating too. Seemed to me an awful way to spend your time."

I wondered if I could find her profile on any of these websites. Maybe if I found one, Goro could look into it on her computer and find out if anyone contacted her. I knew they had her computer and were going through the email. He probably already knew more than I did.

Murata rose from her chair, looking beat.

"Are you going to nap?" I brought her cane to her.

"Yes. Lock up when you leave?" She had complained that she was sleepy when we went out for a walk earlier. The air was cold and she was yawning puffs of steam, but the walk had woken her up long enough to teach me to make bread.

"Of course."

I helped her to her room and closed the door behind me before putting on my coat, grabbing my purse and the recycling, and locking the door. I glanced at Etsuko's apartment and imagined her coming and going from an international flight or saying goodbye to someone she met online right at her door. But that didn't seem very safe. I didn't know many women who would invite a strange guy into their house on a first or second date. If she had done any dating, it was out in the open, and Kumi would've known about it because they were best friends.

Then who were the men Murata witnessed?

I dropped off the recycling downstairs and headed out into the cold, early evening. The sun had set and the block was dark and quiet. I remembered the way Takahara propositioned me at the funeral — how bold he was even though Yasahiro was seated two tables away. He had seemed to think I would consider his proposal because we'd make a good match somehow. But I had seen the women he dated, and I couldn't imagine why I would be any better than them. He was a playboy, dating any woman with a pretty face and a solid bank account. That did not describe me one bit.

I took a step towards Yasahiro's building and stopped, movement out of the corner of my eye catching my attention. Turning around slowly, I looked into the shadows across the street but didn't see anything.

"Hello?" I called out, but my voice bounced back to me. I had probably seen a cat or something.

I kept walking, my scalp prickling as I turned the corner. I felt like I was being followed, but I looked around and no one was there. Huh. I was being paranoid.

Who would follow me?

Pushing my paranoia to the side, I hastened my steps and headed to Yasahiro's as fast as my legs could carry me.

CHAPTER
FIFTEEN

I entered Yasahiro's building and shut the door behind me, pressing my back to it and sighing with relief as I flipped the lock. I peered out the window, both up and down the street, but I didn't see anyone. *Stop being so paranoid, Mei.* Who would want to follow me anyway? I knew who. Tama or someone acting on his behalf. A chill seized me from head to toe, causing my hands to shake. I counted to ten and looked out the window again. Nothing but regular people walked to and from the open businesses on the block. I let the air leak from my lungs slowly. Tama was in jail, and I was safe here at Yasahiro's. There was no need to be this stupid.

Inside his apartment, the lights were low and Yasahiro cooked at the stove. The apartment smelled of potatoes and fried onions, and my stomach growled in response. I shook off the feeling of being followed and pushed thoughts of Etsuko and her possible secret life aside. As much as I wanted to help every person around me, I had to help myself too.

"There you are! I hope Murata is doing well?" he asked, coming to me to take my coat. To the left of the door sat three large cardboard boxes that weren't there that morning.

"She's fine. She was tired, and I left her so she could take a nap. What are these?" I angled my head at the boxes, but he just smiled. "Are we putting together furniture later? That sounds like fun." My voice obviously indicated that would be far from fun.

"It does require a little assembly, but what's in there is not furniture. Although you *could* call it furniture." He bobbed his head side to side. A riddle? What was he getting at?

"You have me intrigued." I slipped off my boots and let him hang up my coat before lifting up a flap of the biggest box to see what was inside.

"Hey! Don't touch," he said, swatting away my hand. "Come into the kitchen. I'm making pork chops, mashed potatoes, and green beans for dinner. A meal wholly un-Japanese-like, but I miss what I used to eat in France."

At the kitchen island, I leaned over to examine the pork chops. "Mmmm, those smell amazing. There hasn't been much meat in my diet lately."

"We're going to change that." He turned off the stove, grabbed a large wine glass, and filled it with red wine. "You wanted wooing, and I always start with wine. I brought this bottle back from France the last time I was there. No label. Just a little family vineyard I would go to on the weekends."

I had hoped the evening would go in this direction, a date and some flirting. We originally planned to go into the city, but Mom and I moved in and Etsuko's funeral was earlier today. This was a nice compromise. But I forgot! Mom would return soon to spend the night as well. Too bad, but I guess I would take a little wooing while Yasahiro was willing to give it. It's not like we were going to have a lot of private time.

He drained a big pot of potatoes into the sink, and I sat at the table, sipped my wine, and sang along to the Brazilian jazz music he had playing. I didn't know the words (they were in Portuguese) but I'd heard these songs a dozen times before.

Yasahiro grabbed butter and milk from the fridge but paused at the kitchen island to stare over at me. I stopped singing and paid attention, thinking he wanted to talk to me. He shook his head.

"No. Don't stop." He closed his eyes as I picked up the melody again, swaying his head side to side. When the song came to an end, he brought the bottle of red wine around the island to me at the table.

"You have no idea how nice it is to have somebody else here. I enjoy seeing you in my space, like you were meant to be here, and I'm going to have a very hard time when you leave."

As he smiled sadly at me, my breath caught in my chest. He was so forthright and charming, and I once again had trouble believing this was my life. I should've pinched myself to make sure I wasn't still back in my old Tokyo apartment, dreaming of this alternate life. One moment I was freezing and starving, and the next I was warm and well taken care of by a seriously handsome man.

"I don't want to leave," I whispered, "but you know I'll have to when the time comes." Because there was no way I would let Mom live alone when so many things were uncertain.

Yasahiro's buzzer rang, and he pressed the button asking who it was. Mom's voice answered, and he buzzed her in.

"Wow! I can't believe how cold it is out there," Mom said, stomping into the apartment and dropping her purse by the door. "But I heard it should warm up and snow by Monday." She slipped off her shoes and patted down her coat, looking between us. A smile grew on her face as we smiled at each other, my face flushed from the wine and feeling comfortable at the kitchen table.

"Please, take off your coat and make yourself comfortable," Yasahiro said, returning to the mashed potatoes. "Dinner is almost ready."

"Actually, I came to grab my bag." Mom walked past both of

us and into Yasahiro's bedroom. He wiped off his hands, his eyebrows drawn together, but I waved him off, getting up from the table to join her.

"What are you doing? The house is still too cold to live there." I stood over her with my hands on my hips. She was not leaving the warmth of Yasahiro's place to live in an icebox. That was out of the question.

"You should stay here with Yasahiro. I'm going to go live with Chiyo until we receive the insurance check. She's overjoyed to have me live with her." Mom lowered her voice. "This way you can have time with Yasahiro. Go snag him and don't let him go." She squeezed my shoulder as I laughed.

"Mom, don't be ridiculous. You should stay here." I inched back and closed the door behind me, aware that Yasahiro was eavesdropping in the other room.

"Don't you be ridiculous. This is the perfect chance for you two, and I'm not going to stick around and get in the way."

"Mom," I insisted. "Listen. I think…" I sat down on his bed. "I think he's still in love with Amanda. He was talking about her this morning, and I could feel it, his regret. Whatever was between them, it's not over. And while I have hope for us, I'm not going to… you know, until I'm sure."

"Mei," she said, sitting next to me and taking my hand, "it's over between them. He still needs closure with her, but it's definitely over."

"Since when do you know anything about 'closure,' Mom?" I snorted a laugh and she patted my hand.

"I read a lot of books. Trust me on this one."

"Do you know why they broke up?" I asked, because she seemed so sure.

She nodded. "But it's not my business to tell you."

"Mom, I'm not the right person for him to move on to. I'm rebound material. She'll come back, all pretty and talented, and I won't stand a chance. I can't do that to myself."

"Tell me something. What's important in a relationship besides love?" Mom turned her face to me and prompted me to answer by bumping her shoulder into mine.

"Uh... Trust. Chemistry. Having things in common? Laughter?"

Mom laughed at me and I smirked in return.

"Yes, all of those things, but trust especially. I loved your father and we had so many things in common. He made me laugh, and he was a great dad. But trusting him was the most important thing. I put my trust in him and he in me. I wish we'd had more years together." She sighed as she rubbed the top of my hand. "Yasahiro trusts you. It was wrong of me to ask you to keep him in the dark about our situation, and I've told him that I made you do it, otherwise he may have lost faith in you." Mom's eyes watered, and she sucked in a short breath. "And I didn't want that. Be true and honest, and you will be fine. He didn't get that from Amanda, and that's why you'll succeed where she failed."

She stood up from the bed, letting go of my hand, and dabbed at her eyes. "Yasahiro," she called out as she opened the door. She ended up yelling directly in his face because he was right on the other side. Sneaky, that one. "Help me bring my suitcase downstairs? Chiyo will be here in a moment. We're going to pick up Mimoji and go back to her place."

He scurried to the kitchen, dropping the potato masher into the sink, and grabbing Mom's suitcase, he hauled it through the door. "Be right back!"

I was left alone in the apartment to contemplate and consider my options. Mom insisted that Yasahiro and Amanda were over, and I had no reason to doubt her even after the morning conversation with him. This meant I had a real chance, and the thought of that sent my heart racing and flushed my cheeks. Because here I was, living in my boyfriend's apartment, we'd been dating for almost three months, and we still hadn't slept together. And wow, I was ready. All the little looks, gestures, and flirtatious jokes had been building up to this. There was still one more thing to overcome, though.

Yasahiro returned to the apartment, cold and shivering. "I'm glad you're no longer at home because there is no way you both would make it through a night like this." He slipped off his shoes at the door again. "Well, we have a lot of food because I cooked for three people, so let's eat."

I spent the entire dinner loose and happy, drinking wine and telling stories. We both talked of school and growing up on a farm, and Yasahiro wanted to hear about the jobs I had, even though I had been fired from every single one of them.

"You weren't fired," he said, clearing away our empty plates. I ate everything and could've had seconds. "You were downsized. That's a whole other ballgame. It's not like you were fired because you were horrible at your job."

"Well, I would argue that I actually am horrible at those jobs and that was the reason I was let go. I know I'm a good project manager, but being a salesperson was too difficult for me. That, and it was unfair. I came into three of those five jobs as a project manager, and they piled on the sales positions later when they let other people go. I was always working more than one job, and only being paid for one."

Yasahiro filled up my glass with wine again. I was already warm and giggly from the amount of wine I'd had. I was sure at this point he was just trying to get me drunk. I giggled and then covered up my mouth to hide it.

"What's so funny?"

I remembered Mom told me to be honest and true with him. "I think you're trying to get me drunk, and you're doing a good job of it."

Yasahiro was going to stop at the halfway point, but he upended the bottle and filled my glass almost to the top. "There. Now we're getting somewhere." He set the empty bottle down next to the sink and grabbed a new one from the pantry. "It wasn't your fault that other people managed their businesses poorly. You got caught in the middle." He dug the wine key out of the drawer of utensils. "While I'm opening this, you should take a look at what's in the boxes."

Hmmm, I'd been wondering about what was in the boxes all dinner long, and now I had the chance to investigate. I took my glass of wine and headed over to the pile of cardboard boxes, being careful not to show how tipsy I was. I'd lost enough weight in the last two months to make me a cheap date, and the wine was so good, it went down like water.

I slid my finger along the flap of the biggest box, but this one was sealed shut with tape. The other three boxes were open so I squatted down, set my wine aside, and opened one of the smaller boxes.

"Ahhh! These are beautiful!" I plucked out a clear glass ball about the size of my hand with a loop of string on top. The sphere glittered with an iridescent sheen much like an oil slick. I held the bubble of glass up to the light and peered through it, wondering about the talented person who crafted it. "Where did you get these?"

"In Italy, from a woman who makes glass art." He poured himself another glass and joined me. "There's more inside."

I set the sphere gently in the box and touched the other dozen ornaments, just as beautiful as the first.

"Wow. They must've been expensive."

"Not really," he said, shaking his head. "She was an apprentice and learning the trade. I was in the right place at the right time."

I set that box aside and opened the next one. Fluffs of silver garland and lights filled the box to the brim. I saw where this was going.

Yasahiro grabbed a knife from the kitchen island and cut open the largest box. I squealed and clapped my hands as he pulled out a fake Christmas tree.

"Oh, this is so wonderful. I haven't had a Christmas tree since I was a kid. When I was a teenager, and we had just gotten Mimoji, he attacked the Christmas tree one winter and broke a bunch of ornaments. My mom refused to put it up the next year. And I never had room for one in my tiny apartment. Instead, I would roam Ginza and be sucked in by the decorations."

"I love this time of year. In Paris, the city is lit up and holiday parties happen every weekend in December. We always had a tree." His face fell into a moment of melancholy. "So I wanted to revive this tradition."

I knew he was thinking of his apartment with Amanda. *Quick! Change the conversation.*

"You were right. The tree is not really furniture but it could be. I should've guessed." Moving on from whatever memory he was having, I tried to butt myself in and make a new one. "We should put it up."

We left our wineglasses on the table and got to work. He set up the tree in the corner at the end of the couch. I opened my computer and navigated to the Internet radio, finding a station that played Christmas music. With festive music in the background, we decorated the tree, and I told him about the last Christmas I remembered with my dad.

"He died the spring after, but I'm glad I remember that Christmas. He bought me my first bike and told me he was going to teach me how to ride it in the summer. My older brother taught me instead two years later. Mom could never bring herself to do it."

I hung one of the last glass bulbs on the tree and stepped back.

Yasahiro put his arm around my shoulders. "I remember getting my first bike for Christmas too. Now I love to ride. It's my favorite form of exercise."

We both fell silent and stared at the glittering tree.

"Do you want me to sleep on the couch tonight?" he asked, leaning over to kiss below my ear.

His lips were soft and warm, sending my scalp prickling and making me smile. My insides melted into a pool of jelly, churned on by the wine I drank, and my conversation with Mom earlier faded away. I wrapped my arms around him, answering his question with a kiss, one I didn't hold back. For the first time since we met, my body, mind, and soul believed he was into me, that I was the only one he thought of when he thought of his "girlfriend." That other woman may have entered his thoughts every now and then, but only as a regret. I was the one who had his full attention now.

He clutched my back and squeezed me to him, our lips fully engaged with each other, and any space we had between us was obliterated by the closeness of our bodies. I pulled away from his lips and caught my breath, and he didn't let go. He held on tight, almost as if he was afraid to let me go because I'd run away. I wasn't planning on it.

"There's one more thing," I whispered into his ear. "Will you come with me?" I tried to turn out of his grasp because I wanted to pull him to the bedroom, but he held on tighter.

"Don't," he said, his breath rushing over the top of my head. "I don't want to let go."

Smiling, I lifted my arms, wrapped them around his neck, and jumped up to wrap my legs around him. "Then carry me."

He took long strides to the bedroom, catching the door in his hand, and shutting it behind us with a slam. He tried to set me on the bed and lay me down, but I put up my hand.

"Stop." Admirably, he did, like I'd zapped him into a frozen state. "You sit." I angled past him and turned around, putting him in my place. His face fell into a frown once he was disconnected from me, but I ignored his pout and soldiered on.

My hand hovered over the light switch. "No," I said, pulling my fingers away. The lights needed to stay on.

I turned to face him. His chest heaved beneath his black shirt and realization crawled over his face like ice across a pond.

Tremors invaded my hands as I reached down for the hem of my sweater and pulled the heavy knit over my head. I had another layer of t-shirt to shed as well because the weather was too cold not to dress warmly. I stepped to him so we were within arm's reach.

"I need to show you first... I need you to see."

He stayed silent, but his eyes spoke when his voice could not. He was frightened. He knew this day was coming, and my stomach cramped with worry. What if this ruined everything? Everything had been so perfect. I hesitated with my fingers at the hem of my shirt.

"I'm scared," I whispered, my lips trembling. I had wanted to be strong for this moment, but I was afraid of everything slipping away. "My last boyfriend broke up with me when he found out. He never even saw the scars. He said he didn't want to date someone damaged, and he could find someone prettier than me." I dropped my hands to my side, my eyes filling with tears.

He darted his hand out and took mine in both of his. "Don't cry. It's not going to be that bad. I promise."

He stood up, grabbed my shirt, and pulled upwards before I could protest. I still had my bra on, but I was immediately cold, so I folded my arms to my chest and leaned into him, pressing my forehead to his shoulder.

"Oh, Mei," he breathed, dropping his lips to my shoulder and lightly stroking the fingertips of his right hand down the landscape of my back.

I inhaled sharply, picturing his face as his fingers took everything in. From the tops of my shoulders to my shoulder blades, the skin was puckered like gravel, pale and knotted, swirling towards a swath of slick, three centimeter wide skin. The skin graft eventually healed but it left a line of scarred tissue in a diagonal from my right shoulder blade, across my spine and ending in my left ribs. From there down, the skin was like a rough day at sea, waves cresting in an endless ocean to my waist.

"Who did this to you?" His voice cracked and I flinched as a warm tear fell on my skin.

"I never saw who pushed me, and the whole night was a blur. I sometimes say I fell in because I don't want to believe anyone would have done that to me." I closed my eyes and remembered the campfire. It had been going for hours so the coals were blazing hot. Kids were running everywhere. I twirled around, laughing and shouting, someone pushed me, and I fell in. "I was sedated for so long after, I doubt I'll ever know. No one ever admitted it."

He sniffed up and pulled away from me, settling his hands on my shoulders and turning me around.

He placed his entire palm and fingers of his right hand on my lower back. "It doesn't hurt?"

"No," I said, shaking my head and trying to look over my shoulder at him. "Most of the skin healed a long time ago. But the area of the skin graft is permanently numb. I've gotten used to it."

"This here?" I assumed his fingers were on the graft area. It wasn't hard to miss because the skin looked so different, stretched and alien.

"I don't feel your fingers." My brain had always tried to fill in the sensory data that belonged to that skin, heat from the baths, the scratch of my bra strap, or the touch of a lover, but my mind could only do so much.

He sighed and hugged me from behind, pressing his chest to my back. "Have you ever considered getting tattoos to cover them up? I bet there are some tattoo artists in Kyoto that would do a beautiful job."

I blinked and perked up. "I have! I used to spend hours looking at photos online. But I've never been able to afford it."

He nodded against my head. "This changes nothing. You're

all I think about. I'm a man obsessed, imagining days, months, and years into the future with you. I'm not scared off by this."

I fell into a canyon of relief, and it swallowed me whole.

"You're becoming everything to me. I thought I lost you the night of the barn fire. We pulled up outside and you were on the ground, motionless, your clothes smoking."

I turned around and ran my fingers through his hair, my thumbs over his cheeks and across his bottom lip.

"I get irrationally upset when I imagine you gone, and I don't want that to ever happen." He squeezed my waist between his hands and blew out a long breath.

Leaning in, I closed the distance between us, touched my lips to his, and inched my fingers into the waist of his jeans.

He had passed the test.

CHAPTER
SIXTEEN

The kitchen was quiet when I slipped out of bed in the morning. Yasahiro was still asleep, so this was the perfect time for me to get some work done before he was up. I paused at the refrigerator door, closed my eyes, and remembered everything that happened last night. It had felt good to be held by somebody again, to experience that intimate skin on skin connection, and sleep next to a man I was falling in love with. I couldn't have asked for a better outcome especially since I was so frightened to bare myself to him.

I grabbed a bottle of cold water from the fridge and sat down at the kitchen table with my laptop. It was Friday, and I doubted anyone would write me back over the weekend, so this was my last opportunity to apply for more jobs before Monday.

Tucking my knees up under my chin, I reached around my legs and sifted through my inbox. Great, nothing but rejections. I leaned over, grabbed my purse, and pulled out my notebook that was nearing its last few blank pages. Making my way down through a list of employers, I struck a line through the rejections and circled places I would try next. My life would be so much easier if I could find a job here in town. But despite Yasahiro's new restaurant and the Midori Sankaku, job growth was slow in this part of the country. Considering how many jobs had been eliminated in Tokyo, job growth was slow for the *entire* country, not just this area. I had legitimate fears about being able to hold my head above water through the rest of the winter without significant income.

Sorting through the open tabs on my browser, I navigated the local news for all of the Saitama region. Looked like snow was coming this week! And there were plenty of year-end festivals going on. I scrolled down the page and found a news item about Fujita Takahara's father passing away in hospital. Oh no. He had said his father was close to death. Though I didn't like him at all, I felt bad for him. Takahara's father had been a wealthy man, made his fortune in banking of some sort. Though I was pretty good with small businesses, the stock market and big banking was something I never got into, so I skimmed through that portion of the obituary. Takahara's mother was deceased too, and that left him the sole heir. Well, I guessed I shouldn't feel too bad for him. He was coming out of the deal pretty well off.

I sighed and rubbed my face. It was too bad Yasahiro had this fancy coffee machine that I didn't know how to work because I really needed some caffeine.

I spent twenty minutes searching several job websites and submitting my resume for anything remotely like what I used to do. This was a recipe for disaster, though. Hadn't I already learned my lesson with my last job? I was only good at project managing, and I didn't have enough experience in straight-up business to apply for business management jobs. I could've applied my skills towards being a tour guide or running an office, but that was about it.

Turning to the next page of my notebook, I found the list I made about Etsuko's murder suspects and why I thought she was killed. Not surprisingly, the page was mostly blank except for Hisashi's name at the top. I slipped my pen from the elastic holding it to my notebook and chewed on the eraser. What was it Murata had said about Etsuko? She was always lonely and complained about how empty her apartment felt. I jotted that down on the page and add a question mark. If she was lonely, why didn't she advertise for a roommate? That's what most people do. Unless they have something to hide from other people. Then there was the observation that Etsuko traveled often on her small budget. How had a waitress with rent and bills to pay afford to leave the country? Goro had said she paid her bills on time. She must've had supplemental income.

The bedroom door opened and Yasahiro emerged, half asleep and his hair everywhere. I smiled at his shirtless form and baggy pajama pants. Wow. I had sex with that guy last night. My smile broadened.

"Why didn't you make coffee?" he asked, rubbing his head and yawning.

"I don't know where the coffee is, and I don't know how to use your machine. I figured I should wait until you got up. That way you could teach me." I rose from my chair and joined him at the monster machine.

He hummed and wrapped his arms around me. "I don't have to teach you anything." He kissed my neck, and I laughed and squeezed him.

"I guess I'm lucky that way." I raised my eyebrows at him and he laughed. "But the coffee machine I'm truly terrified of."

"Okay." He opened the cabinet above the machine and pulled out a bag of beans. "I buy these already ground." He grabbed a measuring spoon from the drawer, showed me where the grounds went, where the water went, and what buttons to press. Coffee began to appear magically not long afterward.

We sat across from each other at the kitchen table and sipped quietly, and it was companionable and easy, the kind of relationship I'd been looking for for years. I liked when I could just sit in silence with somebody else. Silence did not always have to be filled with conversation.

"What do you have planned for today?" he asked, sitting back in his chair.

"I have to leave in an hour to go help Shigimo get to the doctor and pick up his prescriptions. Then I'm free for the rest of the day. But I thought I might come by the restaurant for lunch and then go visit Goro at the police station. I'm hoping he'll let me talk to Hisashi." I swiped on my phone, sitting next to my computer, and scrolled through the messages from Kumi. "Kumi is taking the day off from the bathhouse, so I'll call her too."

"Okay. Any ideas about Etsuko?" He folded his legs crisscross and sat forward to place his coffee cup on the table. "I've been thinking a lot about her especially after the funeral. I hope the police can catch whoever killed her because I don't believe Hisashi did it."

"Me neither. Murata had some ideas that I thought were interesting. She said Etsuko traveled a lot and often complained about being lonely. That she tried online dating for a while."

Yasahiro raised his eyebrows at me, no doubt as dubious about online dating as I was.

"Yeah. I know, but I heard online dating is getting more popular here."

"I was going to try it when I was living in France, but I regularly met so many people, it didn't matter."

"Murata said Etsuko and Hisashi broke up for a while a few years ago, and she dated other men at the time. Perhaps she never stopped once she got back together with him, though. So this brings me to my idea. I was going to open accounts on all the local dating websites and see if I can find Etsuko. If I can figure out which sites she was using, Goro can do a search of her computer or email. Maybe she met somebody and something happened? I was thinking that if she had a guy on the side who wanted her to himself, wanted her to dump Hisashi, then that would be motive to kill her if she refused."

"It's worth a shot." He shrugged his shoulders and sipped.

"And I'm telling you this now, so you don't think I'm cheating if you ever see me on a dating website." I laughed at the absurdity of it.

"I'll keep it in mind," he said, winking at me. "Why don't you get started on it now?"

I opened my browser and Googled for Japan online dating websites. Scrolling through the results, I found a blog post on the top five Japan dating websites, clicked on the link, and opened each of the recommended sites. I didn't have to make it much further than the homepage before I found what I should have been looking for in the first place.

"Oh my God," I gasped and covered my mouth with my hands.

"What?" Yasahiro circled around the table and peered at my laptop.

I pointed to an advertisement on the page, an advertisement with the logo of two sleeping foxes and text above them that read, *"Lonely? Is your bed cold and empty? We have just the man for you."*

"Ne Kitsune. Etsuko mentioned this more than once according to Murata, and she even said it to a man who left her apartment."

Yasahiro sat down next to me. "An escort service?"

I clicked on the link and scrolled through the Ne Kitsune website. "It's like an escort service. No sex — just some guy who comes and sleeps in your bed with you at night." I immediately understood the appeal of this. What if you just wanted to sleep with someone without sex? Gone in the morning. No problems or relationship issues. It wasn't what I wanted out of life, but I got it. I could sympathize.

Yasahiro shook his head. "I've been away from Japan for too long to think this is a good idea."

"Well, not if there's something else going on here." I bit my lip and scanned through the rest of the page. They didn't have any real photos of the guys who were on offer, just manga-like drawings and descriptions. That was a fantastic way to protect their identity, but it didn't help me.

"You'll definitely need to go see Goro now." Yasahiro stood up and wrapped his arms around my shoulders. "I'm so glad I met you."

"Me too." I laid my hand on his arm and sank into his warmth for a brief moment.

"I'll make us breakfast. Why don't you shower now while I'm cooking? Then I'll get ready and take you over to Mr. Shigimo's place before I head to the restaurant."

I had a sudden flash of showering with him, and I sucked in a breath and closed my eyes against the assault on my heart. I'd save that for another day. Instead, I used the time in the shower to hash out this new development.

Ne Kitsune, I have you now.

CHAPTER
SEVENTEEN

t'd been awhile since I was last at the police station. I burst through the doors, armed with purpose and a fresh idea on what to try next. The police station was so small that only a few staff members kept it occupied at all times. I didn't recognize the young man at the front desk, but past him in the open desk area, Goro stuffed a large rice ball in his face and stared at a computer monitor.

"I'm here to see him," I said, pointing to Goro, and he waved to me.

"Sign in please." The young man twirled a clipboard around to me. I wrote my name in, dug through my purse to find my *hanko* name stamp, stamped the paper, and twirled it back to him.

The door to the right of the desk buzzed, and I let myself in right past Goro's partner, Kayo Mitsuwara. She smiled as she looked up from a pile of papers in her arms.

"Hey, Mei. How are you?" Kayo's hair was matted down but pulled into a bun at the base of her neck. I betted she'd been out all morning with a hat on.

"I'm good. You?" I bowed and continued with the pleasantries, though small talk like this killed my momentum.

"Good. It's freezing out there. Goro told me your pipes froze at home. When the weather gets better, I'd be happy to come out to the house and help you thaw them out."

I blinked and tried not to cringe. This was as likely a story as any as to why we weren't living at home.

"Sure. Thank you for offering." I bowed again. "It's been a cold winter."

"Are you really living at Yasahiro's apartment now?" She leaned forward, her eyes as wide as her smile. "I've heard it's gorgeous."

"Yep." I rocked on my heels and tried to ignore her eager look. She could've easily been drooling.

"I can't believe you guys are dating," she lamented, shaking her head. This time, the rage boiled up from my toes, through my belly, to my chest, and I had to swallow several times to keep it down.

"No. We're not dating. We're just sleeping together," I deadpanned, but she missed my sarcasm. Sarcasm was a foreign language in Japan, and I only knew it from watching Western TV shows. She blushed and shied away from me, and I immediately felt guilty. "Sorry. Yes, we're dating. No one seems to believe it. I'm beginning to not believe it."

"Forgive me," she said, bowing.

"Kayo!" Goro growled from the other room. "Why are you holding up Mei?"

She beat a hasty retreat for one of the conference rooms. I tried not to sigh, but I was a horrible person for saying that to her. I should apologize next time I saw her.

I rounded the corner and sat in the chair next to Goro's desk. He popped the last of his rice ball into his mouth and chewed. "What were you and Kayo talking about?"

"Nothing. Did you get my email?"

"Yeah. What's this Ne Kitsune business? Are you looking to cheat on Yasahiro already?" He snapped his fingers, his face lighting up. "Wait. You haven't really been dating and you're checking out escort services? What? You want me to vet these people or something?"

I picked his clipboard up from the table and whacked him over the head with it. Two other people in the room snickered.

"Eh! What's the matter? What did I do?"

I tossed the clipboard onto the desk.

"I've had it with you, with everyone." I stood up and all the activity in the room paused. "I am dating Yasahiro Suga," I bellowed out. "We're living together, and it's the real thing. If you don't believe me, you can ask him yourself."

I looked around at everyone staring at me, frozen, and the back of my neck began to sweat. I should have been more discreet but I'd had it. A phone rang and everyone unglued, returning to their tasks. I sat down in a lump.

"Sorry," he said, obviously not sorry, before he laughed and rolled his eyes. "Wait till I tell Yasahiro about this."

I reached forward and grabbed his shirt. "You tell Yasahiro I did this, and I swear I will prank you till the day you die."

He swallowed, his face paling. I loved a good challenge and he knew this. I would make his life miserable if he breathed a word of this to Yasahiro. "Okay, Mei."

"Now..." I let go of his shirt and smoothed out my own. "Ne Kitsune *is* an escort service. No sex. They hire out men to come and sleep with women at night if they're lonely. Mrs. Murata said she heard Etsuko mention them more than once. Don't you remember this? It should be in your notes."

"Really?" He opened up his browser and navigated to the website. "So I *should* be looking into them." He scrolled until he found the contact information and wrote down the address in his notebook. "They're located in Kokubunji, west of Tokyo. It'll be a drive, but I should go visit in person. They won't talk to me over the phone."

A wave of relief crashed over me. I was glad he could drop the joking around quickly enough to get to work. I pulled out my phone and went to my email. "Just to start the process, I opened an account with them and they're doing a background check on me now."

"What?" He pulled away from looking at the email. "I'm not sure that's safe. What if one of these guys is the killer?"

"I plan to meet him in a public place the first time, and I'll let you know how it goes after that."

He glanced between me and the computer. "Does Yasahiro know about this?"

A little lie. "Yeah. He looked at the website with me." He didn't know I was going to meet anyone yet. I thought I'd have him tag along somehow, have him watch from a distant location, but I wanted to wait until the details were figured out. "Anyway, they said they'd reply to me tonight, but I'll set something up soon. Maybe Monday night."

He stood up from his computer and grabbed his coat. "I'll drive out there today and have a look around. Ask the neighbors about the business, that sort of thing. Kayo!" He called out, and Kayo poked her head out of a conference room. "Keep an eye on Hisashi while I'm gone. I'm heading to Kokubunji to nail down a possible suspect."

She nodded and returned to the conference room. I grabbed Goro's arm. "How is Hisashi?" I jerked my head in the direction of the hallway. The police station had only one jail cell, and saying it was a jail cell was an overstatement. It was basically a room with a couch, bed, and its own bathroom. They only used it for people they didn't consider dangerous. Really dangerous people got shipped off to Tokyo.

"He's fine. He's been questioned every day for the last five days and hasn't confessed. He doesn't seem to know anything.

And our coroner's report says it's possible Etsuko died *after* he boarded his train back to Tokyo. We have him on video at the station, so..." He shrugged his shoulders. "But his work place said that he'd been taking days off and acting suspiciously."

"How so?"

"They couldn't put their finger on it, just lots of strange absences. What if he had been planning her death all along and had been socking away money to flee?"

My mind raced through this scenario. I couldn't imagine him with his hands around her neck, crushing her to the point of death. But then, I could imagine him working a second job to make more money. In my head, I saw him leave work every day and work a night shift someplace. It wasn't like he had to come home to Etsuko every night. She had said they talked on the phone all the time, but he could have been talking from anywhere.

"Mei?" Goro waved his hand in front of my face. "Hello, daydreamer!"

"Sorry," I said, refocusing on him. "Even if he was making extra money on the side, I still don't think he would do anything to Etsuko. Maybe he would break up with her, but kill her? No. If anything, he was keeping a secret second job to pay for the move here. They were talking about his move on our last group date, remember?"

"Yeah, but I don't know." He rubbed his chin. "After what happened with Tama, I would think you'd be more suspicious."

In that case, I had been the only one suspicious of Tama, and everyone else had him pegged as the golden child.

"It's interesting that I'm *not* suspicious." I shrugged my shoulders. "But I'm not a detective."

Goro pulled open the door to the lobby, and we each bundled up in our coats. "You should consider becoming one. There's no time like the present to make a career change."

As fun as it might have been to be a real detective, I didn't have it in me to go back to school. I wanted to help out the community, but I could find another, less tiresome and costly way to do it.

"Maybe. I have another idea of what I can do, though."

I followed Goro outside, and he approached his police car. "Need a ride?"

"No, thank you. I'm going to Sawayaka, and it's only a few blocks from here."

Goro waved as he got into his car and drove off. I headed in the direction of Sawayaka, a six block walk (five in one direction and then one over) along the town's outer road. The sun dipped low near the horizon, and in another hour, twilight would begin to fall. I glanced over my shoulder at the sky in the opposite direction and a young man was walking behind me a block back. He ducked his head and walked into a store, so I proceeded on to Sawayaka.

I sped up, unsure of my instincts. With everything going on, it was only natural for me to feel paranoid, right? I passed a gift store, a place that sold local knickknacks and sweets, and abruptly halted to look in the window.

From the corner of my eye, I caught the young man less than a block behind me again. He couldn't be more than twenty-five, his long bangs and shaggy hair, dyed blonde at the tips, fell over his face. He clutched a messenger bag, thrown across his chest and over one shoulder in his gloved hands. This time, he made eye contact with me, panic washing over his features. We both stood in our spots, staring each other down.

Who was going to move first?

He did. He whirled around and sprinted for the end of the block.

"Hey!" I unstuck my feet and ran after him. I hadn't properly exercised in weeks (sex didn't count) and my legs tired after a short dash to the corner. Oh no. I was going to lose him! "Hey!" I yelled again after him. He didn't stop. His legs pumped at a breakneck speed, and my legs slowed down, burning from unaccustomed exertion. I sucked in a deep breath and began to cough. The doctors had told me not to run because of the smoke inhalation, and now I knew why. The young man, dressed in a dark charcoal gray coat with a red and black scarf waving in the wind, rounded another corner, startling a few young women walking the opposite direction. In a blink, he was out of eyesight.

Great. Either I had scared off a random person by yelling at him or someone really was following me.

CHAPTER
EIGHTEEN

"Come on. Let's go on a road trip," Yasahiro said, grasping my hand and pulling me off the couch. After breakfast, we had spent the whole of Sunday morning on the couch, drinking coffee and reading. I loved this about our relationship so far. We were quiet and easy with each other, no rushing to go out and be active, just spending the time together.

"A road trip? Where?" I carried my coffee cup into the kitchen and placed it in the dishwasher. It only took one day for Yasahiro and me to settle into a housekeeping routine. He cooked, and I cleaned, which was a lot like my routine with Mom, but I was trying not to dwell on that. I rolled up my sleeves and grabbed the soapy sponge, ready to take care of the morning's dishes.

"Leave that. We should head out soon since I need to be at the restaurant later." He tugged on my arm again, a playful smile dancing about his scruffy face. I had the urge to drag the back of my fingers along the beard growth because it'd be gone in an hour, but my hands were already wet.

"Are you sure?" I held up the sponge and waved to the pile of dishes in the sink. "I hate leaving these here."

"Yeah, I'm sure."

Forty-five minutes later, we were on the road, heading west. Yasahiro had the heat blasting and the music playing, his GPS turned off.

"Are you going to tell me where were going?"

He glanced at me as we merged onto the highway. "I figured it was best to spring this on you. We're going to visit my parents."

I sighed and flipped down the mirror so I could check my makeup. "I had a feeling you would do this. It would have been fine to warn me, you know. I'm ready to meet them. You and my mom are the best of friends now, and I'd like to make friends with your mom." I evened up the makeup around my eyes and patted down my hair. "I'm glad we got *some* sleep last night." I smiled over at him. Some sleep? I could honestly say I'd never been so happily sleep deprived in all my life. At least the sleep I had at his place was warm, deep, and comfortable.

"We've been dating for almost three months. It's time. And I wanted to go visit before the holidays, before things get crazy around town." He drummed his fingers on the steering wheel. "And there's something else..."

The way he avoided looking at me made my brain flood with worry.

"Out with it, Yasahiro." I folded my arms across my chest. He'd been on the phone a lot the last two days, speaking in French, and shrugging off my questions whenever he hung up.

"I was waiting for the final confirmation, but I have to fly to France for three days to teach a class. This is my old school, so I feel obligated. They'll pay me a high fee, and they'll pay for my airfare, too. I'm glad I can finally do these things, now that the restaurant can function without me for several days in a row." He glanced my way, to the road and back several times. "Do you want to come with me?"

I concentrated on the scenery out the window, watching the

world speed by. "I wish circumstances were different, and I had the money to come with you."

"I'll pay," he insisted, running his hand through his hair. "I'd really like for you to come. I want to show you Paris at Christmastime. It's nothing short of magical."

I laughed, a short huff of a breath. This was just my luck, wasn't it? "I don't even know if my passport is current." I tried to think of where I had seen it last. Possibly in a box in my room. "I got it when I was sixteen and it only lasts five years."

"I thought you said you've never left Japan."

"I haven't. I wanted to go to Australia for a foreign exchange program so I got the passport, but then Mom said we couldn't afford it. Anyway..." I returned to looking out the window. "I just got these new clients this past week, and I would hate to abandon them after offering to help. When do you leave?"

"Tonight. 00:30 flight out of Haneda. It was the best they could do." He kept his eyes locked straight forward on the road. "I'm nervous about this trip, and I was hesitant about what you would think of it. I want you to come. I, um, suspect Amanda will be there. Last I heard, she was still living in Paris. And we share some same friends..." His voice wavered as he changed lanes.

This was the moment that I knew he belonged to me. Any other guy would have gone and not told me about the ex-girlfriend being there. Any other guy would have done the deed and cheated, or hoped to avoid the drama entirely by not saying anything to anyone. That he cared enough to be honest with me before he left was crucial.

"Don't worry about it." I slipped my hand across the seat and rested it on his knee. "I understand. I'm sure she's going to be hard to avoid if you share the same friends. I'll have to grin and bear it." I popped a small smile at him and turned to look out the window.

"I'll be busy the whole time. There are classes, and meetings, and dinners to attend. If I'm lucky, she's out of town for the holidays."

"If you're lucky?"

"Of course." He blew out a long breath. "I've done a good job of avoiding her since we broke up. I really don't want to see her again. And if I do see her again, I want you right there next to me."

"Okay." In a way, I was ready to encourage him to meet up with her. It might have been good for him to get the closure he needed. But I was selfish and I wanted him to never see her again. Since I rarely got what I wanted, I was sure she wasn't gone from our lives.

Yasahiro pulled off the road into a small farming town, mostly homes in smaller subdivisions surrounded by fields. Kilometers worth of farmland zipped past the window as he wove through the back roads. I'd never been to Chichibu before, so I soaked in the surroundings and cataloged them away in case we ever came here again. Yasahiro slowed the car and pulled into a dirt road that led to a farm house.

My stomach shrank to the size of a soybean, and I swallowed to stop a wave of nausea. I was suddenly so nervous my hands were shaking. What if they didn't like me? What if this was so awkward Yasahiro got discouraged? But there was no time to gather myself and prepare because as we came to a stop, the front door opened and a woman walked out, her hair streaked with gray and tucked behind her ears, wearing jeans, a sweater, and an apron over them.

"You're here early," she said, opening her arms to her son, and Yasahiro walked right into them. I could tell how much he loved her by the way his guard was so fully down.

"Hi, Mom." He hugged her, and I was surprised to notice they were both tall. I came up to Yasahiro's shoulder, but his mom was taller than me.

I stood next to the car and tried not to intrude on their

moment, though my ears were ringing and sweat pooled on my lower back. This, coupled with the knowledge he'd be gone and within striking distance of Amanda, made me feel sick. I gripped the car door handle and squeezed, trying to ground myself.

"Mom." He stepped away from her. "This is who I wanted to surprise you with. Mei, this is my mom." He grabbed my hand and held on tight, smiling at me, but I watched her reaction. It was exactly what I thought was going to happen. Her face was a riot of confusion before settling into a frown.

"When you said you had a surprise visitor coming, I assumed it would be somebody different."

Yasahiro's face fell, as he realized at the same time I did, his parents were expecting Amanda. Not me.

———

"This is what I get for trying to surprise people," Yasahiro whispered to me inside his parents' house while sitting at the kotatsu. I was so angry, the sound of his voice irritated me to the point of snapping.

"Don't talk to me," I growled at him and he dipped his head, shamed for a moment. I sifted through the last ten awkward minutes and tried to find something to make it better. Yasahiro's mom had been so surprised she couldn't even speak to me. If I were a gambling woman, I'd bet Yasahiro never mentioned me to them prior to this day. But I didn't believe he was a liar, so I couldn't take that bet.

I was surrounded by Amanda. Up on a cork board on the wall, printouts of online articles about Yasahiro and Amanda filled every square centimeter of available space. All the images I had seen on Google were right there, taunting me. I'd been good and stayed away from my search history the last two weeks, but now I wanted to stare at them again, remind myself I'd never be as pretty, smart, or talented as her. When my life was uncertain or in upheaval, I had this masochistic desire to hate on my own life, and Amanda was my go-to weapon of choice. I had been so proud of myself for staying away. Now, I felt the pull again. To my right, along with framed photos of Yasahiro's family, a large print of Yasahiro and Amanda at the Cannes Film Festival stared down at me. If I walked into the other room, I wouldn't have been surprised if her photo was up in a shrine.

"Listen here, Yasahiro." I dropped my voice low, and Yasahiro paled at the use of his whole, proper name. "You have five minutes to go into the kitchen and explain this to your mother before I stand up and walk out of here. Your father will be home soon, and I want to try to make a good first impression on him. I can't do that if your mother has no idea what's going on."

"Yes, Mei."

"And another thing," I said as I grabbed his shirt, "if you ever do this to me again, we're through." I nodded at him and he nodded back.

I'd never understood this about some people, wanting to surprise others. Surprises usually led to heartbreak.

I sipped on the tea in front of me and strained my ears to listen to their conversation in the kitchen.

"Mom," Yasahiro's voice filtered in from the kitchen. "I need for you to give Mei a chance. I told you Amanda and I broke up over a year ago. It's over and I've moved on."

"I always thought you would get back together." Something clanged into the sink with such force that I thought it'd been thrown there. "When you told me you were dating, I didn't think it was serious. How can this be serious enough to bring her here?"

I cringed and stared down into the cup of tea, hoping something was said that I could use to my advantage. Because I denied it all the time, but I was falling hard for this man, and I could tell he was falling for me too. I wanted this to work.

"Because I said it was serious. Did you not believe me?"

"You proposed to Amanda. That was it for me. No one with

honor proposes marriage and then breaks up. I did *not* raise my son to be dishonorable and loose."

Yasahiro sighed. "It wasn't me who was dishonorable."

They fell into silence except for the noise of chopping, a metal knife hitting a wooden butcher block in rhythmic thumps. Honor meant something to this woman? She sounded pretty old-fashioned for someone wearing jeans with a modern haircut. Okay, then. If this was something she valued, I could do that. I chewed on my lip and stared out the window as the sound of a car approached the house. An older man drove up and parked behind Yasahiro's car. This was the same man in the photos on the wall, so it must have been Yasahiro's dad. Time for action.

"No one is more honorable than Mei. If you give her a chance, you'll see what I see."

His mom stayed silent for another minute, which gave me the impression she was stern and tough.

"Can I help you with anything?" he asked. Good move.

"Set up the burner, please."

Yasahiro emerged from the kitchen and set a portable gas burner on the table right before the front door opened and his father entered the house. They smiled and embraced swiftly, one of those manly, fast hugs that involved a swift pat on the back and a laugh. I pulled my feet from under the kotatsu and sat on them, seiza style.

"Dad, I've brought Mei today to meet you both." Yasahiro stepped back from his dad and gestured to me. I put on my sweetest smile and bowed forward in *keirei*, one of the bows you're only supposed to pull out of your arsenal for high bosses at work or your in-laws. I inclined forward, my forehead thirty centimeters off the tatami, and placed my hands on the floor, careful to create a triangle between my thumbs and forefingers.

"I'm honored to meet you, Mrs. Suga." I added a cheerful note to my voice, pausing in the bowed position for a count of four in my head. Then I slowly came up for another count of four. My mom would've been so proud. She had taught me the polite ways to bow when I was a kid and we practiced them all the time.

When I lifted my head, all three of them stood aghast with their mouths open, Yasahiro's mom holding a steaming hot pot in two oven-mittened hands. I doubted anyone had treated them as nicely as I was about to. I knew what it was like to grow up in a low-income household and have people treat you like the dirt you work. I would never do that to anyone else.

I jumped up from my spot. "Can I help bring anything from the kitchen?"

"No. No." Yasahiro's mom snapped out of her shock, shaking her head. "Please sit down."

"It's nice to meet you, Mei." Yasahiro's father smiled at me and his son. "I'm sorry our home is a humble farm house and we don't have anything fancy to feed you."

"Your house is lovely," I said, ignoring Amanda staring at me from the photos on the wall. "And I've come to love all kinds of food, thanks to Yasahiro."

Yasahiro set bowls and spoons on the table, not saying anything. I wished I could read him better, but I supposed that would come with time.

"I'm happy to serve up. What a lovely hot pot you've made, Mrs. Suga." I distributed a bowl to each spot after ladling in a large portion of soup, then I waited while everyone else sat before we said "Itadakimasu" and began eating. I stayed silent as much as possible during the meal, listening and nodding where appropriate, or answering questions if they were directed at me. But the three of them mostly talked about the farm, Yasahiro's business, and family matters, leaving me out of the conversation. I noticed, though, that the questions directed at me came from his father while his mother often looked over at the news clippings on the wall.

After lunch, Yasahiro's dad asked him to go outside for a walk around the property. It was well above freezing, so he obliged and left me to his mom. I tried not to worry and instead I bid them a happy farewell with a big smile and a wave. Then I did what I always did after a meal, I cleaned up.

"Please, Mei. Sit. You're our guest." Yasahiro's mom wanted me to stay behind by myself in the living area, but I shook my head and followed her to the kitchen with the bowls anyway.

"I enjoy cleaning, and I'd like to help. Please allow me to do the dishes." I barreled past her to the sink, sought out the cleaning sponge and dish soap, and turned on the faucet, waiting for the water to turn hot. As I picked up a bowl, I glanced over my shoulder at her, and she was peering past me to the sink, a nervous twitch to her lip.

"Yasahiro tells me you farm mostly soy here." I soaped up a bowl and arranged her dish rack so I could stack clean dishes there. "We've never farmed soy, but I hear it's lucrative."

She came to stand next to me, dumping anything left in the dishes into the burnable trash. "Does your family farm?"

"We cultivate greens and tomatoes during the summer. Sweet potatoes, squash, and a ton of other root vegetables during the fall. Mom likes to grow wildflowers and chrysanthemum as well in the spring and summer."

"And your father...?"

"He died when I was five." I added another washed bowl to the drying rack. "My older brother lives with his family in Osaka. It's just me and Mom now."

She tilted her head to the side, not asking any questions except for the ones via body language.

"I had a string of jobs and a small apartment in Tokyo for years, but my company let me go this fall." I shrugged my shoulders. "I moved home with Mom and decided to stay and help out. I met Yasahiro not long after."

I finished off by scrubbing the chopsticks and spoons in the sink, adding them to the utensil basket, and wiping down the surrounding area. When I turned around, she was very still, examining me with an intense shrewdness one reserved for a principal disciplining a rowdy student.

"There," I declared, gesturing to the clean dishes, taking a towel, and drying off my hands. How many other girlfriends of Yasahiro did the dishes when they came over? I was going to guess, hmmm, none. "Can I help with anything else?"

"No. Thank you." She twisted her towel in her hands, so I saw an opportunity to make a statement.

"I want to say that I know I'm not pretty or famous like Amanda, but I'm kind and loyal, and Yasahiro can trust me. He's been so good to me." I clutched my hands to my chest and smiled, remembering all the little things he does, like how he brings me water at bedtime, or the time I was caught in the rain and he helped get me dry again, or the extra cream and sugar in my coffee when I needed both. "And I plan to be good to him, forever, if we get that far."

"Shhh." She stepped forward suddenly and grasped my arm in her right hand. She squeezed, glancing behind me. I turned my head and Yasahiro was in the doorway with his father. "What is it you plan on doing, now that you no longer have a job in Tokyo? You don't plan on taking over your family's farm, do you? My son is a successful businessman. He wasn't meant for the fields."

"Mom..." Yasahiro's voice contained a note of warning.

Ah. This was where I truly differed from Amanda. She would have been a good match for him because she was successful like Yasahiro. I suspected I may have had an advantage over her because I was not a foreigner, but that wasn't enough.

"No. I was never meant to be a farmer —"

"Mei is an artist. Her work is beautiful," Yasahiro interrupted.

"And I want to work with and help the elderly," I blurted out. Even Yasahiro was taken aback. "I... This is a new thing for me." I shrugged my shoulders. "I have new elderly clients I help a few times per week, and I enjoy it. I wish I could do more. I wish it were my real job."

Everyone's eyes were on me, and I squirmed inside from their attention.

"That's a noble idea, Mei," Yasahiro's dad said, breaking the silence. "Why don't you come and have a drink with me at the kotatsu, and I'll tell you about my father?" He waved to me, and I hesitated a moment before slinking past Yasahiro's mom.

Yasahiro stopped me at the doorway. "Be careful. My dad can put away saké like no one else." He dropped his voice. "Let's talk about your idea when I return from Paris."

"Okay," I whispered, and then gave him a quick peck on the cheek. "Thanks."

When I reached the table, Yasahiro's dad already had the saké waiting for me.

CHAPTER
NINETEEN

"You look so worried," Yasahiro said as he set down his bag at the bottom of the stairs. "I promise I'll be back on Thursday, and it will feel like I never left to begin with."

Cold air leaked under the door, frosting my socked feet. I didn't have the heart to tell him that this was not the reason I was worried. I had received email that I was approved to meet up with a boy from Ne Kitsune, and I didn't tell him about it because he wouldn't be there to help anyway. Now I was second-guessing my decision. It could have been dangerous or just plain stupid, but I wouldn't know until I tried. I had promised Kumi I would help find the person who murdered Etsuko. I liked to keep my promises, so I was going forward with my plan in the safest way possible.

"I'll be fine." I produced a half-smile for him, memorizing his face so I could daydream about him over the next few days. "I have a safe place to live, with plenty of food. I'll miss having a warm body to sleep next to, though." I pinched his arm and he laughed.

"That's it? I'm nothing but a warm body to you?"

"I think you're a lot more than that." I wrapped my arms around him and buried my face in his coat. I wished he wasn't going. Our relationship had just begun, and I hated having to put everything on hold so he could go to Paris and leave me here. But I prided myself on being an independent girl, so I sucked it up and dealt with it.

"The car's here." A flash of headlights swept through the vestibule as a car pulled up to the curb, right on time. There was nothing like leaving for the airport at bedtime to make one happy about taxi services.

"Remember what I said," he whispered, taking my face in his hands and looking me straight in the eyes.

"Eat a lot, get lots of sleep, and be careful," I repeated back to him his "instructions" as if I needed to be reminded to eat when I had actual food in the house. Cooking it would be another story. Maybe I'd call Mom to come hang out with me the next few days.

"And don't worry about me or Amanda. I probably won't even see her."

"I understand. And I'll be fine with it even if you do see her." Jealousy was a horrible emotion on me. I tried not to succumb to it as much as possible.

He leaned in, touched his lips to mine, and kissed me goodbye like he wouldn't see me for a year, forever. I threw my arms around his neck and squeezed, pressing my body to his. Who knew? If we ended up dating for years or even getting married, in the future, he'd leave on trips like this, and I'd wave from the door or not even get out of bed. But the first absence was the hardest.

He buttoned his jacket and shouldered the door open, grabbing his suitcase and wheeling it to the curb. We waved to each other as the car sped away, and I pressed my face to the door to catch the last sight of the red brake lights at the corner.

Going to sleep was tough without him, but after I calmed my brain down, I managed to sleep until nine, have a quiet morning at home, and ate leftovers for lunch. Just as I was about to walk out to meet up with Murata at her apartment in the afternoon, my phone rang. It was Goro.

"Hey, you still at Yasahiro's place?"

"Yeah," I said, hesitating. "Please don't give me a hard time about dating him. I don't think I could take it with him out of town."

"Is he out of town?" A squawk of a police radio interrupted him. "Where did he go?"

"He's in Paris until Thursday."

"Is he going to see his ex?"

"Goro, could you be a little more insensitive, please? I'm not feeling vulnerable enough."

Silence. "What, Mei?"

"Never mind! What's up?" No one got my sense of humor but Yasahiro. I paced back and forth near the door, my coat already on, my shoes waiting.

"I wanted to report in about the Ne Kitsune business."

I stopped in my tracks. "What did you find out?"

"I'm downstairs in my car. Want to come down and chat about it?"

I took three long strides across the living room, and standing on the couch, I saw his police car downstairs.

"Now I know why you asked me if I was at Yasahiro's. I'll be right down."

I pulled on my boots, grabbed my bag, and turned down the lights in the apartment, being sure to lock up behind me. Down on the street, Goro's police car idled at the curb. I opened the door and slipped into his heated car.

"It's actually warmer out today," I said, a note of excitement in my voice. I was desperate for spring.

"It's a heatwave!" Goro chuckled. "You got out the door fast."

"I'm on my way to meet up with Mrs. Murata. We have a regular thing Mondays through Thursdays."

"Okay. I won't keep you then. So I did some searching on the Ne Kitsune organization. They're legitimate. Their men are only escorts. No sex. The businesses around them seem pleased with their presence. They pay bills on time, conduct their business quietly and discreetly, and never give anyone cause to complain. The woman who runs the main office did say that they hire a majority of gay men for this."

I raised my eyebrows at him and he shrugged.

"Makes sense when you think about it." Goro turned down the radio that suddenly switched to a high-energy pop duet. "They have regular clients all over the Tokyo and Saitama area, and most of their guys travel by train so they can save money. They're almost all broke college students."

I stared out the window towards the empty retail space under Yasahiro's apartment. I'd still not been in there, and with the steel shutters down, I'd never been able to look inside from the street.

"If you were a broke college student and trying to pay your bills, wouldn't you do just about anything to keep your head above water?" I asked, turning to Goro.

He rubbed at the shadow of a beard on his chin. "Well, it would depend on how broke I was. Would I kill, though? No, obviously."

"Right. But you may take bribes or do work on the side?"

He shifted in his seat.

"Hypothetically speaking, of course. Maybe you're not cut out to be a detective," I said, chuckling.

"Perhaps." He blew out a long breath and gripped the steering wheel. "Okay, I may take bribes or do work on the side if I was desperate."

"So, we need to find the desperate ones and question them." I waved my hand as if this was a foregone conclusion.

"Uh, Mei. They *all* seemed pretty desperate to me. I watched them come and go during the course of a day — young, hip guys. I followed several to apartments in run-down sections of

Takadanobaba. One shared an apartment with five other people. Five," he stressed.

Ugh. I couldn't imagine. Tokyo apartments were tiny to begin with.

"Well, if he's getting money, then Etsuko was getting money too, right?"

The area between his eyebrows creased. "Her bank accounts were dry."

I looked at the retail space below Yasahiro's apartment. If I were going to hide anything anywhere, I'd hide it in the last possible place someone would look, right in front of their face.

"Then she squirreled it away somewhere. Buried it in the park or it's in her apartment." I nodded my head, certain this was the answer.

Goro ran his hand through his hair and sipped coffee from an insulated mug in his cup holder. "We only did a cursory search because we didn't want to damage the property. I'll have officers come in and tear the place apart."

"Great. Let me know if you find anything." I grasped the door handle, but then stopped and threw my weight into the seat. "What about Hisashi? Are you going to release him?"

"No. We still have no motive for anyone else to kill her. The evidence against him isn't strong, though, so he'll be let go next week if we don't find anything else. I feel bad for him. I see him every day, and he's slowly sinking into a depression." Goro shook his head again. "I wish he could have gone to her funeral."

"Such a shame." We both sat quietly for a moment before I opened the car and swung my legs outside. "Text me if you hear anything else. And I'll be at Yasahiro's until spring."

"I'll be sure to let him know you took good care of the place while he was gone!" He yelled at me as I shut the door. I smiled as I walked away and around the corner to Murata's apartment.

"We're going to do something a little different today," I said, grabbing her coat and scarf once I was inside. "I want to go have coffee at the café a few blocks from here. We'll walk there together, and I'll treat you to tea. It'll be a good way to get out of the house and exercise."

Murata raised her eyebrows at me. "How cold is it outside?"

"It's above ten degrees today, a good day to walk and stretch our legs."

"Fine. Fine. But I'll treat for coffee and tea."

"Now it was my idea..."

"Don't argue with me, young lady. I have the money, and I'm happy to get out anyway." She glanced around her apartment before we left, noting the lights and space heaters were off. "Hey, wasn't your police officer friend going to send someone by to pick up this box?" She pointed to the cardboard box of bentos meant for Etsuko.

"Yeah. I'll call him and remind him." I ushered her out the door.

I helped Murata down the stairs, and we walked, arm in arm, to the café. Along the way, she smiled and waved to everyone she knew. People were happy to be outside. The sun was shining and the weather was the nicest it'd been in weeks. I almost felt bad for Yasahiro. It was supposed to be colder in Paris than it would be in Tokyo. But tomorrow night called for snow, and I was sure I would be shoveling for hours the next day. I needed to contact my clients and make sure they had someone to take care of snow removal. I would hate for them to be cooped up at home because they couldn't clear their walkways.

"You're awfully quiet today." Murata patted my arm.

"Yasahiro left last night to go to Paris for three days. I miss him already."

"Are you still living at his place? What about your mom? She's not living at home, is she?"

"No, no. She's living with her friend, Chiyo. We promised we'd stay out of the house until spring. All of the pipes froze, and we have to save our money."

We approached the café, and I held open the door for Murata. Inside, the space was warm, bright, and steamy. Happy people sat at tables or on couches, sipped coffee or tea, and chatted.

"I haven't been here in ages!" Murata glanced around and waved to a few people. I swore she knew at least half the town. "It was a good idea to get out of the house."

"I'm glad you approve. We'll hang out here for a while and then go back later, and I'll finish cleaning out your front closet."

I helped Murata order tea and coffee, and we found a table to sit at.

"So..." Murata blew on her hot teacup. "Have you given any thought to your next job?"

"What do you mean? I submit resumes for new jobs every day. It's beginning to look like submitting resumes *is* my job."

She chuckled. "What I mean is have you thought about relocating to another part of the country? Or entering a new profession entirely?"

I dumped a packet of sugar into my coffee and stirred. "No. I haven't thought of doing anything that drastic yet. Originally, I didn't want to move home. I dreaded it. But now, I like being home and helping my mom, so I'm hoping I can find a local job. Mom is set with work for the time being. She's good until spring when she wants to get the farm up and running again. I'd like to help her with that." I sipped on my coffee and thought for a moment, glancing out the window. "If only I could find something part-time, then I'd be set."

I'd been thinking a lot about what I said at Yasahiro's parents' house and how I could deliver on my idea. I wanted to help the elderly, but I wasn't sure how to do it.

"If only I could do for others what I do for you, as a real job." I sat back in my chair and stared at the woman making coffee behind the counter. "I don't think I have it in me to be a nurse, nor do I have the qualifications to work in a nursing home, but there has to be something else."

Murata hummed, picking at the napkin on the table. "You know what's missing in Chikata? A gathering place for us older folks. It used to be that the community center was that for us."

"Right," I said, perking up. "You were telling me that last week."

"What about a central place where people can do crafts?"

"Maybe they could do crafts, or sit and talk, or have tea. They could even have family gatherings there some days."

"Yes, yes," Murata said, nodding. "If you could figure out how to sell discounted meals there, too, that would be ideal."

I slipped away into a daydream of this place. Several low tables and easy seating, crafts on designated days, birthday parties, and grandkids coming to visit, hot tea and discounted bento boxes. A place like this, central and catering to anyone over sixty-five, would be hopping with people. What if it also sold specialty items to help cover the rent?

"Mei?" Murata sat forward, trying to get my attention. "Your smile is as wide as the ocean." She laughed. "What are you thinking about?"

"I'm thinking about making dreams into reality." I picked up our empty cups and brought them to the counter. "Let's brainstorm some more on this on the way home. I just had a fantastic idea, and it's going to involve a lot of planning."

"Planning, young lady, is what I do best." She snapped her hat on her head. "Let's go."

CHAPTER
TWENTY

The cafe was busy at 18:00, and for once, I was there and not hungry for the pastries in the case. Yasahiro had left me a huge bowl of curry and all I had to do was make rice for it. Bless him. He knew I was only capable of handling a microwave. I was stuffed to my chin with dinner and sipping on the cafe's cappuccino was the perfect way to end my night.

I told the Ne Kitsune administrator that I would meet their candidate between 18:00 and 18:15. I was nervous, but I was in a busy, well-lit place, and no matter what, we wouldn't be going back to Yasahiro's place. I was there to question him, and this would be my only shot. Once I started asking questions, I wouldn't be able to hide my intentions.

Instead of bouncing my leg and glancing out the window every two seconds, I pulled my eReader out of my bag and got back into my latest novel. It was hard to concentrate because I kept thinking about the ideas I had with Murata. We talked about building a little tea house slash community space for elderly Chikata residents, and she was as excited about the idea as I was. But right now, it was just a dream — a dream I wanted to make a reality, but that was it. I would need funds, an investor, space to buy, capital... Ugh. A lot of stuff I wasn't sure I could accomplish on my own. I had the knowledge to start a real business, but I didn't have relationships with investors or any savings of my own. For the time being, I had to be happy dreaming about it.

I focused on my book, and after five minutes, I was sucked into the story while sipping my coffee and not paying attention to the world around me. This was what I loved about books. Even when my life was low, I was happy to lose myself in fiction and forget about it for a short while.

"I love girls who read." A voice broke into my world, shattering the fantasy universe of knights and fair maidens to pieces and bringing me right back to reality. A young man slipped into the seat across from me. My brain was slow to register all of his details and kicked into high gear to keep up.

Oh no. We made eye contact across the table like we had on Saturday when he followed me through the streets of Chikata. He smiled, pushing his long bangs and shaggy hair, dyed blonde at the tips, away from his face. His eyes were changed, an unnatural violet color, and he was better dressed than most men I'd ever met, his skin smooth and perfectly even.

"Hi," he said, his voice quiet and soothing. "I'm Jun, and you must be Mei."

I glanced left and right as I turned off my eReader and slipped it in my bag. "Uh, didn't you...?" I stopped, thinking that maybe I imagined that.

"Sorry I ran away the other day, but I had a feeling we'd meet again."

"Jun..." I tested out his name on the tip of my tongue; it didn't sound familiar. No one I knew had ever spoken of a Jun, never even heard the name in random conversation. "How long have you been following me around?"

"Just that one time, and it was an accident. You walked past me, and I was sure I had seen you before, and I was right. We have a mutual friend in common. He's pointed you out on more than one occasion, at that restaurant in town."

"Who?" I leaned forward, almost knocking my cup off the table. Was he talking about Yasahiro? Did Yasahiro know this young man? My scalp began to crawl, and my heart beat swiftly.

Jun smiled, but none of the warmth of it reached his cool, violet eyes.

"When I saw your name come through at work, I volunteered for the job."

"You did?"

My thoughts were a tangled mess of confusion. Who was this guy? How did he know me? Why had he followed me? What the hell was going on?

"Yes, absolutely. I think you're perfect, actually." He waved his hand in a flourish. "You're single and you live with your mother who is hardly ever home during the day."

I wanted to interrupt and ask him how he knew this because I hadn't been home for almost a week. And hello! I was dating Yasahiro!

I growled under my breath. No one really believed me, did they?

"Did I say something wrong?"

"I'm confused. Who is the friend we have in common? Yasahiro Suga?"

Jun sat back in his seat. "Never heard of him."

Relief rushed through me even though I didn't expect him to tell me the truth anyway.

"Do you want to test me out tomorrow after your mother leaves for work?" Jun extracted a small notebook from his bag and clicked a pen. "I do day jobs too when I don't have other things to do."

"Really?"

"Of course. Plenty of people have night jobs and sleep during the day. I have to remain flexible."

I swallowed hard, wondering what kind of life this was. Goro said most of these guys were broke, but he seemed well put together. Perhaps he was one of the more popular escorts.

Who did we have in common? I thought back through the people I knew in town.

"Did you sleep with Etsuko Hiyasa?"

"I'm not obliged to talk about my other clients."

Anger boiled up in my gut. "She's dead, you know? Murdered in her apartment. Her family and her boyfriend are devastated."

His face paled, all the heat of it lost in a swift intake of breath. "What?" He pulled out his phone and typed furiously on it.

"She died a little over a week ago. Didn't you know?"

Jun jumped up from his seat so quickly the chair fell over with a sharp crack. Everyone in the café turned to look at us, and I began to bow and try to correct the chair as he spun from his spot and leaped for the door. I lunged from my chair, grabbed my bag, and ran out after him.

"Wait!" I sped up to catch him. "What's going on?"

"Deal's off, lady," he said, as his phone pinged at him. "I should have known he'd get me into trouble."

"Who?" I grabbed his arm and pulled hard. *Talk to me! Tell me what's going on!*

He cursed at me, throwing his arm wide, and pushed me down with both hands. My feet slipped out, and I crashed to the concrete sidewalk, knocking my arm and head on the ground. All the air from my lungs burst out in a puff of vapor.

"*Busu! Kutabare.*"

My mind blanked; I was in such shock. A moan rumbled through my lungs, trying to refill with air. Jun's hands searched all over me, patting my pockets and then he yanked my purse from my hand. I tried to open my eyes and get up, but nothing was working. A moment later, my purse landed on my chest and footsteps ran off into the distance.

"Hey!" Someone else yelled. "Stop him!"

I rolled to my side and clutched at the back of my head. My hand came away unbloodied but the point of impact throbbed. When I finally looked around, an older man was crouched over me.

"Did that young man assault you? Are you hurt?" He pulled me to my feet and I swayed to the side, resting my body against the building nearest me. "I saw him push you down. I was taking out the garbage across the street." He motioned to the apartment building he must have lived in, his eyes wide. "I haven't seen a crime committed around here in twenty years! What happened?"

"I... I'm not sure what happened." I gathered my wits and squatted down to pick up the things that fell out of my bag. My purse exploded on the sidewalk. Ugh. I hated when that happened. Most everything was there, thankfully. My phone had been in a zippered inner pocket and was unharmed, but I grabbed my wallet, opened it, and my cash was gone. Tears erupted instantly. I had worked hard for that small amount of money, and *he just took it.*

"Oh no. Young lady, are you okay?" The old man patted my arm.

"He mugged me." Everything I made Thursday, Friday, and today with Murata was gone. It was cold and dark outside, but I slumped down against the building, my butt freezing on the icy sidewalk. This was what I got for trying to be helpful.

"Should we call the police?"

"Great idea." I pulled my phone from my purse and dialed Goro. He arrived in three minutes exactly, lights flashing.

"I guess that wasn't so smart, Mei," he said, pulling me off the ground. "Whatever happened to meeting in a public place?" He turned to the old man, who stuck by me the whole time we waited. "Thank you, sir. I'll take it from here."

"I hope you feel better." The old man bowed and returned to his building across the road.

"Are you hurt?" Goro asked, ushering me to the car.

I probed the back of my head again with my fingers and noticed a small knot where there didn't use to be one. "I need ice for my head, and I banged up my elbow pretty bad." I sank into the seat of his police car as he drove off. "And I'm broke now because he also mugged me. He probably figured he wasn't going to get work out of me so he took everything I had."

Goro pulled up outside of Chiyo's bathhouse, leaned to the side, and yanked his wallet from his pocket. "Here, Mei. This should hold you through till Yasahiro returns."

My eyes filled with tears again.

"Don't refuse it," he said, pushing a wad of cash at me. "We've been putting money aside so you can start painting again, and it's my fault I didn't come with you tonight. You're doing the job of a police officer, you don't have the training for it, and you're not getting paid for it. It's the least I can do."

I took the money with a shaking hand and mumbled my thanks.

"Let's go inside. We'll get you ice for your head and you can relax with your mom and Kumi."

My phone, sitting in my lap, started to flash and ring. Yasahiro's face popped up on the screen, a photo I took of him in the kitchen one day when he was looking extra handsome.

Goro glanced at the screen and opened the door. "I'll give you a minute."

I took a deep breath and answered. "Hi! I was wondering when I'd hear from you."

"I made it to my hotel in one piece early this morning. It felt like the middle of the day, though, so I took a nap before my first class, and now we're about to have lunch. I'd really like to go back to bed."

I sniffed up and calmed my voice. "Jet lag is such a pain, or so I've heard."

There was a moment of silence on his end of the phone. "Mei, your voice doesn't sound right."

"I'm fine," I said, but my voice cracked and gave me away.

"You are not. What's wrong?"

"I... uh, I was just mugged outside of the café."

"Mugged?" His voice climbed.

"Some young man pushed me down and stole all the money from my wallet." My voice broke, and I hung my head. I didn't have the heart to tell him I had brought this on myself. "I'm glad he didn't take my phone."

"I'll be on the next flight home tomorrow."

"No! No. Don't do that. I called Goro right away and he's taking care of things."

"Mei," he said, wounded. "My heart is breaking listening to you."

I sniffed up again and stared at the ceiling of the car. "I'll be fine."

"I can't believe I have no cash stashed away in the apartment. I usually do but I grabbed it before I left since there was no time to go to the bank."

"It's okay. Goro is lending me some."

He was silent again and I imagined him pacing around like he did when he was upset or worried.

"Don't worry about me. I just seem to attract bad luck, that's all." I switched my phone from my right hand to my left and noticed blood on my pants. I flipped over my right hand and the heel of my hand, near the wrist, was scraped and bleeding. Fantastic. "It's better off you're in Paris or my bad luck would be rubbing off on you."

"I wish I was there. I'd rather have you and your bad luck than be here in Paris right now."

I laughed, my tears going everywhere. "I highly doubt that. Paris before Christmas? I'm sure it's spectacular."

"My room has a view of the Eiffel Tower. I'm looking at it right now."

"Of course, it does. I wouldn't expect anything less." With a continent between us, he felt farther away than ever.

"Are you sure you don't want me to come home? I want to hunt this guy down and make him pay." I shivered at his words because I knew he meant it.

"No. Stay. If you leave now, they'll think you flaked out on them. You'll have trouble getting more of these gigs in the future. And I'd like to go to Paris someday."

"We could come for a vacation. I don't have to come for work," he insisted.

"Stay," I whispered back. "I'm going to head into Kutsuro Matsu for the evening and then off to bed. Tomorrow will be better."

"Okay. I miss you already."

My heart ached. No one had missed me for a long time. "I miss you, too."

I hung up the phone and stared off into space. This was all such a bad idea. Why did I never see these things until it was too late?

───────

WITH THE BATHHOUSE IN ITS LAST HOUR OF THE DAY, AND most people packing up to go home, Kumi, Mom, and I took advantage of the baths, while Chiyo ushered the last of the stragglers out the door at 21:30. Most bathhouses in Tokyo stayed open until midnight or later, but out in Chikata, 21:30 was more than enough time to get in a good soak after dinner and head home, warm and clean, for bedtime.

"Here. For your hand." Kumi handed me a length of gauze,

antibiotic ointment, and tape. She sat down next to me at a washing station and groaned onto the stool while turning on the hot water spigot. "I've been standing all day. I love the new standing desk, but I am so tired by the end of the day." She splashed hot water on herself and sighed, then pumped soap onto a sponge and got to work soaping up.

I was already done washing, babying my right hand and keeping it away from the water, so I slathered some ointment on the cut and wrapped it in gauze. "Thanks. I'll have to keep it up out of the water."

"Go join your mom." Kumi jerked her head at the bath where Mom was already sitting in the water, her eyes closed, her breathing measured. If I hadn't known better, I would've guessed Mom was asleep. But she displayed her peaceful face, the one that told me she was content, despite everything going on around her. I envied that. Everything about my life was a mess.

I gingerly stepped into the tub of hot water and sank into the steamy relief. If there was one thing in this world I couldn't live without, it was baths. A hot bath could make anything bearable.

I sat quietly since Mom didn't budge, and I didn't want to admit how badly I had been failing lately. What with the resume rejections, or just plain silence from employers, Yasahiro gone and succeeding at his job, and me getting in sticky situations and getting mugged, I was a big barrel of fail. If I hadn't had my elderly clients, I would've sunk into a deep depression.

The water level changed as Kumi got in and sat beside me.

"Ahhhhhhh," she breathed out, long and satisfied. "I love this bath. I never thought I'd be married and part owner of a bath-house. Life is strange."

"Indeed it is," I replied, my eyes closed.

"Speaking of strange lives, have you, uh... talked to Akiko lately? I saw her the other day, at the pharmacy and we spoke a little about you."

I opened one eye and stared at her. "Really? What about?"

Kumi shrugged her shoulders. "She seemed, I don't know, sad about how things turned out with you."

I sighed and closed my eyes, resting my head gingerly on the tile. "Well, after what happened with Tama, I lost some faith in us, in our friendship. We're talking a little more, but it's taking some time."

I could have said more, how, deep in my gut, I felt betrayed. I had stood by Akiko through everything in her life, been there in good times and in bad. I had been more than family to her. At least, that's what I believed. I believed in our friendship, and she let her killer of a brother almost end it all.

"I guess I don't blame you." Kumi's voice was succinct, true. "You should give her a tiny break, though. I know she feels bad."

Without opening my eyes, I reached out my hand in the water for hers and she took it. Kumi had become my best friend over the last few months, and I valued her opinion and insights. I wished the awful feelings I had for Akiko would go away, but they hung over my head like a thundercloud ready to rain. "Thank you," I whispered. "I've done all I can do. Now, I wait to see what happens next." I squeezed her hand and let it go.

"Akiko is lucky to have you as a friend, Mei," Mom said, startling both Kumi and me. She hadn't said a word in at least ten minutes.

"Considering how unlucky I am, that's not saying much."

She harrumphed and closed her eyes again. "You'll see. Good fortune is around the corner for you. I prayed at the temple and washed the Arai Kannon to heal your spirit. Have faith."

"Thanks, Mom." I would take all the faith I could get.

CHAPTER
TWENTY-ONE

woke up to the sound of snowplows scraping up and down the street. That was a sound I hadn't heard in a long time! Rolling over in bed, I yawned and stretched, my aching body protesting any movement. At least my head and back didn't hurt, but my right hand still throbbed.

I pulled Yasahiro's covers up to my chin and stared at the ceiling. What could possibly happen today? I certainly hadn't started out the day before thinking I would be mugged. It was just my own luck that had gotten me into that mess. And despite telling Yasahiro he didn't have to come home, I missed him enough to want him to return. I hadn't thought our first separation would be so tough, but if the time had been uneventful, it would have been easier.

Throwing my legs off the bed, I jammed my feet into house slippers, grabbed a robe, and headed out into the main area. The morning light was cold, bright white, and fluffy snowflakes floated past the windows. It had finally decided to snow. I wrapped the robe tighter around my body and stood at the window so I could look down at the street. The sidewalks had accumulated a significant amount overnight, at least ten centimeters, and I was going to have to shovel before I left for Yamida's house. It was her morning to go to the physical therapist at 10:00. It was 07:30, so I had a little bit of time to eat before I got moving on the snow removal.

I took a long moment to prop my hip on the window ledge and watch the snow fall. I was a summer gal, through and through, but there was something magical about the first snowfall of the season. The world seemed new and quiet, in a way only a blanket of fluffy ice crystals could provide. The clouds hovered low and morphed from white to gray and back again. Looking up the street towards Izakaya Jūshi, I spotted several neighbors already outside shoveling. Plenty of people woke up early around here, so I had better get moving. I didn't want to look like a slacker.

I managed to cook up two eggs and toast without burning anything (score!), and I ate them at the table with a hot cup of coffee and my usual morning ritual of rejections. Sigh. Maybe it was the time of year? This was not the best time to be without a job. Most companies were dealing with year-end parties and the upcoming holidays, and they weren't hiring anybody. I may have had more luck in January, but it felt like failure to give up now. I opened my notebook, ran through my list, and realized I had no one new to apply to. I was either going to have to come up with something totally new or make my way through the list again, and I couldn't do that without waiting a few weeks. Well, that solved that. I'd take time off from submitting resumes and come back to the search later when I'd hopefully have more places to apply to. In the meantime, I had plenty of work to do.

I dressed in several layers, leggings under yoga pants under jeans, and I bundled up with both a hat and scarf and my boots. Putting on my gloves was difficult. My right hand was scraped up enough to be hot to the touch, and my bandage wouldn't stay on for long. Akiko would be at Murata's apartment later today, so I'd ask her to dress the wound for me. Remembering the conversation I had with Kumi the night before, I needed to be a better friend to Akiko. Letting her be a nurse to me, which she loved to do, was a good place to start.

I grabbed the shovel from outside the door and headed down the stairs. Pulling the door open, a small wall of snow fell into the vestibule, so I had to brush it back outside. I pushed the shovel against the sidewalk and cleared a section of walking space, one meter at a time. I hadn't done this much physical exercise since the fall harvest, and my shoulders and back ached from the exertion. It felt good, though, to be out and active. As I slowly made my way down the front of Yasahiro's retail space, I stared at the metal shutters over the windows and door, wondering what it looked like inside. What had been in there before he purchased the building?

"Do you need help, young lady?" A middle-aged man from the building next door waved to me with a shovel. I didn't recognize him.

"No, thank you. I'll be fine." I smiled and bowed to him, getting back to the shoveling. Push, lift, turn, repeat. This repetitive motion reminded me of the way Murata kneaded dough. I still hadn't tried to bake bread of my own yet, and I wanted to try that tomorrow.

The man ignored me anyway and came to my section of the sidewalk with the shovel. "I can help. I'm already done with my shoveling, and this one is twice as long as mine." He walked to the other end of Yasahiro's property and began to shovel. "I don't know you," he said, lifting his voice above the scrape of our shovels. "Are you Yasahiro's sister?"

Here we go. "No. I'm his girlfriend, and I'm staying in his apartment for the next month or so. He's in Paris right now or he would be out here doing this instead of me." I pushed a shovelful of snow into the pile near the curb.

"Ah! He mentioned he was dating somebody new. It's nice to meet you. I'm Koshiro Hasé. This is my cobbler's business right next door." He waved to the small building next to Yasahiro's, and I tilted back my hat so I could read the sign. His store was only open a few days a week when I was never around, so I hadn't noticed it.

"You fix shoes?"

"Yep. My father taught me, and I took over the business five years ago."

"How long has your business been here?"

He ceased shoveling and scratched at his beard. Several snowflakes were caught in his hair and he brushed them off. "Twenty-five years?"

I shoveled some more snow and edged closer to him. "You've been here a long time then. Do you know what used to be in this space?" I waved at Yasahiro's building.

"Yes, yes. A store for brushes! The man who owned this building used to be a brush maker. He made brushes for calligraphy and for makeup. He was bought out about five years ago by a bigger manufacturer up north that was looking to lessen competition. They made him a sizable offer, and he was happy to retire. Moved his family and sold the whole building. I hear he's doing well now. Became a fisherman or something, just to pass the time, you know? They made more than enough to live off of until they die."

A brush shop? I would've never have guessed. But the metal shutters didn't have any windows, so I hadn't ever seen inside. It could have been a butcher shop or a salon for all I knew.

My phone in my pocket vibrated and rang. I set my shovel against the building, pulled off my gloves, and answered it. It was Yamida.

"Are you coming today?" she asked, her voice shaky. "There's a lot of snow outside, and I'm worried about making it to my appointment on time."

"No worries, Mrs. Yamida. I'm on top of it. I'm shoveling my own walkway right now, and I plan to be there thirty minutes early so I can shovel your walk before taking you to the physical therapist."

She sighed into the phone, and I could feel her smile on the other end. "Oh good. I was worried."

"That's why you hired me! I'll make sure you make it to your appointment on time. I'll see you soon. Feel free to call me if you need anything else."

I hung up and dropped my phone into my pocket. "Thank you so much for helping me, Mr. Hasé," I said to the man from next door. "I have to go help my elderly client now. She needs to have her walkway shoveled before I take her to her physical therapy appointment." I bowed and smiled to him, and he bowed back.

"What is it that you do? Are you a nurse?" He leaned on the handle of his shovel and tilted his head to the side.

I pulled one of the business cards Kumi made for me from my pocket and presented it to him with both hands. "No. I'm not a nurse, I'm just an elderly helper. It's a part-time job for me. I charge an hourly rate, and I help them with whatever they need help with. I can shop or help them get to appointments, or I can clean. Whatever they need except cooking. I'm a horrible cook," I said, laughing and covering my mouth.

He examined both sides of my business card. "My parents live around the block, and I don't always have time to go over and help them. They sometimes need little things done like changing a light bulb in the ceiling or carrying something heavy. I feel bad that I can't drop everything to be there for them."

I smiled and bowed, nodding my head in sympathy. "If you ever need assistance, my information is on the card. I charge 900 yen an hour, and I'm available most days. I can do all those things and more. Thank you again for your help! I really have to go!"

We waved to each other, and I headed back inside, only to change and return to the snow outside of Yamida's house.

"Here, Mei!" She waved to me from the doorway, and I

stomped through the snow to get to her. "The shovel is right here."

"Okay." I cleared off her porch. "This should take me about twenty minutes. Why don't you get ready to go while I take care of this?"

"Are the busses running?" She wrung her hands together in worry. I loved Yamida because she was sweet and generous, but she worried over everything.

"The busses are running on time. I got here super fast. Can you take my bag?" I handed her my bag that contained my book and some snacks for while I waited at her appointment. Later, I would go to the bathhouse, too. A good soak after all the hard labor would be perfect.

Thirty minutes and a hundred shovels full of snow later, we were on and off the bus and at her physical therapist. I cleaned off my boots and left them at the door, jamming my wet, socked feet into provided plastic slippers and slumping into a chair in the waiting area while Yamida was ushered to the weight room to exercise. The physical therapist was a Swedish woman who spoke perfect Japanese. Her voice never ceased to amaze me. I needed to get out more.

I texted with Yasahiro who should have been asleep but, due to the jet lag, was up at an early hour.

"You're missing all the snow!" I texted to him.

"I'm missing you. How are you today?"

"Sore, but I'll be even more sore tomorrow with all the shoveling I've done."

"No. No. How are you doing with the whole being mugged thing?"

"I'm okay. Really. It was a freak occurrence, and Goro is on the case. No need to worry."

"Okay. I'll take your word for it. I have a busy day ahead of me. Classes this morning, then a restaurant opening this afternoon and evening. I'll text you later when I can."

"Have a great day!"

"You too."

I stared at his last text, ended with a heart emoticon. I missed him too and I hadn't even said so. I brought my thumbs over the screen of my phone to text him back, sighed, turned it off and put it away. No need to get too mushy because I'd just start crying, and crying was the last thing I needed to do while on the job.

I relaxed into the chair and recalled the prior evening. Jun had known who I was. He said we had someone in common. He was visibly upset and bolted when he heard Etsuko had died. This coupled with Etsuko's strange phone call the night we went out together, her on-time bill payments and international travel, and on-the-side boyfriends meant that something shady had been going on, but I was missing a piece, or even a few pieces, to tie everything together. Still, I was unhappy to report everything to Goro and Kumi last night at the bathhouse. They had loved Etsuko and had a hard time believing she was involved in anything improper.

I pulled my book from my bag and settled into the fictional world from where I left off last night when Jun interrupted me. I loved a good historical romance, and I was immediately swept into a scene of fighting on the battlefield, swords swinging, and the consort of a high prince was being held by the enemy.

"I told you I love girls that read, right?"

For a moment, I thought I might be imagining his voice, but I looked up, and Jun stood over me with a wad of cash in his hand. I opened my mouth to scream and stopped as he lunged at me.

————

"No! No, stop." Jun waved his hands in my face, and I clamped my mouth shut over my scream. Looking past him to the woman at the front desk, her head bopped to music pumped directly to her ears via headphones, and her head was bent over her smartphone. She hadn't noticed my squeal.

"What the...?" I tried to scramble backwards but only knocked my head against the wall behind me. "Ouch!"

"Wow. You're awfully touchy."

I stared at him for a moment to make sure he wasn't about to kill me, but his face was compassionate, not murderous.

"Considering you mugged me last night, I'm sure I'm not overreacting."

Jun shoved the money at my hands and sat down next to me. "Here's your money minus some train fare. I had to pay to get back out here again."

I counted the money and I was short 1000 yen. Great. I was paying for my own mugger to travel back and forth from the comfort of his home in Tokyo. That seemed entirely unfair. I stuffed the money in my wallet and clutched my purse to my chest.

"You hurt me pretty badly yesterday. I bumped my head on the sidewalk and scraped up my hand too. What do you want?" I asked him, keeping my voice down. I wasn't negotiating with him if he was going to continue to harass me.

"I didn't mean to hurt you, and I'm sorry I freaked out on you. I had no idea Etsuko was dead." He stared out the window, his eyes unfocused and sad. "I loved her, you know? In my own way. She was one of my first clients, and I always felt bad that her boyfriend lived so far away. She loved him so much. She missed him. Being apart from him was the hardest thing she ever did." Jun sighed and hung his head. "I never meant for things to get out of control."

I held my breath, unable to believe what I was hearing. Jun loved Etsuko. Etsuko loved Hisashi. Hisashi loved Etsuko. When you looked at the triangle, Jun was the one left out. What role did he play in all of this?

"So... Did Etsuko cheat on her boyfriend with you?" I sat

forward in my seat and turned to him, looking him in the eyes, determined to catch him in a lie.

"No. If anything, the love was only one-sided. I cared about her, but she only saw me as someone to sleep next to. After a while, I couldn't take it anymore. I wanted to be with her, but she wanted to be with her boyfriend."

Roaring in my ears turned my vision black. Couldn't take it anymore? I jumped up from my seat and pointed at him. "You killed her!" I whirled away from him and dug in my bag for my phone.

"No!" He lunged for me but this time I was quicker. I sidestepped him, and he crashed into the line of seats across from us. He groaned but straightened up quickly. The receptionist didn't move; she was absorbed in her music. "No. I never hurt her," he said, clutching his hand to his chest. "I loved her, but I had to let her go. There was no use trying to tell myself not to get attached. I was attached and there was nothing I could do except to stop seeing her."

He was probably lying, but the pain and anguish on his face made me believe him. This had happened to me once. I had fallen in love with a guy in one of my college classes. We studied together all the time, and I even slept in his bed when we were up too late cramming for a test. But he hadn't loved me in return, and eventually, I had to stop being his friend because it hurt too much.

I stretched out my hand to Jun and pulled him to our seats, stroking his back as he cried into his hands.

"I told her I couldn't do this anymore, so I would recommend somebody else from the agency for her. He's gay, so I figured there would be no attachment. It was better for all of us this way." He pulled a handkerchief from his bag and wiped up his face.

"Maybe it wasn't so great for Etsuko." I considered their situation. If she hadn't been seeing Jun anymore, she must have fallen into a bad deal with somebody else. "Who was the next person she started sleeping with?"

"Look. You have to promise me I'm not to get in any trouble…"

The hair on my head stood up. "Why? What do you think happened?"

"Remember how I said we had a friend in common? You and me?"

"Yes?"

"He'll kill me if he finds out I've been speaking to you. He's a very powerful man with a lot of secrets, and I can't say anything or else I'm dead. I got involved with them once when Etsuko called me for help, and it was enough for me to tell her to leave me alone for good. I called her one evening a few weeks ago, and we had an argument over him. I think that may have been the day before she died." More tears fell down his cheeks.

My brain ran through every possible man I could think of, but besides Goro and Yasahiro and Hisashi, I couldn't think of anybody. *Who was this powerful man?* I hadn't lived in Chikata long enough to know many other people.

I grabbed his shirt and shook him. "You need to tell me. Etsuko's boyfriend is the main suspect. And if he didn't kill her, we can't let him sit in jail. We need to put the right person behind bars."

Jun's face whitened. "He follows me around. It's a miracle I made it here today without being caught. But the snow was on my side today." He stood up, ready to leave. "I said that I stopped sleeping with Etsuko, but I still saw her. I kept getting dragged into things, and she was desperate for help. She was in the middle of one triangle after another. There was no escaping." He headed to the door, and I followed him as he put on his boots.

"If you won't help me, what can I do?" I was ready to sink to my knees and beg because I didn't understand what was going on. It sounded like Etsuko was in a whole lot more trouble than I had thought she was.

Jun leaned in my direction, lowering his voice. "She was paid, a lot, for what she did. Cash. And sometimes the meetings were hurried and ill-timed. If you find the money, you may be able to trace it back to him." Jun zipped up, threw his scarf around his neck, and tromped out the door without looking back.

Find the money. Find the money, I repeated in my head. It was the only clue I had. I checked my phone and only ten minutes remained until Yamida was done. Perfect.

I dialed Goro. "You won't believe who I ran into just now," I said to him as soon as he answered.

"Well, you can tell me all about it in person. We're heading into Etsuko's apartment right now. Come on by and help us out."

"I'll be there in thirty minutes."

CHAPTER
TWENTY-TWO

Once I got Yamida back home, I stomped through the snow and ate instant ramen from the convenience store. I scowled down at the styrofoam cup as I slurped up the last of the noodles. This stuff was awful! How had I eaten this all those years living in Tokyo? I tossed my chopsticks into the empty cup and then recycled the different pieces of my lunch, angry at myself for a hundred reasons. I used to love junk food. Cheap ramen and cold green tea on my thirty-minute lunch break were a part of my life. I adored it. I craved it. Now, I stood in front of the recycling bins at the convenience store and realized my few months with Yasahiro had changed me. His love of food — quality, local, healthy food — had transferred to me. And I couldn't even cook it. Turning on a burner on the stove made me sweat and my heart race. I had cooked eggs the other day, and it had been the most harrowing fifteen minutes I'd had since I almost died in the barn fire.

I wondered... I wondered if I asked him, would Yasahiro teach me how to cook? He was in Paris right now teaching other young students to cook. Would he do that for me? I stepped over to the window of the store and stared out at the snowy chaos on

THE DAYDREAMER DETECTIVE BRAVES THE WINT...   185

the streets of Chikata. The buses were running and people were walking around in high boots and carrying umbrellas. I let my eyes blur and imagined being taught to cook by Yasahiro. In my mind, he showed me how to handle a knife, his arms wrapped around me. I chopped vegetables slowly, and he complimented me on how good I was doing. My chest constricted when I imagined the two of us working in the kitchen together. But the scene immediately devolved into us tearing each other's clothes off and having sex on the dining room table.

I shook my head and tried again, but we ended up in the bedroom. Clearly, my brain had other ideas about what I could be doing with Yasahiro in our "spare time."

"Can I help you find anything else?" the store clerk asked, passing me on his way to stock the shelves. I blushed, sure he could read my dirty thoughts. I should've bought a sponge and dish soap to clean up my brain.

"No. I'm just psyching myself up to go back out there." I waved at the wintery mess outside.

"Only way to do that is to charge right out. Thinking about it too much will only make it worse."

I buttoned up and put my hat on. "Story of my life. Thanks!"

I plowed through the streets, avoiding clumps of people, and puddles of dark, slushy water that could swallow me whole. When I reached Murata's building (Etsuko's old building), three police cars and a van were parked outside, and an officer I didn't recognize guarded the front door.

"Only residents are allowed inside right now," he said, blocking my way with his arm.

"Goro Hokichi told me to meet him here." I stepped to the side while he conferred with someone inside on his radio. Pulling my phone from my pocket, I found a text from Yasahiro checking in on me. I smiled as I texted him back that I was good and keeping busy. I hesitated, but I gathered enough courage to admit that I missed him too. I didn't want to seem needy, but I also didn't want him to think that I didn't think about him while he was gone. These are the things I always had difficulty with early in a relationship. Sometimes, I came on too strong. Other times, I was too distant. This relationship was different because I hadn't even believed it existed in the first month! I had trouble accepting that I was really dating Yasahiro, though clearly we were a couple now.

"You can go up," the officer said, knocking me out of a daydream about Yasahiro coming home from Paris and sweeping me off my feet.

Outside of Etsuko's old apartment, a long, neat line of boots sat on a meter long piece of brown heavy paper. I added my boots to the end, glanced at Murata's door, and entered Etsuko's instead. I hadn't been here since the night she was murdered, but the place didn't feel anything like that night because it was crawling with police officers. A trio of people sifted through her DVD collection, her desk, and cut open her couch. From her bedroom, bits of cotton fluff trailed out into the hallway. When they had said they'd take the place apart, they'd meant it.

"Goro?" I called out. Everyone's heads snapped up and the young man cutting up the couch jerked his head at the bedroom. I bowed multiple times as I made my way down the hall. The place was a mess. Etsuko's bed linens were stuffed in large evidence bags and another officer used a knife to cut open her mattress. Goro was half in her closet, pulling out boxes.

"Mei! Welcome!" The excitement on his face cratered my stomach. No one should be this happy tearing up someone else's life.

"Ugh. How can you guys even do this?"

"Do what?" They both asked, their hair dusted with cotton and purple nitrile gloves on each hand.

"Destroy someone else's house. It just doesn't... It doesn't feel right." This bothered me to my very core. One of the principles we were taught growing up was to show respect for others, their property, and their privacy. A search this intense violated every single one of those tenets.

Goro left his post and came to me. "This is part of the job. We want to find the person that killed Etsuko, right?" I nodded my head in agreement. "Finding him requires a thorough search. She would be okay with this. Besides, the sooner we do this, the sooner her parents can have everything."

"Right. Makes sense." I swallowed and accepted that Etsuko would be okay with us going through her underwear drawer, though I wanted to destroy everything I had so no one could paw through it when I was gone.

"We need to search for money," I blurted out, and both men stopped. "Jun, that guy from the escort service, followed me this morning and talked to me while Mrs. Yamida was getting her physical therapy. Whatever happened to Etsuko, it involved a whole lot of money."

"Wait wait wait... You don't think...?" Goro rubbed his face, his eyes darting around the apartment, landing for a long time on the bags of her bed linens. There may have been DNA evidence in there.

"I don't know what to think," I said, my shoulders slumping. "What if she was a prostitute on the side? Or she had a gambling debt? Or she was handling money for the mob? I don't know."

"Whatever she did, she was careful. I never had any clue she was doing anything but working and seeing Hisashi. I don't think Kumi did either. And we never found fingerprints in the apartment of any felons or foreign nationals."

"It could be anybody. Anything."

"Right." Goro slipped past me into the main room. As I followed him and passed the bathroom, I waved to his partner, Kayo, standing at the sink.

"She had expensive taste in makeup," Kayo said, showing me Etsuko's stash. I focused on a bottle of moisturizer I knew to be at least 9000 yen at regular price. Expensive was right.

"Listen up everyone!" Goro yelled in the main room and everyone shuffled to be within eyesight of him. "We're looking for money. Possibly large sums of cash." He sighed, glancing around the room. "This means that if you haven't found anything yet in obvious places, we're going to have to be creative and start looking for hiding spots in the walls. Be sure to open every single one of those bento boxes too."

Everyone nodded and got back to work.

"Mei, grab a pair of gloves and search the kitchen, will you?"

I set my bag on a small kitchen table and snapped out a pair of gloves from a box sitting there. "Do I get paid for doing this? I have to go across the hall to Mrs. Murata in two hours."

Goro smiled. "I'll let you keep the money I gave you yesterday."

"Okay!"

"Perfect," he grumbled as he walked away.

Since everyone else was making a huge mess of the place, I forced myself to make a mess of Etsuko's kitchen. It was a small space with only a few cabinets, a half-size refrigerator, a toaster oven, and two electric burners. I started with her refrigerator, which was pretty bare to begin with. Most of her food had gone bad, so I left it since I didn't know what to do with it. What if it was against some police search procedure to trash or recycle things? Despite wanting to clean and bleach everything, I moved on.

I opened the top cabinets and emptied out the plates, bowls, and glasses making stacks along the far wall. Once everything was out, I hopped on the counter and looked inside the bare cabinet. Nothing — nothing in the corners or taped to the walls. I did the same with the bottom cabinets, taking out the pots, pans, cleaning supplies, dry food goods, and random stuff Etsuko had shoved in there at some point. I even found a few packs of unused nylons and a desiccated carrot. As far as I could tell, there was nothing more in the cabinets.

All the searching and organizing made me break out in a sweat, so I shed my coat and started in on the area around her stove. I pulled up the top and looked inside. I searched through her baskets of utensils. I opened every box of dry goods and cereal on her shelf to the left of the stove. Nothing.

I sat at the kitchen table to think. The guys in the living room had moved the couch away from the wall and were tearing off the trim with crowbars. I winced at the sound of nails squeaking against the wood.

Goro exited the bedroom and grabbed a bag from next to the door. "Any luck?" he asked, opening a thermos and drinking from it.

"Nothing." I pointed to the plates, pots, and pans lining the one open wall. "I looked in everything."

"Did you go over the cabinets with your fingertips and a flashlight?"

"No. I didn't. Should I?"

He laughed. "Amateur. You know, normally, you wouldn't be able to do this kind of thing. But because I'm here supervising, it's fine." He pulled a flashlight from his belt and handed it to me.

I knelt on my hands and knees and shined the flashlight into the empty cabinet.

"Look up. Were you able to open the drawers? If so, then the money isn't attached to the bottom of them, but it could be taped up along the rear of the drawer." Goro stood behind me and tapped his foot against mine.

I lit up the drawers, sliding each out and looking at the wall. Nothing.

"Sides?" he asked, and I examined them too, not seeing anything.

"Now the bottom. Tap it. There's usually a space under the cabinets, between the cabinet and the floor." I tapped along the bottom shelf of the cabinets, hearing the same echo — *thonk, thonk, thonk.* But the sound began to change, becoming duller, less loud, as I neared the side next to the stove. I tapped again and the wood rattled.

"Wait," I said, being careful not to hit my head on the inside of the cabinet. I ran my fingers along the wood and detected a seam, so I pushed on a few spots, but it didn't move. "I need a knife or something thin." I ducked out of the cabinet for a breath of fresh air and Goro slapped a kitchen knife into my hand with a smile.

Heading back in, I put the flashlight on its side, slipped the knife into the seam, and pushed down. The piece jumped up with a pop. Inside, underneath the cabinets where Etsuko kept her pots and pans, where she cooked every day, a dozen stacks of cash were lined up neat, like pencils in a brand new box.

I honestly hadn't thought I'd find anything! And my blood cooled, looking over all the money. There was a lot here, way too much for someone working at their family's izakaya. Her izakaya salary had probably gone into savings. This money wasn't supposed to belong to her. To the side of the plastic-wrapped stacks was a manila envelope. I was afraid to open it.

"The search is over," I said, backing out and shining my light down at the jackpot.

"Kayo!" Goro called and she ran over.

"*Sugoi!*" she cried, covering her mouth. The other men and women in the apartment halted and joined us.

Goro knelt on the floor and handed each stack to Kayo. She placed them on the table, grabbing her notebook and making notes about everything. She unwrapped one bundle and flipped through it, her eyes flicking as she followed the 10,000 yen notes. She set her hand on each, moving her lips and muttering numbers.

"My guess is each of these is about fifty bills and there are... Forty bundles. *Chikushō*. That's 20,000,000 yen."

Everyone forgave Kayo's burst of profanity and stared at the money. Goro reached into the cabinet and grabbed the manila envelope. He pulled out a cluster of papers, a thin booklet, photographs, and a key.

Goro studied the papers and photos, beads of sweat forming on his brow, before he put them back in the envelope, showing no one.

"Kayo, clear the room. Everyone returns to the office. Leave the place as-is, just take your stuff with you when you go."

The men and women grumbled but obeyed, slowly filing out the door. Kayo spoke to them in the hallway and then shut the door behind her. I helped Goro up off the floor and we sat at the kitchen table. He placed the key next to the envelope.

"We're in a lot of trouble on this one…" Goro stared past me to the window and the snow falling outside.

"What's in the envelope?" I whispered, though my heart told me I shouldn't ask. My brain had other ideas.

Goro opened the envelope and pulled out the photos. I averted my eyes immediately, counting to three, and looking again. Kayo, over my shoulder, gasped and swore again.

It wasn't so much the pictures of two men in bondage that bothered me. That stuff was all over the internet, and I understood that people had kinky tastes in sex. But it was the man in the submissive position that caused the wave of shivers to fall over me.

This was the person Jun and I had in common! *"He's a powerful man,"* Jun had said.

"Fujita Takahara," I whispered. The ladies' man, the bachelor of the year, the Midori Sankaku regional manager, the one who kept propositioning me every time I saw him. "Oh… My…"

"And that's not all," Goro said, flipping the stack of paper and the booklet around to me. The booklet was an accounting ledger, columns of numbers lined the top graph paper with dates and yen amounts. On the front cover, *Bento Number Nine* was printed in neat characters with an address in Sumida ward, old town Tokyo over by the Skytree.

Goro tipped over the envelope and Etsuko's passport fell out. He thumbed through the pages and groaned, clutching at his forehead. "Singapore, several times over the past two years."

"What does that mean? I thought she was visiting Hisashi." I craned my neck to look at the passport.

"Apparently not. What's he going to say when I ask him about this?"

This seemed like a rhetorical question so I didn't answer.

"So...?" Kayo asked, her voice indicating she needed information from Goro.

"Definitely money laundering. Possibly some blackmail too. We'll have to give this to a forensic accountant and see what he or she thinks. I wonder if Hisashi is involved too?" Goro stroked his chin.

"No. No way. He doesn't strike me as the type."

But I doubted the words as they came out of my mouth. I didn't know him that well. Could he have done something like this? I picked up her passport and looked through the pages. She'd been going to Singapore every couple of months for the past two years. He had to have noticed.

I tossed the passport on the table. "I don't know," I said, sighing. "What about the key?"

"A safe deposit box. It has a number stamped on it. We'll have to go through the ledger and search this place in Sumida to find out."

Goro put everything in the envelope but the ledger. He looked between the ledger and the money on the table. "The money has to be hers. Damn. Why didn't she spend it? That's what you're supposed to do."

"What do you mean?"

Goro rubbed his face again, his eyes tired. "When you launder money, you're supposed to take your cut and spend it on luxury items... At least, that's what I was taught." He glanced at the piles. "She must have been saving it."

"Well, now we know how she afforded to pay her bills on time and travel, too. Plus, look at her bento box collection and expensive taste in makeup."

Goro laughed. "You're supposed to spend it on cars and diamonds, Mei. Not makeup."

"Well, I doubt she was very experienced at laundering money. Hisashi was only a few months from living here. If I were her, I would have saved the money too. For things like a wedding dress, a honeymoon... Baby items." I swallowed, my throat dry. "She was probably saving for her future. And I'm sure she wanted out of the mess before he moved here. What if she tried to quit and whomever she was working with freaked out and killed her?"

Goro glanced at the envelope again. "I'm betting it was Takahara." He stood up and adjusted his belt. "I'm going to arrest him."

"Wait," I said, grabbing his arm. "We should gather more evidence first." I pointed to the envelope. "Right now, Etsuko looks really bad. Everything's in her name, and all we have are photos that could have been manipulated."

Goro bit his lip.

"We need more," I insisted. "Hisashi looks bad too. He was dating her. How did he not notice a whole business she was running? This Bento Number Nine, whatever it is."

"Mei is right," Kayo said, and I jumped. I had almost forgotten she was there. "This is bad for Etsuko. What if Hisashi *was* involved? What if Takahara is just an accomplice? The real motives could be anything."

"Fine." Goro sat back down. "But we need to get to work right away. Right now. You in?"

I glanced at Kayo and we nodded. "I'm in."

CHAPTER
TWENTY-THREE

Since Goro and his crew had to return evidence to the police station and question Hisashi again, I volunteered to come by the station once I was done helping Murata for the afternoon.

"What's going on out there?" she asked, waving her cane at the hallway as I entered. Goro waved back to her, and I closed the door on him, laughing.

"A more thorough search of Etsuko's apartment." I left my boots at the door. "We may have some leads. Did someone ever come by here to do a police sketch of the men you saw coming and going from her place?"

"Yes," she said, sitting down on her couch. "I did give descriptions, though I'm not sure how well I did. My eyesight isn't the best anymore."

"Okay, fine. Can I get you some tea?"

She nodded, so I filled up a mug from the hot water boiler in the kitchen and dunked her favorite green tea a few times, bringing the mug out to her in the living room. As I set the mug down on her kotatsu, I spied the cardboard box of bentos again. I couldn't believe I had forgotten about this! I was about to open it when a soft knock upon the door stopped me.

"It's Akiko!"

I changed directions and opened the door. "Oh good! I was hoping I'd see you today."

"Mei, you look much healthier now. I haven't seen you around the neighborhood. Where have you been?"

I sighed as I took her coat and she sat next to Murata on the couch. "She's been living at Yasahiro Suga's place," Murata said, tattling on me.

Akiko gasped and I nodded. "It's been a crazy week. He has heat and food." I shrugged my shoulders. "And he insisted I stay."

"Oh, please," Akiko said, unconvinced by my aloofness. "He's smart, talented, handsome, and rich, and you're sweet, pretty, and resourceful. I'm sure you'll be married in no time." She said this without an ounce of bitterness, so I believed she meant it. But married? Really? I couldn't imagine myself married. I could barely imagine myself with a real boyfriend.

I stared out Murata's window at the back of Yasahiro's building and imagined us there in the summer, having a barbecue on the rooftop deck, him proposing on one knee. How had he proposed to Amanda? I'd never asked though I had seen the ring in photos.

I shook my head. No. We had a lot of work to do before we ever got to that point. His parents had to let go of Amanda, and I had to kick her out of my head. I needed to get a real job so I could contribute to an equal relationship. I wanted to be able to travel with him and go the distance.

"What are you thinking about over there?" Akiko asked, sitting next to Murata, placing her stethoscope on her lap and opening her blood pressure monitor.

"Oh, nothing. I'm going to clean the kitchen." I edged past Akiko and Murata, but Akiko caught my hand.

"What happened here?"

I had forgotten that my right hand was scraped up. The injury had been under gloves for the past few hours, and between the search and the shoveling, the bandage was falling off and the scrape was still bleeding.

"I slipped on some ice yesterday. No big deal."

"Sit," she directed. Murata shook her finger at me.

"I already have a mother, thank you very much," I warned Murata, but she laughed and made me smile.

I sat patiently while Akiko swabbed the wound with antiseptic and antibiotic and placed a new bandage on it. "Wear gloves," she said to me, and I nodded. Murata had dish gloves and I'd wear them.

My phone buzzed in my pocket with a text from Kumi. *"Goro called to say they have leads and you found the evidence! So excited! Come to the bathhouse tonight after the police station. Have a hot bath and sushi, my treat."* My chest tightened and I held back tears. I loved Kumi. I wished I could do even more to prove that Etsuko had been doing some of this against her will. She had been too nice to be a criminal. Perhaps this business was legitimate? We were thinking the worst, instead of believing she was a good person who would never do this kind of thing.

"Sure. I'll be there!" I texted, and then continued to look at my phone.

Opening my browser and navigating to Google, I searched for Fujita Takahara again. The top stories about him were about the death of his father and how he was now one of the wealthiest people in the prefecture. He'd inherited his father's fortune, and in one interview, he made a statement that he would be leaving the Midori Sankaku Board of Directors.

I glanced at Murata and Akiko, and they were checking her blood sugar, so I continued. Sitting on the Board of Directors for Midori Sankaku, he had been involved in new store placement for the past five years among other things, like buying up land and planning out new business strategies. This is why he'd been in town so much the last two years. He had helped place a Midori Sankaku store in Chikata and got us the greenhouse too, both of which had revitalized the town to a point I hadn't seen in twenty years. His decisions had impacted our community in a positive way. How was he involved in all of this? I didn't care what kind of sex he had on his own time, but apparently, Etsuko had reasons to keep those photos. Why?

I pulled up a photo of Takahara, dressed in a tux, zoomed in and sat down next to Murata.

"Mrs. Murata..." I showed my phone to her as Akiko took notes in her journal. "Have you seen this man before?"

She squinted at the photo and pulled back. "Of course I know him. Mei, that's such a silly question."

Akiko raised her eyebrows at me.

"Why is that silly? How do you know him?"

She blinked at me. "He owns the building. He's my landlord. Well, sort of. There's a management company that takes care of the place, but I often see him in the building a few times per week. Especially when they were renovating the apartment under Etsuko."

My hearing rang, the new information knocking me over the head. "He owns the building?"

"Yeah."

I glanced at his photo again. He was entrenched in this town, wasn't he?

"Okay. Thanks." I slipped the phone in my pocket.

This was something I could never wrap my head around — rich people and their money, and what they do with it. I was sure I only knew a tiny, infinitesimally small part of what Yasahiro does with his money, and he wasn't half as wealthy as Takahara. When you had that much money, what did you do with it? Especially if you didn't want to pay taxes?

While Akiko tested Murata's reflexes and watched her walk, I cleaned the kitchen, snapping on dish gloves, and gathering dirty dishes and glasses from the rest of the apartment. I let my mind wander while I scrubbed, imagining the web of lies that surrounded Etsuko, the young men from Ne Kitsune, Takahara's proclivities, and the stacks of cash hidden under her kitchen cabinets. I began to sweat as I stacked up dish after dish and cleaned the counters.

"I'm heading out," Akiko said, right behind me, and I jumped, almost dropping my sponge. "Hey…" Her hand rested on my shoulder. "Are you okay?"

I sighed. "I'm tired, and I've been busy with my new clients. Yasahiro's in Paris, and he told me he might run into his ex-girlfriend, Amanda, while he's there. And I've been trying not to think about it… I haven't been thinking about it, actually, but it must be there in the back of my head because everything feels wrong without him here." I yanked off the gloves and hung them on the sink to dry.

"Well, your eyes look better and your skin is flush and pink again. So whatever he's doing for you, keep it up." She winked at me and I blushed. "If he knows what he's got going for him, he won't cheat."

"He doesn't strike me as the cheating type." But then, Etsuko could be a criminal. Takahara could be into men. And I hadn't believed I'd ever be in this situation. I bit my lip and stared at the floor. I didn't know what to think anymore.

"Me neither." She squeezed my arm. "It's Amanda you'll have to watch out for." Before I could ask what she meant, she turned away. "I've gotta go. Lots of paperwork to take care of today. Mrs. Murata is fine. Make sure she gets out later this week." She threw on her coat and stepped into her boots. "And be careful out there! So much snow. My car was slipping everywhere."

Car. I wonder if Mom had sold the car?

"Want to bake some bread? I have a loaf in the oven rising."

Murata rose from her spot on the couch, and I compared her apartment to Etsuko's in my head.

"How do you have a real stove and oven, and Etsuko had neither?"

"My son bought the stove for me and had it installed. I've lived here for twenty years. I do what I want." She winked at me as she hobbled by, and I smiled back.

My gaze fell on the box of bentos again in the corner. I needed to remember to take it with me when I left later.

———

I ARRIVED AT THE POLICE STATION, WHEELING THE BOX OF bentos on a luggage cart. The warm air of the station welcomed me, and my clothes, wet with snow, steamed as the door closed behind me. Murata had been happy to let me borrow her cart especially since I was getting rid of the big box.

"Mei!" Kayo shouted as I approached the front desk. "Come on back. We're almost done cataloging the evidence."

The man at the front desk buzzed me in, and I wheeled the box to Goro's desk.

Kayo waved at me. "I'm off for the night. See you both tomorrow!" She walked off, bundling up against the weather outside.

"What's this?" Goro asked, pointing to the box.

"This was addressed to Etsuko's bento box company and had been sitting in Mrs. Murata's apartment for the last week. She signed for it the Friday before she died and had forgotten about it." I sank into the chair next to Goro's desk and melted into a snowy puddle. "So had I. I saw it the last few times I was there but forgot to say anything." It had been tough getting the box to the police station, what with the snow on the streets, and I was exhausted from all of the hard labor I'd done. I needed a large meal and a hot bath, and at least ten hours of sleep. I groaned as I pushed into the chair. "I feel like I've lived ten days in the last one."

Goro grabbed a letter opener and cut the box open after glancing at the address label on top. Inside, twelve stacks of five bento boxes apiece lined the available space. A paper invoice sat on top, and the sender's address was from an area north of Tokyo.

"Huh. It's just bento boxes." Goro folded his arms across his chest.

"It was safe to assume it would be bento boxes considering." I rifled through the boxes on top. One box immediately felt out of place — too heavy. "Well, here you go. Not just bento boxes after all." I pulled a stack of money from the box and handed it to Goro. It was hard to watch it go. Thinking back on all of the cash I had seen at Etsuko's apartment, and the money in front of me now, I couldn't help but be jealous. Did you have to be dishonest to make this kind of money? I was barely scraping by because I played by the rules, and playing by the rules didn't pay like this did. But this business had killed Etsuko, and I didn't want that kind of danger in my life. It was bad enough when Tama tried to kill me because I wanted to help Akiko. There was no way I could handle an illegal money-laundering business.

I licked my lips as the money was dropped into an evidence bag, and one of Goro's coworkers took it from the room.

At the next desk over, several men examined the photos of Takahara. They snickered and giggled, pointing to one after another. It was like they'd never seen porn before.

"You gonna let them do that?" I pointed to them and rolled my eyes. Goro walked over, snatched the photos from their hands, and told them to get back to work. He handed the photos to me, but I placed them face down on the desk. "I have no idea why Etsuko would even have these photos."

Goro returned to his desk chair. "Blackmail, obviously. The real question is how did she get them in the first place."

"Ew. I don't even want to think about it." I was hoping, for everyone's sake, that she wasn't involved in a sexual relationship with them. I had a feeling that would be the last straw for Goro and Kumi. Kumi had always thought the best of Etsuko. As it was, she was going to be crushed when she learned about the money laundering.

"So, do you have everything?" I wasn't sure where to begin asking him questions about evidence since I knew nothing about police procedure.

"Well, we have a lot. We have her phone, computer, bank statements, bills, her journal, and everything we found and cataloged today." Goro scrolled through a long list on his computer. "But now that we have to look into this side business she had, that will open up a whole other line of investigation. Because we'll have to trace the money, trace her suppliers, and figure out why she got involved."

"That's a lot..." I remembered that night we all went to Izakaya Jūshi together, and my thoughts clicked into place like a newly oiled gearshift. "Wait. Her phone? She had two phones."

He turned to me. "Are you sure? We only ever found one phone."

"I'm positive. The night we went out together, remember? The day before she died. She took a call while we were out to dinner. I remember her outside talking on the phone while her other phone sat on the table. She had two phones. I'm sure of it."

"Great," he mumbled, rubbing his face. "More missing pieces." He slammed back the last of some cold coffee in a can. "It's already 18:00, and I have at least two more hours of work to do. We'll go to the office space in Sumida tomorrow morning. If it hasn't been cleaned out by now, we may find more clues there."

"Don't you think they would have closed down the office right when Etsuko was found dead?"

"I would have, but we don't know how stupid these people are. Etsuko was smart enough to hide things. It looks like she did billing out of her apartment," he said, waving at the cardboard box I brought in. It had her home address on it. "The only thing with the office space address is her bank ledger. We would never have found it otherwise."

"I always thought she was a smart girl." I raised a weak smile and nodded. I had liked Etsuko, and I was sad this was the way I would remember her.

"Want me to drive you anywhere?" Goro asked, grabbing his coat and locking his computer. "I'm going to head out to grab some food and more caffeine."

"Yeah, if you don't mind. Your lovely wife invited me over to the bathhouse for dinner tonight. I'm going to take her up on the offer." I hoped I didn't fall asleep in the bath. I was hoping to text with Yasahiro before bed. I hadn't heard from him all afternoon. I missed him.

Goro placed a hand on my shoulder. "If you wouldn't mind, I'd appreciate it if you kept everything we learned today a secret. I told Kumi we made a breakthrough and we found some more evidence, but I didn't say anything else. I don't *want* to say anything else until we know the whole truth."

I nodded in response as I buttoned my coat. "I'll be honest. I don't want to tell Kumi. She loved Etsuko so much. That should be your job."

It must have been tough, being married and having to break bad news to your spouse or a loved one. I remembered when my mom had found out Dad was dead from the neighbor who found him in the fields. My heart had broken for her.

"I understand. Let's go."

CHAPTER
TWENTY-FOUR

rolled over in Yasahiro's bed and groaned. I was so sore, I was ready to die. Everything hurt. Everything. My legs, my arms, even breathing hurt. I had really overdone it yesterday, and I'd be lucky if I could hobble around the rest of the day. I dragged myself to the bathroom and rummaged through Yasahiro's medicine cabinet until I found a bottle of Eve, Japan's version of ibuprofen. It was right next to a bottle of Advil, its bottle covered in English. Hmmm, I guessed that had been Amanda's. I filled a glass of water, popped the pills in my mouth, and swallowed, hoping they didn't give me a sour stomach. My digestive system was pretty hardy, though, so I wasn't worried.

I placed the bottle of Eve and Advil on the counter and looked at them while I brushed my teeth. Even when I thought Amanda hadn't invaded my head space, she had. I continued to brush my teeth and pawed in the drawer of Yasahiro's vanity, looking at things he had in there, but nothing struck me the way the American bottle of Advil did. He could have bought the painkillers on a trip to California or New York, though. It didn't have to be *hers*.

Ugh, what was wrong with me? I tossed both bottles in the

drawer, pulled my hair into a ponytail while whimpering (My shoulders! They were on fire!), and headed into the kitchen to have breakfast. Being as inept at cooking as I was, I made coffee and ramen, which both tasted amazing if I didn't eat them together in one bite. I sat at Yasahiro's giant dining table, listened to the clock tick, watched the clouds race by outside, and felt the hot air currents from the furnace waft by me. I loved Yasahiro's apartment, but I wasn't used to it yet.

I slurped noodles while I spent some time in my head. How long would I stay here before I had to return to the farmhouse and live with Mom again? If I made this place mine, wouldn't I regret it later when I had to leave? A lot of the walls were painted but bare, except in the bedroom, and I began to imagine my own artwork up on the wall. I dreamed up a giant landscape to hang to my right, something surreal. I'd been thinking about painting landscapes and substituting the colors for something more alien and jarring — purple trees, green skies, pink clouds. I closed my eyes and wondered if I should change my focus to something almost science fiction. I could paint landscapes with moons or other planets in the background! I'd never done that before. Lots of people designed landscapes like this with graphic design programs, but I hadn't seen the concept done with oils. I should search and find out what other people had done.

I picked up my phone on the table, disconnected the charge cord, and the first thing on the screen was the conversation I'd had the previous night with Yasahiro. I scrolled back through the texts and started at the beginning.

"Are you busy?" I'd texted him around 22:00 my time, knowing it was 14:00 in Paris and he could've been busy with either a class or that restaurant opening he had been talking about. He didn't write me back, so I got in bed to read.

"Are you awake?" He'd texted around 0:15 my time. The phone buzzed on the nightstand and jolted me out of a half-sleep, my eReader sitting on my chest, and the lights still on.

"*I am! Hi! How are you?*"

"*Oh good. I was hoping I would catch you still awake. I've been trying to get away from people for the last two hours so I could text in peace.*"

Smiley face. "*I miss you.*" I finally had the chance to say so.

"*I miss you too.*"

"*What are you up to?*"

"*That restaurant opening I was telling you about. One of my more famous fellow graduates just opened his third restaurant in town. Michelin star. All that stuff.*" *A sticker of a dog rolling his eyes.*

"*Oh come on. If you had a Michelin star, you would be pretty happy too.*"

"*Lol. I DO have one. That's why I roll my eyes.*"

"*Oh. I totally forgot! Sorry!*" *Sticker of an anime girl banging her head against a desk.*

"*Anyway, tell me about home.*"

"*Home misses you. It's quiet here without you. There's lots of snow on the ground. I spent a lot of time shoveling.*"

"*I'm going to hire someone to do the restaurant and the apartment building.*"

"*It's okay. It's good for me. Builds character.*" *Sticker of a man flexing his muscles.*

"*I'll come home and you'll be all buff.*"

"*Don't count on it.*" I remembered laughing here and wishing we had chosen to Skype instead.

"*What else?*"

"*I'm getting creative with the microwave and the packaged goods you have. Mrs. Murata has been teaching me to bake bread, but I'm scared to turn on the oven.*"

There was a long pause here. "*Do you want me to teach you how to cook?*"

"*Hmmm. Yes? Maybe? I'm sweating just thinking about it.*"

"*We'll talk about it when I'm home. I leave tomorrow and I'll be home around 10:00 on Thursday. I can't wait to see you!*"

"*I have to take care of Mrs. Yamida on Thursday morning, but hopefully, I'll see you right after.*"

"*Hey, so, I wanted to let you know that Amanda is not here. She's in the States. And I'm glad I didn't run into her. I don't want to see her, as much as you don't want me to see her.*"

"*Okay.*" Smiley face.

"*And there was a camera crew at the pre-party at the restaurant, so sometime tomorrow, you should check the Paris news and see if you can find me.*" Smiley face.

"*Okay! I'll look tomorrow afternoon!*"

"*Good night. Keep the bed warm for me.*"

"*I will. Night!*"

I set my phone down on the table, as a wave of jealousy rolled over me. He was so lucky. He was practically made of luck. He had a good, strong family, and he had a wholesome, easy upbringing. He got to live and study in Paris. He'd already made a name for himself in his field and made money with investments. He had a Michelin star and a famous restaurant. People paid him to travel the world and teach students what he'd learned. There were days when I was afraid to touch him or even look at him, that I would taint him with my eternal, bad luck.

To drive the point home, I checked my email and my inbox did not contain job offers or even responses to my resume. Right. That was the balance of the world, right there. I was here by myself and he was in Paris without me. I knocked my head on the table a few times. Why hadn't I just gone with him? I needed to renew my passport and be ready the next time he was called on to travel or I'd be bitter and unhappy forever.

I glanced around his apartment again. I had to live here one more day without him — just one more. I picked up my phone again, dialing Chiyo. She answered the call immediately and greeted me by name. "Hi, Chiyo. I know my mom's at work, but did she turn her phone back on?"

"No. She's determined to save every cent. She even sold the car yesterday."

My stomach sank to my toes. That was news I was hoping never to hear.

"Oh, really?" I stood up from the dining table and plopped onto the couch. "That was fast."

"She put the money right in the bank."

"Of course she did. Anyway, I was wondering if you could bring her over here to Yasahiro's this afternoon or for dinner tonight? I miss her and wanted to spend some time with her."

"Sure, Mei. She misses you too. I'll be sure to let her know you want to see her."

"Thanks. Call me when you're on your way, okay?"

"Yes, sure. She'll see you later."

My phone didn't stay silent for long. Goro called me a moment later.

"Are you up and dressed?" he asked, abrupt and direct.

"I'm up and fed. I can be dressed in five minutes. What's going on?"

"I'm pulling up on your block. Get dressed. We're going to Sumida Ward to have a look at Etsuko's place of business."

I jumped up from the table and put my coffee mug and soup bowl in the sink. "I'll be down in ten minutes."

I brushed out my hair, braiding and pinning it over my ears, and put on jeans, a shirt, and sweater. I grabbed my boots by the door, hat, scarf, and coat, and got dressed on my way down the stairs.

When I pushed the door open, I immediately groaned, and Goro rolled the window down on his car. "I need to shovel the sidewalk." At least eight centimeters had accumulated overnight, and if I didn't shovel, the neighbors would complain. I couldn't leave Yasahiro with that earful when he came home from Paris.

"Don't worry about it," Goro said, waving to me and picking up his radio. "Kayo!" I was sure this was not the correct way police officers were supposed to talk over the radio, but whatever worked for Goro.

"Yes, boss!" Kayo's voice echoed through the car and bounced off Yasahiro's building.

"I need you and one of the new recruits to come and shovel the sidewalk outside of the building at Kawamida-dori and Twenty-three."

"Yasahiro's place?"

"Yeah. You'll be doing me a huge favor. I'll bring back doughnuts."

A chorus of happy cheers screeched through the radio. Goro turned it down and rolled his eyes as I got in the car. "Don't tell them I was going to bring back doughnuts regardless."

I laughed and buckled myself in. "Thanks. My whole body hurts from shoveling."

He threw the car into gear. "Don't mention it."

He peeled away from the curb and followed the signs leading to Tokyo.

———

WE ARRIVED IN SUMIDA WARD AN HOUR LATER. THE streets of Tokyo were slushy and gray, the snow almost gone from the roads and sidewalks except in little mountains near street corners. I wished Goro was a less angry car driver, though. Riding with him was an exercise in patience because he was constantly weaving in and out of other vehicles, laying on the horn, or swearing at other drivers. At one point, he threatened to turn on the sirens and lights to get us to Tokyo faster. I rolled my eyes and concentrated on my phone the entire trip. I never got carsick, so I was lucky to read in the car and have this distraction.

Goro slowed down in the shadow of the Tokyo Skytree, the

tallest structure in Japan. Sumida was an interesting enclave of artists and craftsmen. The ward was a collection of one and two-story buildings, absent of high-rises. Tokyo Skytree was the highest thing around here, and whatever street you ended up on, your eye was always drawn to it in the distance. I'd only been here two times prior, and only ever to the area around the Skytree. A restaurant up in the tower was worth checking out. Great views, and all that.

"I think it's around this corner..." Goro mumbled, making a turn and pulling up to the curb. He threw the car into park without even caring where he was.

"Do you never have to park your car in a garage?" I craned my neck to look out the window at the stretch of small factories that lined the street. Some were open for business. Others were closed up and appeared as if they'd been that way for years.

"Nope. I get a special exemption." He patted the dashboard of the car and smiled. "It was one of my happiest days when they finally gave me a car. Kayo is jealous, but I keep telling her she's got to work hard, and she'll get one too someday. That's the way it works."

That's the way the system worked for most of Japan. Work hard, work late hours, work on the weekends, spend the night at work, anything for work. I had worked a lot when I had an office job, but it never seemed to be enough. People would sleep at their desk overnight, and I just couldn't. There was something alien about giving away so much of my personal life for a job. So, it was my own fault I kept getting downsized and fired. I should have cared more about the companies I worked for.

"Goro, what do you think of my idea to help the elderly around town? I actually like working hard, putting in the hours, as long as it's for a good cause. I don't think I had it in me to slave away for a corporate job, but I could work hard for people who need me."

He sighed as he pulled on a pair of knit gloves. "This is why I wanted to become a police officer. I couldn't see myself in a suit and tie, commuting to work in the city, and doing the same thing every day for the next fifty years. As a police officer, I'm doing something new all the time, I'm helping people in our town, and I'm solving mysteries. It's the best job on earth. You should think about joining us."

"That's not the first time you've mentioned this."

His smile was smooth. "Because I mean it when I say I think you have a gift for this stuff."

"Really?" I had always thought of the police as being peace-makers, but before moving home to Chikata, I'd never spent any time with a police officer, and I appreciated how varied Goro's job was. "A gift?"

"Don't take it lightly. I mean it."

"Okay, okay. But I... I don't want to go back to school." I had believed that part of my life was over.

"That's understandable. Anyway, I like your idea. More involvement with the town and the elderly is a noble cause. They often need more than their families can provide. Let's go." Goro cut the conversation off and opened his door, swinging his feet out onto the street. A noble cause? Pride swelled in my chest. I wanted to help. I wanted a bit of nobility.

I followed him along the sidewalk as we examined each building and tried to figure out where Etsuko's shop was amongst the tiny factories. A lot of the places manufactured small hand goods like bags or cups, and they recycled cast-off materials from larger facto-ries. Three-D printing and die cutting were popular around here, and I peeked in doorways to see if I could spot anything cool or inter-esting. I let Goro take the lead, and he muttered to himself as he glanced up at each building we came across. He stopped, looking at a piece of paper in his hand, and pointed across the street.

"There it is."

Etsuko's office was one of four in a squat, brick building.

Goro pulled open the glass door and headed into a short hallway that divided the building in half, two offices on each side. Inside the door, on the wall, a directory listed Etsuko's business, Bento Number Nine, as office number four, in the back right corner of the building.

We were halfway down the hallway when one of the offices opened and a young woman called to us.

"Who are you here for?" she asked, waving in our direction.

"Not to worry, ma'am," Goro said, bowing to her. "We're here to check out office number four."

The woman softened as Goro pulled out his police officer badge.

"Is Etsuko in trouble? I haven't seen her in over two weeks, and she's usually in the office at least twice per week."

"Well, I'm afraid to tell you that she died two weeks ago."

I was glad I didn't have to deliver this information because she gasped and covered her face with her hands, a distraught moan leaking between her fingers.

Goro didn't move to comfort her, so I took a few tentative steps forward and patted her on her arm. "Did you know her well?"

"Yes, we were friends." She brushed her long bangs away from her teary eyes. "She's had this office for two years, and we would often go out to lunch together. Does her boyfriend know what happened? They lived apart."

I glanced at Goro and he nodded. "Yeah. He knows. Did she have any business partners or anyone else she worked with here? Anyone else we should inform of her death?"

The young woman shook her head, dabbing at her cheeks with the sleeve of her sweater. "No. She worked alone. She told me once that she only keeps the office so she has space to box up orders and store her inventory. She still did a lot of business out of her own apartment because that's how she started."

She took a deep breath and let it out. "Was there a funeral? Did I miss it?"

"Yes. I'm sorry," I said, stepping away and giving her space.

"That's too bad. I would've contributed to her family for the funeral. She was so nice, and I liked hanging out with her. Do you need to open her office?" She fumbled at her sweater's pocket, keys jingling inside.

"We have a key."

The young woman retreated into her office as we approached Etsuko's. Goro shuffled through a ring of keys until he decided on one he was willing to try first. Three keys later, the door opened and he turned on the light.

The office space was small, about fifteen square meters in total. Every available centimeter of wall space was packed with cardboard boxes, from floor to ceiling, minus room for a tall filing cabinet and a table and chair. To the right of the table, Etsuko had carved out space for packing boxes and supplies. Folded up cardboard boxes, packing tape, a box knife, and a stack of labels were ready and waiting to be used. There were no windows for natural light and the only door to the place was the one we had come through. The office didn't feel miserable or neglected, but the place lacked cheer or any kind of personalization — no photos on the table, posters on the wall, or anything I might associate with Etsuko.

Goro and I slipped on the purple, disposable gloves he kept in his pocket and searched the place in silence. He headed directly for the table while I peeked in the boxes along the wall — bento boxes, hundreds and hundreds of bento boxes. She had such great taste. I loved that she collected a variety of shapes, sizes, and colors, and she hadn't been short on inventory. Picking up the top two or three bento boxes from each box, I opened them. No money. Perhaps she hadn't taken deliveries of money here? She might have only done that at home.

"This looks legitimate," Goro said, rifling through the papers on her desk. "If we had never come here, I would've believed her bento box company was a front. But she has invoices from several companies and individuals. It's funny that she never told Kumi about this. I knew she liked bento boxes. You saw them in her apartment..."

I nodded as I closed another cardboard box.

"What if she thought it was silly?" he continued. "She had a job at her parents' restaurant. Perhaps she was afraid of people telling her that having her own business was too much? You know how people can be."

He moved on to the filing cabinet, pulling on the top drawer but it didn't open. Taking the key ring from his pocket again, he found a smaller silver key that opened the filing cabinet. The two bottom drawers were filled with hanging files of paper. He glanced through them, not finding anything interesting. I looked over his shoulder, and the folders were labeled "inventory," "taxes," and "past due." The next drawer up contained a folder for each of her suppliers. The third drawer from the bottom was filled with teabags, ramen noodles, napkins, and feminine hygiene products. Goro didn't even flinch as he shuffled through her personal goods and closed the drawer. The top drawer contained a cashbox.

He placed the cashbox on the table, unlocked it with another key on Etsuko's ring, and inside the box, neat stacks of bills took up the available space. Goro eyed each stack, mumbling and counting on his fingers. I suppressed a smile.

"Looks like... She had about 300,000 yen on hand. That's not a little bit of money, but it's also not a lot of money. Not the kind of money we found in her apartment." He hummed and drummed his fingers on the table. "I bet this was her legitimate storefront, and that she got into money laundering later after her business was already established. She probably kept the legitimate business coming in and out of here, and everything else happened in and out of her home."

I looked at the money, all that money. Etsuko had worked hard, trying to build a future for her and Hisashi. Getting caught up in the money laundering was secondary, as far as I was concerned. There was no reason her money should get caught up in this investigation, especially if the police had already confiscated the cash in her apartment.

I grabbed a stack of money and held it between us. "Hisashi deserves this money. They were going to marry and start a family. She was going to use this to take care of her loved ones. If we add this money to the investigation, Hisashi will never see it."

"No way, Mei. That goes against every rule and regulation we have. This is all evidence." Goro's eyes searched mine, probably hoping I was joking. I wasn't.

"No one ever has to know. Etsuko worked alone, and when we came here, the cashbox was empty." I said it with confidence, believing that if I was convinced the lie was true, it must have been. I pushed the cash at Goro. "Hold onto it for Hisashi. There is no way he killed her. He deserves this money. She obviously worked hard for every yen she made." I waved to the room around me. "There's no reason to throw away the money now."

Goro looked between me and the money in my hands. "I have a better idea." He grabbed my bag and threw the cashbox inside of it. "You take the whole thing." Amazingly enough, the box fit in my sack of a purse. "When the investigation is over, you give it to him. If something happens and he goes to jail, you keep the money."

"What?" I drew back with my hand over my chest. "I can't keep this. I'll donate it or something."

"Fine." He opened both upper drawers of the filing cabinet and moved the food and tea to the top drawer, keeping the personal products in the second one. "If anyone asks, this is what we found here." He closed the drawer and pressed his forehead to the cold metal. I immediately felt guilty for suggesting we take the money.

"Goro..."

"Don't, Mei. Don't try to make me feel better." He pushed away from the cabinet. "Everything about Chikata has been falling to pieces ever since the grocery store came to town. Yet, everyone's grateful for the extra jobs and foot traffic."

I shrugged my shoulders. "Yin and yang. I can't imagine it was a challenging job being a police officer in a peaceful town like Chikata before Midori Sankaku."

"No, but at least it was honest."

My face flushed with heat. "*This* is honest, Goro. Don't tell yourself anything different. We look out for our own. I'm not going to take this money and bet it at the track. The invoices are here to prove she did business. For all we know, she could have buried money all over Tokyo. At least this way, Hisashi can have some cash to move on with. I'll bury the box under the clothes in my closet at home. When he's released, tell him to come to me."

Goro glanced around the office again and nodded his head. Good. Because my next step was to put back the box and walk out, and I would rather have kept the money in play until we knew what was going on.

"We have one more stop before we return to Chikata, the safe deposit box."

Goro opened the door and ushered me out as he turned off the lights and locked up behind him.

CHAPTER
TWENTY-FIVE

I left the cashbox in Goro's police car, sliding it under the passenger seat and out of sight. Not that I thought anyone would break into a police car, but better to be safe. I shouldn't tempt someone. According to papers left at Etsuko's office, she had used a local bank located right under the Tokyo Skytree. The high tower loomed overhead as Goro and I entered the bank's lobby. A gust of hot air hit me, and I sighed with gratitude. I was so sick of being cold. How many more days till summer? Too many.

I sat down in a cushioned armchair while Goro asked to speak to the bank manager, a tiny man in a crisp suit with a full head of silver hair. They conversed for a moment, then Goro was directed back to an office.

What I wouldn't have given for a cup of coffee right then. My head was pounding which meant my blood sugar was low, and I was short on caffeine. Ramen for breakfast wasn't my best idea ever. I should have had more protein. I dug through my bag, looking for something to eat when I noticed my phone. I sat back into the comfortable armchair and swiped the screen on.

It was already 11:00, and I'd had a text from both Kumi and Chiyo.

Kumi wrote, *"Hope you're feeling better today! It was good to hang out last night and have dinner together. I've been working on a logo for you. Just a little something to put on fliers or business cards. I hope you like it. I've sent it in an email."* Smiley face.

Oh, that was so sweet. She didn't have to do that for me, and once again I was bowled over by the kindness of my new old friends. I couldn't help but smile down at my phone.

Chiyo wrote, *"I spoke to your mom and I'll bring her by around 17:00. She wants to take a nap before coming over."*

Yay! An evening with Mom. I couldn't wait to see her. I texted Chiyo to thank her and tell her how grateful I was for her help. I was lucky to have these wonderful ladies in my life.

Instead of going straight to my email to check out the new logo Kumi made for me, I decided to take out my book and start reading. The last two times I had tried to read, I was interrupted by Jun. I wondered what was going on with him. Was he safe? Or was he in trouble? I didn't have a lot of love for him, what with the mugging and everything, but I didn't want to see him hurt or even dead. My mind wandered, and I stared out the window, imagining Jun with Takahara and Etsuko. Were they in some kind of love triangle? I was unsure. She wasn't in the photos with them. How did Etsuko, the Ne Kitsune boys, and Takahara end up in a mess together? There must have been some explanation I was missing. I'd gone from thinking that Etsuko had had an affair to thinking Jun killed Etsuko to money laundering and back to a love triangle. It felt like the lies would never end.

My phone rang, and I dug through my bag again to find it. It was Murata. She had never called me before, and my heart beat a panicked pace as I answered.

"Hi, Mrs. Murata. Is everything okay?"

"Everything's fine, Mei. I saw my physical therapist this

morning, and I'm tired, so I'm going to sleep this afternoon. You don't need to come by." Her voice croaked with weariness.

"That's fine! I'm relieved you're okay. Let me know if you need anything."

"I'm glad you're not angry," she said, sighing into the phone.

"No. Absolutely not. I'm here to help you, to make your life easier. Don't worry about me. My mom is coming over later, so I'll be fine."

"You're a good girl, Mei. I'm glad we met." I blushed at her praise and glanced up to see Goro coming towards me.

"Get some rest, and I'll see you tomorrow." We said goodbye, and I hung up. I lost money for the day, but I kept a client, and that's what mattered.

"All right. We're set to go." Past Goro, near the door to the rear of the bank, the bank manager waited for us.

"What did you tell him?" I whispered, trying not to draw attention to ourselves.

"The truth. I have Etsuko's death certificate and a warrant to search anything she owned. The safe deposit box falls in that jurisdiction."

I followed Goro and the bank manager through a hallway to the safe deposit boxes and safe. They both used their keys to open the box, and the manager bowed and left us alone. Goro took the box into a private room, and I closed the door behind us.

"Okay," he said, opening the flap on the long metal box. I held my breath, believing there would be some dramatic evidence inside. We'd come so far, from no clues to finally being within reach of the killer. I wanted to end this as soon as possible so we could put Etsuko's memory to rest and move on.

The giant box had nothing but a few slips of paper and an envelope. That was it.

Goro grabbed the papers, and I grabbed the envelope. Inside the envelope, four numbers were written on a note in Etsuko's handwriting. *"The pin number to an application of locked images on my phone: 8-3-2-8."*

"Did you ever find an application that needed a pin number on her phone? What if she was hiding more images of Takahara, for blackmail use?"

Goro shook his head. "Not on her personal phone, and we still don't have the other phone you saw. I was hoping it would be in this box."

"It couldn't be here," I said, shaking my head. "I saw her use the phone the night before she was murdered, and she spent the whole day with Hisashi. She didn't have time to come into the city and drop the phone in the safe deposit box. It must be in her apartment somewhere."

"We tore that place apart. There's no way it's there."

"Then the murderer must have it."

"Yeah..." Goro relaxed against his chair as his eyes skimmed the paper he was holding. He swore. "Well, here we have a confession."

My scalp tingled as I took the paper from his shaky fingers. Before I started reading, I peeled off my heavy winter coat.

"If someone besides me finds this letter then I know I've been found out. I wish I could turn back the clock and never have gotten involved in this business, but it's too late. The only thing I can do now is come out and confess to everything I've done.

"It was about three years ago I decided I should take a second job. My parents were good to me, always giving me shifts at the restaurant if I needed them, but it wasn't enough to put money in the bank and save up for a future. I had this little hobby that I love, buying bento boxes. I would pick up a new one every now and then, make lunch, and post photos of the boxes online. It was some-thing fun to do and I loved it. Eventually, I had a lot of online followers who complimented me on my collection and clamored for more boxes, more photos. They wanted bento boxes like mine too, and they wanted to know how to find them. That was when I

got my idea! I would start up a little online business selling bento boxes to the people who followed me. At first I wasn't making any money, then word-of-mouth grew, and I had hundreds of orders per month. Hisashi thought I was a little crazy. He didn't want me to tell anybody about it, so I didn't. I figured it would be my little secret only he would know about. I rented a little office space in Sumida and worked on my orders from there and at home.

"Then two years ago my apartment building was sold to Fujita Takahara. I had heard of him because of the work he did with Midori Sankaku, and I knew he was a popular ladies' man, but that was about it. He took delivery of one of my boxes while he was living in the apartment below mine, and that's how we met. He would often stay in that apartment when he had a lot of meetings in town and didn't want to commute back to Tokyo. We got to talking, I told him about my business, and he said he wanted to invest. I was excited! I thought I had lucked out. He told me that because most of his money came from his father, he would have to invest under the table. I don't know why I didn't question that. I should have.

"We set up a system where we would exchange money and invoices, and in the end, I would have money to invest. It wasn't until six months later when he started shifting more money my way that I realized what had happened. He was using me to launder money, and I stupidly stepped right into his trap. But once I was sure I knew what was happening, I couldn't get out of it. He was insistent that we keep things the same, and since he lived underneath me, there was nothing I could do to hide from him.

"Then I did something even stupider. I was lonely and I wanted someone to hang out with, to spend the night. Hisashi traveled all the time, and I hadn't seen him in three months. So I emailed this Ne Kitsune service, a no-sex escort service for lonely women, met a young man named Jun, and he came over twice a week. I had cash from Takahara, so I spent it on this. I had no feelings for Jun, but he fell in love with me. Takahara caught Jun leaving my apartment one day, and I knew that was the end for me.

"Takahara blackmailed me into doing even more money laundering for him. I should've come clean to Hisashi. I should've told him, and we would've worked things out but instead I made things worse. Takahara followed Jun to his apartment and blackmailed him, too. Since Jun was in love with me, he didn't want to see me get hurt either. It was awful. Takahara is very good at blackmailing, and I've since learned this is his favorite tactic, to find lonely women and prompt them to start businesses, take his money, launder it, and blackmail them into staying silent. I am one of maybe a dozen women he's conned into doing this. I'm sorry I don't know their names.

"Eventually, I found out he met another young man through Jun and the Ne Kitsune service. I could hear them in the apartment below mine! Takahara was sleeping with this young man and right under me most nights. I figured I would turn the tables on him. I had Jun plant a small camera in Takahara's apartment, and I took videos and photos. They are all in a locked folder on my work mobile phone. I change the pin often, so I'll leave the number in an envelope next to this letter.

"I'm going to take the photos and video to Takahara and tell him that if he doesn't let me go, I'm going to show the photos to his father. Takahara gets most of his money from his father, and I suspect the money I was laundering was from bribes, though I can't be too sure. He never told me. Hopefully this will be over soon.

"Please tell Hisashi I'm sorry. All I wanted was for a little business to myself, and I was stupid. I screwed it up. I was hoping to save the money so we could have a family, and if I'm lucky, I'll come here when this is over and burn this letter. If someone else is reading this, it means I'm in jail. I regret my decisions, and I hope my family can forgive me. Signed, Etsuko Hiyasa."

"Oh," I breathed out, shutting my eyes against the pounding

headache. It was worse now. "I don't think she ever believed her life was in danger. She thought she would be arrested." Instead, she was killed. In my head, I could see Takahara wrapping his hands around her neck and squeezing until she was lifeless, limp. I reflexively touched my neck and swallowed.

"Threatening to go to Takahara's father was, most likely, going too far. His father was extremely wealthy, and now Takahara is extremely wealthy since his death. He's untouchable, Mei. I've heard his family comes from the samurai class, and they guard their relatives with everything they have. This will be tough."

"It's her word against his unless we find some accomplices. Jun, this other young man, and the other women he conned into doing this. We'll need all of them to come forward. But what do we do now?"

Goro put the papers back into the box and closed it. "We put this back, and I call it in. The office and the safe deposit box both will be searched today."

Relief washed over me. With the whole department on the case, we were sure to have more evidence soon. We put the box away and locked it closed.

"Wait for me in the lobby. I'm going to go talk to the manager, and then we'll head back to Chikata after picking up doughnuts."

Goro walked to the bank manager's office, his shoulders stiff and face creased with worry.

This case had just become ten times more complicated.

CHAPTER
TWENTY-SIX

"I brought food!" Mom said, climbing the stairs to Yasahiro's apartment. "We had leftover chicken at Midori Sankaku today, so I purchased it at a discount."

Mom, ever the lover of a good sale, smiled at me as I ushered her into the apartment. I was glad her shoes were free of slush or snow which meant the sidewalks outside were clear. I came home earlier, and the snow had been shoveled thanks to the young officers of the Chikata police department. Goro brought them two dozen doughnuts from a place called Mister Donut on the other side of the Skytree. The place was ridiculously filled with plastic lion statues and lion chairs. It was super *kawaii*.

I grabbed the bags of groceries from Mom's arms and waited while she took off her shoes and placed her purse on the kitchen table.

"This place never ceases to amaze me," she said, glancing around at the apartment. I had the Christmas tree lights on, the blinds down, and the overhead lamps dimmed. I even turned on Christmas music, and the place was warm and dry. "He has such great taste. When will he be back?"

"Tomorrow afternoon." I placed the groceries on the counter

and began to unpack vegetables and chicken meat. "What are you going to make? Can I help?"

Mom's eyes widened. "Mei, since when do you work in the kitchen?"

I opened my mouth a few times before responding. "I'm trying. I really am. I made eggs the other day. I broke into a sweat while they cooked, but I did it and didn't kill myself or set fire to anything." I gripped the edge of the counter and took a deep breath. "Mrs. Murata has been teaching me how to make bread."

"Really? You do remember the time you set fire to a wooden spoon, and I found you passed out on the floor of the kitchen while the spoon set a dish towel on fire?"

I swallowed past the lump in my throat, remembering the incident that led me to avoiding the kitchen for the next twelve years. All I remembered was fire and then blackness.

"I'm feeling brave. I want to overcome this fear. I'm in my mid-twenties and I can't cook anything but rice." I separated out the vegetables like I'd always seen Mom do, and I placed the chicken in the fridge until she was ready to use it.

Mom joined me at the kitchen island, squeezing me around the waist and smiling. "I'm proud of you. You've been working so hard, and I know you don't have much to show for it, but everyone's noticed how strong and helpful you are."

"Oh, stop," I said, squeezing her back. "I'm barely making a few hundred yen per week at this rate, enough to pay for a bus pass, and that's it. I would be starving and freezing if it weren't for Yasahiro. I wouldn't call that brave." I glanced over at my bag near the door, containing the cashbox I took from Etsuko's office today. Some would call what I did stupid, considering the police could arrest me for tampering with evidence, but I liked to think of myself as strong for protecting what Etsuko would have wanted for Hisashi.

I teetered on the edge of good luck and bad luck at all times. Even on days I was lucky, everything could turn around in the blink of an eye. I was either falling prey to a string of bad karma or my head was stuck in the clouds daydreaming how different things could be.

"You've been brave lately. Surviving the fire, a new relationship with Yasahiro, and starting a new business? All of these things show how tenacious you are. Whatever happens, you need to pick yourself up and keep going. That's what I did during even my worst years as a farmer, and I had some rough years." Mom reached into the cabinet to the right of the stove and pulled out two cutting boards. She then opened a drawer, took out vegetable peelers, and pulled a knife from a knife block next to the stove. She knew Yasahiro's kitchen better than I did. I'm sure she had come here to teach him too. She'd known him a lot longer than I had.

"Now, we're going to make a chicken and dumpling soup. You can begin by peeling and cutting the vegetables, and I'll start the soup stock. We'll work together, and you'll learn knife skills first. Even if you never cook at the stove, the knife skills will come in handy. You could always prep vegetables for Yasahiro." She winked at me and laughed like she could see into my happy future to where I would be in five years. I hoped she was right.

We cooked together for an hour, enjoying the easy chatter about her interim job and some of Yasahiro's wine. Mom taught me how to hold the knife correctly and angle my fingers so I didn't chop them off. She handled the chicken but left the dumplings to me. It was good to be cooking with somebody else here. The apartment had been empty with Yasahiro gone, and I'd missed my mom.

While the soup bubbled away on the stove, we sat at the table and tended to our own hobbies. Mom hemmed an old shirt with a needle and thread, and I opened my computer to check my email. I'd been away most of the day, neglecting my inbox when it was finally seeing some traffic. Kumi's email sat at the top of the list, and I remembered she had drawn a logo for me. I opened the email and smiled at her creation, a sweet illustration of an old lady with a cane and me next to her, guiding her by the elbow. Kumi had even drawn my flyaway hair right. I turned the computer to show Mom, and she laughed and clapped.

"It's perfect! Are you thinking of expanding your business?" Mom tried to ask nonchalantly, but her smile was too big.

"You've been talking to Goro. I'm considering it. Definitely. I'd like a few more daily clients, but I've had bigger ideas in mind, too." I paused while I stood up to stir the soup. "Mrs. Murata had an idea that I thought was genius. She said there was no central location for elderly people to meet up. No place for them to do crafts, eat or spend time together. Perhaps a little, old-fashioned tea shop with extra space for families or gatherings would be perfect. It would need a handicapped-accessible bathroom that was easy to move around in."

I let my eyes blur, imagining such a place, how happy and alive it would be. "I thought I would write a business plan, and I would ask for investors. But I don't know how someplace like that would work. How would it make enough money to provide me with a salary and pay the rent? I need to talk about this with someone who is better at business than I am."

"Yasahiro is a successful businessman. He's the person you should be speaking to about this." Mom set down her sewing. "Because this is a fabulous idea. We need more community spaces for the elderly and their families. Tiny apartments just aren't enough, especially if they want to do other activities." I tapped the wooden spoon on the pot, set it on the spoon rest, and sat down across from Mom. Her face was full of mirth.

"We could do sewing classes, origami classes, maybe even tai chi? I have a lot of ideas. I need to write them down... But I don't want Yasahiro involved." I shook my head. "I don't want to make him feel like he owes me anything. I'm already indebted to him for all of this." I swept my hands out at his luxury apartment and the wine I was drinking. I immediately felt guilty for opening the bottle.

"That's a mistake, Mei. I bet he would love the idea, and he has the space right downstairs to make this happen."

I couldn't deny that I'd been dreaming about the retail space downstairs and wondering if it would be perfect for my idea, but that was going too far. We had only just started dating, and I was afraid of pushing things too quickly. Everything was going well so far. We'd slept together, he'd seen my scars, and he'd let me stay in his place. I didn't want my bad luck to spoil it.

Because I was sure Mom was not going to give this up, I said, "We'll see," hoping that would placate her.

I turned the computer around to face me and an email had hit my inbox in the last five minutes from Yasahiro. Subject: "Getting on the plane."

"Fuji-ko, I'm about to board the plane, and I wanted to send you the link to this news story from yesterday's restaurant opening. Be sure to watch the video. –Y."

I hesitated, not knowing what he was directing me to. Was it a video of him? The restaurant? If it was on a news site, I was okay to watch it with Mom in the room. While she was at the stove dishing out our dinner, I clicked on the link and was brought to a French news site.

The article appeared to be about the restaurant opening he went to yesterday. I had Google translate the page for me, and I got the basic idea of what his day was like, a lot of photos, food, and celebrities. It was so posh, the restaurant had a red carpet outside the front doors with an area for interviews. I scrolled through the photos, recognized a few movie stars, a famous author, and then Yasahiro standing with some other people, posing for the cameras. His smile was bright and genuine, and he looked like he was having a great time.

My insides squirmed as I leaned in to examine him closer. He was wearing a sharp suit, dark colors accentuated his wide jaw and sparkling smile. His hair was styled, something I hadn't seen in person, only in photos like these and the ones before I met him when he was with Amanda. I found the swoop of his hair ultra sexy, and I closed my eyes to remember how soft and easy it was when I ran my fingers through it.

I had it really bad for this guy.

I scrolled down the page to stop any further arousal and ran right into the video. I pressed play, and a woman's voice speaking French narrated the scene of a busy opening night for a famous restaurant. Images of popping champagne and plates of food with people in fancy outfits cut in and out with English subtitles over them.

"The opening of Les Pivonies in 13th arrondissement today was the talk of the town. The line for entry stretched around the block at one point, and Chef Richard had to pull his friends into the place himself..."

I watched for two minutes, impressed by the sheer display of wealth and popularity on hand. Two American and French stars were interviewed and everyone was sure this restaurant would be popular for the next decade.

"What are you watching?" Mom asked, coming around the table behind me. "Is that French? Since when do you speak French?"

I laughed and pointed at the screen. "I don't, but the subtitles are in English." I pulled my hand back to my mouth as Yasahiro appeared on camera.

"I love what Richard has done to the building and his kitchen is very impressive. I'm sure this place will be hard to get into for anyone without the proper connections." He laughed and I sat stunned, listening to him speak French, reading the English subtitles that I translated in my head into Japanese. It was like listening to a stranger I thought I may know, but I wasn't sure if I did.

"How long are you in town?" the interviewer asked.

"*I leave for Japan tomorrow. Back to my home, my girlfriend, my own restaurant.*"

"*Your girlfriend? Are you and Amanda Cheung back together?*" Hearing her name doused me in cold water. Of course, they all assumed they'd be back together. Everyone had.

"*No, no. Amanda and I broke up over a year ago. I'm dating someone new in Japan, in the town I call home now. She's my life.*" He placed his hand over his heart, and my eyes welled with tears. "*I'm a lucky man.*"

I paused the video on his sincere face and wished I could hug him.

"I think I understand what he said," Mom said, placing her hand on my shoulder. "Though my English is terrible. I'm so happy for you. You couldn't have picked a more reputable man, and he *is* lucky to have such a wonderful person like you."

Mom picked up my hand and squeezed it. "Now we just need to deal with the house and the farm and everything will be back to normal, better than normal."

But that meant sleeping in my room at home, alone. I looked around Yasahiro's apartment and immediately felt conflicted and nostalgic for the place. This luxury was only temporary. Soon, I would have to return home.

I rewound the video and played it again.

CHAPTER
TWENTY-SEVEN

"I t's not going to be enough," Goro said, shaking his head and putting his car into gear. I had just finished helping Yamida with her physical therapy and had a few hours before I needed to be at Murata's apartment, so I decided to join Goro in another excursion into Tokyo. He offered to buy lunch if I came with him out to Takadanobaba, and I relented since I'm low on cash.

I glanced at my phone as Goro sped along on the highway at a breakneck pace. No texts from Kumi or Akiko, and none from Yasahiro, but he wasn't due to land until close to 15:00. If I timed things right, I'd be done at Murata's apartment and back to his place in time to heat up the leftover chicken and dumpling soup and make a fresh batch of rice. That way he'd come home to hot food and a warm apartment, probably something he missed on previous trips. The footage from the news story replayed in my head again, coaxing my eyes closed so I could remember the expression on his face. He'd said, *"She's my life."* No one had ever said that about me. What had I done to deserve such high praise from him? How could I keep doing it so I didn't lose his love and attention?

I opened my eyes and came back to the present, to the sound of Goro honking the horn.

"What's not going to be enough?"

"The evidence we already have. Most of the staff worked through the night to go over everything brought in from Etsuko's office and safe deposit box. They found lots of evidence that she had a profitable business, and she laundered money for someone else, no names. Then we have her own confession as to what happened. But it's her word against his, again. If we confront him with the letter of a dead woman, it will mean nothing, and he'll laugh in our faces." Goro swerved in and out of slow-moving cars and flashed his lights to make people move over.

"Are you allowed to do that?" I pointed to the roof of the car, indicating the police lights and the frantic people trying to merge into the next lane.

"Are you going to tell on me? Because if I remember correctly, you took evidence from the crime scene yesterday."

Suddenly, Goro and I were either locked in a blackmail relationship, or we were best friends. Depended on how you looked at it.

I laughed and rolled my eyes at him. "Nevermind. We're in this together." I sipped on the cup of coffee he bought me, and he turned on the lights again to get traffic moving. "So what's the next step then?"

"We're going to persuade Jun to come forward —"

"Wait, wait, wait." I waved my hands in the air. "He was as skittish as a half-blind cat. There's no way he'll come forward."

"You said he was involved, and I'm going to bring him in. If we're lucky, we'll convince him and the other guy in the photos to be sworn witnesses. If we're extremely lucky, we might even find some of the other smurfs that were laundering Takahara's money."

I slid my eyes to the side at him. "Smurfs? What do little blue cartoon characters have to do with this?"

Goro laughed, throwing his head back before jerking the car into the next lane. "'Smurfs' is a money-laundering term. A smurf is somebody who does the money laundering in small increments for someone else. If an individual or company has a lot of money to launder, sometimes they hire multiple smurfs to do all the laundering. Or they can buy diamonds or other untraceable goods..." He circled his hand in the air. "There are a lot of ways to launder money."

"Interesting. I had no idea."

"I handled one other money laundering case about five years ago when I was working in Tokyo. I learned a lot, and now my skills are being put to work." He smiled over at me. "I may get a raise or maybe a promotion."

"If anyone deserves it, it's you." And I did mean that. Goro loved his job, and he was good at it. If he'd done anything wrong these past few months, it was my fault, and I'd take the blame. But I'd hid my own wrongdoings well, and hopefully, they'd never be found out, especially since the people I lied for appreciated my help. I hoped.

Goro pulled off the highway, and ten minutes later we were in Takadanobaba, an area west of Shinjuku. This was one of the lower rent districts of Tokyo, if that was even a thing. Nothing about the city was even remotely affordable to people like me anymore, but since this was a college area of town, the buildings were more rundown and the rent was cheaper than other wards. When I graduated from high school, I had wanted to go to Waseda University, the university closest to this area, but I didn't get in. I had ended up going to Tokyo Metropolitan University instead, which was an excellent school, but I was disappointed. For the past eight years, I had viewed my rejection from Waseda as the first of many failures.

When I worked in the city, I used to come to Takadanobaba in the evenings to be close to Waseda students, hang out, and eat cheap food. I would dream and wonder how different my life would have been if I had been one of them, the happy college kids eating dinner at the table next to me. What I should have done was gone out with my coworkers and stopped dreaming, but it was hard to learn that lesson when dreaming was the way I lived my life.

We slowly pulled the car into a quiet neighborhood off Waseda-dori. The place hadn't changed much in five years, with its tiny back alleys and artistic counter-culture pumping out of every storefront and cheap izakaya. The street we drove down was one-way, and with snow piled up on the corners, Goro had to work hard to drive his car around the bends.

"That's it, right there," he said, pointing at a three-story apartment building over a café. He pulled his car all the way over to the side of the road, not bothering to notice that he was parked on the sidewalk. I knew better than to remark on it. He had his own ideas of what constituted parking.

Ignoring the café, we let ourselves into the downstairs vestibule of the apartment building. Goro glanced at the mailboxes and mumbled, "Number three." I remembered he had other police officers follow the young men who worked for Ne Kitsune.

I followed him up the stairs, and we stopped in front of door number three. Goro knocked hard on the door, in the way that meant, "I'm not here to sell you something, and you better open the door," but nothing happened.

"What if he's in class?" I whispered to him. "It *is* a weekday after all. Or he could be at a client..."

The door behind us opened, and a young woman poked her head out. "Are you looking for Kenichi?"

"No, we're looking for Jun. Do you know if he's home?" I asked, smiling and being as pleasant as possible.

"He came home this morning." She adjusted her glasses and

pulled up her pajama pants. Ah, to be in college again. I missed it. Well, I missed the pajamas-all-day lifestyle, not the tests and studying. "I had breakfast downstairs in the café near the window, and I saw him come home and into the building. I came in about thirty minutes later. And he hadn't left."

"Who's Kenichi?" I asked, wanting to get down to the real questions. I was starting to get hungry, and no matter how much caffeine I'd had, it wouldn't be enough to keep another headache away.

If Jun was home and he wasn't answering the door, then he was either sick or very asleep because we were loud.

"His roommate, well, one of two roommates. Another guy named Daisuke lives there too, but Kenichi and Daisuke are both in Hokkaido. They left yesterday to visit their families over the holidays."

With Jun's roommates gone, he would've had the place to himself. Goro knocked hard on the door again, this time turning his fist and pounding enough to make the doorjamb shake. The young woman jumped at the sound.

"You know, if you need to get in there, the man who runs the café downstairs is our landlord. He has keys to all the apartments."

"Really? Are there no other exits in here?"

"No. Just out the front door."

"Wait here," Goro said to me, and he took the stairs down two at a time. Where did he get all his energy?

I smiled weakly at the girl, and she glanced at me before wishing me a good day and closing the door. I strained my ears for any sign of life from Jun's apartment. Instead, I heard the TV turn on in the girl's apartment, and I imagined her wrapped up in a blanket, eye-guzzling some new show I'd never heard of while neglecting her school work. Yep, I missed college.

Goro returned a few minutes later with the landlord in tow. I bowed and said hello, but the landlord grunted and opened the door. "Don't stay too long. I don't want any trouble. I have customers downstairs, and I can't be bothered by this around the lunch rush." The landlord slapped a key into Goro's hand and walked down the stairs. "Lock up when you leave and bring the key back to me," he called over his shoulder.

"Pleasant man," I mumbled.

"They can't all be winners," Goro replied, pushing the door open slowly. The apartment was a mess, as I expected it to be. The guys had turned the living area into a bedroom with loft and bunk beds over the tatami mats. The rest of the space was dominated by racks of clothing, a sewing machine in one corner, and scraps of cloth draped over every available chair or bed surface. The kitchen was piled high with dirty plates and bowls, and a computer sat to the right of the beds, powered off.

The situation and the apartment itself gave off a creepy vibe. I suppressed a shudder and began searching. I stepped over a mess of clothes on the floor and flipped through the stacks of paper on the desk, invoices for customer dresses and other clothing to Kenichi Giruhan. Sounded like a fake name to me, but what did I know about those things?

Goro searched through the kitchen briefly before stepping towards the only other door in the apartment, the bathroom.

He swore violently, startling me badly enough to trip over the clothing and stumble, knocking over a dressform along the way. When I reached the bathroom, Goro was on his phone.

"I'm at Jun Nomohiro's apartment in Takadanobaba, and he's dead. Suicide. In the tub. No pulse. Send someone out now."

Kayo's voice on the other end of the line repeated, "Yes, yes. Of course. Yes..." as he hung up.

Thankfully, I closed my eyes as soon as I saw the blood on the floor, a pool of water stained bright red. I turned and pressed my back to the wall, covering my mouth with my hand.

The situation had, indeed, gotten worse.

———

It took a lot of willpower, deep breaths, and physical anguish to keep myself from crying. The tears were right behind my eyelids, ready to pour forth, but I held them, like stopping a flood from a dam with my bare hands. I hadn't liked Jun much, but I didn't want him dead. No one deserved to die for something stupid like this.

"What are we going to do?" I asked Goro as he pulled me away from the bathroom and sat me on a chair in the living space. "Is this our fault?"

It felt like my fault. I had gotten him into this mess by trying to hire him from Ne Kitsune. He pushed me away, told me to leave him alone, and then returned the next day. If only we had never seen each other again after that night.

"This is not our fault. Jun got himself into trouble with Etsuko. He was doomed from the start." Goro brushed aside the curtains on the window and looked out onto the street. I didn't hear sirens, but they would come at any moment. This time, though, it'd be Tokyo Metropolitan Police. Goro being there was expected, but it would look suspicious if I was hanging around. I took stock of everything I'd touched since I had entered the apartment. Why had I touched things?

Goro returned to the bathroom and emerged with a small sheet of paper.

"I saw this in there the first time..." He unfolded the paper. "It's a note from Jun. '*I can't keep secrets anymore. I have no money, no family, and no friends, so I'm going to end it now. Please cremate my body and place the ashes next to my parents.*'" Goro looked at me, the paper in his hand, the bathroom, and back to me. "I'll never understand why some people feel it's better to end their life than to try something new. He could've moved, become a new person someplace else."

A wave of nausea curled up from my toes, and I swallowed hard to keep the bile in my stomach.

Faint sirens in the distance closed in on our location. I began to panic, my heart rate increased, and I flushed deep red.

"Should I go?" If I ran down the stairs, I could've made it into the café and hid out there until Goro came to find me.

He scoffed. "Don't worry, Mei. It's a suicide. He left a note. I'll explain to the Tokyo Metropolitan Police that we were here to check up on him because he was a witness in one of our cases. I'm sure that's what Kayo told them when she called it in." He sat down next to me. "Besides, you touched things in this apartment. If it were a criminal investigation, they'd find your prints anyway."

Just as I had thought. Note to self: keep gloves in your purse if you continue to be an amateur detective.

When the police showed up, everything went the way Goro said it would. An officer took our statements, their team bagged the suicide note as evidence, and we were released before they pulled Jun out of the tub. Good. I didn't want to see him like that again.

Goro and I headed into the café, dropping the key off with the landlord who was mighty upset with the police in and out of his building, and we walked to a noodle shop down the street for lunch. The restaurant was small, with only four spots to stand at a counter, and two main dishes of *tonkotsu* ramen. Goro remained silent all through lunch, and I took that as my cue to stay silent as well, to daydream and try to forget about what happened. Whatever was going on in his head, he needed the time to think it through. I slurped up the hot noodles and soup and tried to erase the blood I witnessed from my brain. Not an easy task for a daydreamer like me.

A quiet rage grew in my chest through lunch. Takahara, this man... He had completely ruined the lives of so many people. If he had been blackmailing Jun, like he was blackmailing Etsuko, he'd probably been blackmailing a dozen other people. Where did he get off destroying other people's lives? Was it all for the money? How much was a life really worth? Right then, I wanted to find him and beat him to a bloodied pulp. To me, his life was worth very little.

When my bowl of noodles was empty, I gave it back to the one woman running the place, thanked her for lunch, and followed Goro out onto the sidewalk. A cold, winter wind whipped around the buildings and froze me instantly. I would have given anything for it to be summer. I zipped up and pulled a hat onto my head. Goro, his hands and head exposed to the cold, but not seeming to care, texted on his phone. After a few moments, he slipped the phone into his jacket pocket.

"We have two choices," Goro said, heading to our car. I sped up my legs to catch up to him. "We can chase down the other Ne Kitsune boy that Jun mentioned..." He glanced at me, hoping I'd fill in the blanks.

"Jun said he found a gay guy who would be willing to sleep in the same bed with Etsuko, and he wouldn't get attached. I bet he's the same guy in the photos with Takahara because that was definitely not Jun."

"I'd bet that as well, but we need to consider his safety. If we go chasing after him, Takahara will know we're aware of the young man, and right now, he thinks we know nothing. Jun chased you down and got in trouble all on his own, without our help."

I shook my head, my stomach twisted into a tiny ball. "I don't want to get anybody else killed."

We reached the car, and Goro started up the engine, turning the heat to full.

"Right. Me neither. We should head back to Chikata and regroup. What we need to do is arrest Takahara first, take him into custody, and start questioning him while we gather up more witnesses. This may keep everyone safe, assuming Takahara was working alone."

"I assumed he was working alone since Etsuko didn't mention anyone else in her confession note." I sank into the chair, pressing my whole body into it. "We can't let him get away with this."

Goro threw the car into gear again. "No, we can't. It's time to show our hand."

CHAPTER
TWENTY-EIGHT

checked my phone for Yasahiro's flight status as Goro pulled up to Murata's building. My phone informed me Yasahiro was ten minutes from landing, and I was getting excited to see him. We were in that early part of a relationship where I almost forgot what he looked like when he was gone. Would I recognize his face? His voice? I closed my eyes and remembered the soft touch of his fingers on my back, the only man I'd allowed to touch me there in years. It was heaven. I'd rather have thought about all these things than Jun, dead in his bathtub. That was something I would never forget, and I wished I could.

I expected a text from Yasahiro at any moment or maybe even a call, so I set my phone to normal mode, since usually I liked to keep it on silent. I slipped the phone into my bag and stared out the window at Muarata's apartment building. It'd be good to see her since she asked me not to come the day before, and I could've used a little normality in my life. Daylight was beginning to wane and the lights were on in her apartment, giving the window a warm glow. I glanced over at Etsuko's old apartment and remembered my conversation with Murata two days ago.

"Goro?" I asked, interrupting him texting on his phone. "Remember that Takahara owns this building? Etsuko said so in her confession letter and Mrs. Murata mentioned it to me."

"Oh right. I do remember that. Didn't she say in her letter that he lived in the apartment below her for some time?" He leaned across to my side of the car and stared out at her building, aiming his eyes at the window under Etsuko's.

"She did." I looked at each of the cars parked on the block, and down the road, a black BMW sat unoccupied. "I think that might be his car right there."

"Could we be this lucky?" He turned his car's computer to face him and started punching in numbers.

"I've never seen you use your computer."

"What do you think I do while I'm waiting for you in the car?" He smirked at me, and I rolled my eyes. It wasn't like I was some high maintenance girl, crushing his dreams of being on time for everything.

"It's his car all right." He swiped on his phone and dialed a number, pressing his phone to his ear and waiting. "Kayo, it's me. I'm at Etsuko's apartment building, dropping Mei off to see Mrs. Murata. Takahara's car is up the block from us, and I think he's here. Send another car around in case we run into him." He waited for a moment chewing on his lower lip and staring at his own fingers drumming on the steering wheel. "How long?... Okay. Call me back."

He hung up his phone and slipped it into his pocket. "Kayo is coming with another officer. They'll be here in five, ten minutes, tops."

"Want to come inside and hang out with me and Mrs. Murata? She likes you," I said, poking him in the chest. "And I'm sure she'd love to talk to you. We can kill time while we wait."

"Sure, why not? I should speak to her again, in case she remembered something else."

We walked inside together, hunched over against the cold.

"She knows everything about everyone. Well, maybe not everything. If only she knew who killed Etsuko, we would've been done with this case weeks ago."

"We can't just expect murderers to be given to us on a silver platter, Mei. You have to work for them." He shook his head in mock displeasure. "You have much to learn."

We were careful to walk through the building quietly in case Takahara was home, but I didn't hear anything from the apartment below Etsuko's as we climbed past it. Maybe he wasn't actually here, just his car. Murata welcomed us into her apartment with a cheerful smile. She immediately tried to serve tea to Goro, but I urged her to sit down and relax since I was there to help out. I poured hot water for us all and served tea in her living area.

"I hope you're feeling better today," I said, sipping on the hot tea. "I was worried about you yesterday."

"I'm fine, Mei. I just needed some rest, and Akiko came by again to check on me. She adjusted some of my medication, and I feel better already. Shall we go out for a walk in a little bit? How is it outside?"

"It's bitter outside," Goro said, getting into the conversation. "I'd watch out for patches of ice."

"We can take a short walk to the café and back," I suggested, hoping this would be enough exercise for her. Murata nodded in response.

We talked of the weather until Goro's phone rang, and he excused himself to take the call in the kitchen. I could hear him mumbling, but I couldn't make out any specific words.

"Mrs. Murata, Mei was telling me that Fujita Takahara owns this building." Goro hung up his phone and slipped it in his pocket. "Have you ever noticed him here, acting suspicious?"

"Suspicious? He's always suspicious." She sipped her tea. "I've never liked him, and I found it irksome that he was always around when he didn't need to be. I heard he was going to renovate the apartment below Etsuko's, but I never saw workers come in and out of there. Instead, it was like he moved in. He bought a couch and a bed at the very least."

I imagined Murata at the front window of her apartment, watching Takahara's every move, cataloging his deliveries, and going so far as to complain to him about the state of the building and his involvement with its upkeep. He'd probably not sunk a yen into this place and was only using it to live in or launder money through.

Goro made strict eye contact with me, and I immediately knew what he was thinking. We needed to figure out some way to confront Takahara, either by camping out in front of the building or right at his door. Perhaps I was wrong and he *was* in there, sleeping or something. I was determined to catch him, and after the morning we'd had, both Goro and I were angry enough to do something about it.

"I'm going to borrow Mei for a few minutes. I hope you don't mind." Without waiting for an answer, Goro grabbed my arm and hauled me up next to him. "We'll be right back."

We left a stunned Murata in her apartment, and I crept down the stairs behind Goro, trying not to make any noise at all. Outside the apartment under Etsuko's, we paused and listened. I strained my ears, and after listening to my own heart beat like crazy, I heard signs of life inside, a box scraping across the floor and paper shuffling. He was in there!

I came up with a plan, my brain speeding forward through time. "This is what we do," I whispered to Goro. "He'll panic if he sees you, so let me talk to him. I'll pretend I'm interested in renting the apartment. I'll flirt with him and get him talking. Maybe he'll slip up and say something? Anyway, I'll keep him occupied long enough for Kayo to arrive and then you can arrest him and continue on with the investigation."

"This is a dangerous idea," he whispered, shaking his head.

"It's the least I can do." Kumi's tear-stained face popped into my head, begging me to help in any way I could. I had promised I'd do what I could. I could do this. "It'll be fine. You do your job, and I'll do mine."

"Your job?" He raised his eyebrows at me.

"Shut up." I smiled back, took a deep breath, and knocked on the door, as Goro hid on the other side of the stairwell.

CHAPTER
TWENTY-NINE

"Mei?" Takahara's face changed from a frown to a smile as he opened the door to me. I had forgotten what a sickly handsome guy he was. All those photos I had seen of him at red carpet events didn't even compare to how hot he was in jeans and a t-shirt. No wonder women got entrapped in his schemes. "What are you doing here?" He looked side to side, and not seeing anyone else, he opened the door wider.

"Hello, Mr. Takahara," I said, bowing. "I work for Mrs. Murata on the next floor up, and she mentioned that this apartment may be for rent soon? I was hoping to take a look. I didn't realize you were here, but I thought I'd knock anyway since the light is on." I smiled at him, trying my best to appear calm and inquisitive, not nervous and scared as I really was. I glanced past him into the apartment. "Can I come in? I heard you own this building, is that right?"

"Yeah, sure." He moved to the side, and I gained entrance to the place, mentally pumping my fist into the air. I was in! He had taken the bait. I kicked off my shoes next to the door. "Yeah, I do own the building, for the last two years. How have you been? I haven't seen you since Etsuko's funeral."

"I'm fine. Things are a little cramped at home, and I thought I'd see what's on the market for apartments." That was a huge lie. I couldn't think of anyone who would voluntarily give up free room and board at home, but hopefully he wouldn't question the statement. I needed to make it look like I wanted to see the apartment, not him.

I tried to act casual, poking my head into the kitchen and sizing the place up like I would if I was interested in renting. I took note of the empty shelves and bare counters indicative of a vacant apartment. He was living a sparse existence, though I was sure if I had opened the fridge, I would have found beer and condiments at the very least.

"It's got a good size kitchen. Was this renovated recently?"

Takahara stood dumbfounded amongst the boxes in the living area. "Um, no. I planned on renovating the place but hadn't gotten around to it. Did you say you're working for Mrs. Murata? Upstairs?"

I walked past him to the front window, pushing aside the cheap, vertical blinds and looking out at the street. Parked half a block away, Kayo and another officer sat in a police car. I let the blinds go and turned to him.

"It has a nice view. This is a great street." Those were the only adjectives I could come up with, "nice," "good," "great." I always talked like this when I was nervous. I set my purse on a stack of cardboard boxes with labels indicating bento boxes were inside. "Yeah, I work for Mrs. Murata. She's one of the many clients I have. I started a business a couple of weeks ago helping elderly citizens in town." I began to sweat as I realized he was between me and the door, and the door was locked. "I needed to make some extra money since the barn burned down. My friend, Akiko Kano, helped me find my clients. You remember her, right?"

I was sure he did. He tried to buy her land right out from under her when her dad died, and Akiko admitted once that he asked her out. I pushed down the rage in my chest and quieted the impulse to leap across the space between us and choke him with my bare hands. I wasn't usually a murderous person, but if anyone screwed with the people I loved, they were dead to me. I wasn't done with him yet.

Takahara folded his arms across his chest and appraised me from head to toe. I didn't like the hungry look in his eyes, like I was his next meal. "I didn't realize you had such an entrepreneurial spirit, Mei. Starting your own business is hard work."

He edged towards me, slowly at first and then stopping within my personal space bubble. I suppressed the desire to push him away, but I couldn't help the blush of fury that rose to my cheeks. He smiled, probably mistaking the blush for desire instead of anger.

"This is a fortuitous meeting. I honestly hadn't thought we'd run into each other again anytime soon. Have you given any thought to my proposal? The one we talked about at Etsuko's funeral?"

I swallowed in a dry throat and averted my eyes to the floor, trying to seem shy and flattered even though I was anything but. I took a small step backward, away from him.

"I've thought about it, yes. Yasahiro and I have gone out on a few dates, but we're not serious." I waved my hand and hoped this conversation was not overheard by anyone but Goro. I suspected he'd pressed his ear to the door or wall outside and was waiting for me to give him a sign. What sign? We hadn't discussed this ahead of time. I may have been screwed. "You mentioned we'd make great partners? How so?"

I tore my eyes from the floor and glanced around the living space again. This time I noticed the cardboard boxes were not just filled with bento boxes, but there were other boxes labeled "shirts," "bags," and one labeled "gerbil food." My God, how many people did he have laundering money for him? And was this where he kept the extra goods?

"Well, you see, I like to invest in small companies and help people grow them so the owners can make a living. Helping others is one of my favorite pastimes."

In any other situation, this would've sounded truthful and impressive. No wonder he'd managed to get away with laundering money for so long.

I licked my lips and cautioned myself. *Mei, if you're not careful, you're going to give everything away.* I wanted to confront him about his shady business practices, but I couldn't just yet.

"Can I take a look at the bathroom and the bedroom?" I tried to point in the direction of both, but my hand shook so I stuffed my fingers into the pocket of my jeans.

"Sure," he said, his voice husky. Oh no. He was possibly thinking of seducing me, but I couldn't back away now. I needed to stall and keep him talking. I went with my original plan.

I walked past him on unsteady legs and flipped on the light in the bathroom. "What kind of businesses have you invested in? Anything I would know about?"

"Actually, I was invested in Etsuko's business before she passed away. That's how we knew each other. Did you know she had a bento box company? She sold bento boxes online and from a store front. If your current business model doesn't work out, I could show you how to do what she did instead."

I had my back turned to him, examining the tub and medicine cabinet, so I wasn't ready for his fingers to brush along the back of my neck. If I had seen them coming, I would've been prepared. Instead, my instincts kicked in, and I shrank away from his touch. His smile dissolved to a frown, and I pushed past him to continue my tour, but his hand came down on my upper arm in a vice-like grip.

Warning sirens blared in my head. We had gone from friendly and chatty to possessive and prone to assault in less than a minute.

"Don't run away from me, Mei. I can show you the bedroom, if you like."

"Uh, no. That's okay." My voice warbled, and I jerked my arm, but he held on tight. My heart beat like a *taiko* drum in my ears.

This was about to barrel into dangerous territory. If I didn't signal the alarm soon, Takahara would overwhelm me, and he'd rape or kill me while Goro sat out in the hallway. I couldn't let that happen. My mom depended on me. My new clients needed me. And I had too much life to let this guy take it, like he took Etsuko's.

"Tell me, *Fujita*—" I stressed his first name since he dropped the honorific with mine. "How upset were you when Etsuko died? If she was such a good friend, and you were invested in her business, I should have heard more about you through her. She never said a thing to me."

He squeezed my arm even harder, and I winced in pain. "What do you care?"

"I cared about Etsuko." I steeled my voice and hardened my body. "So, where were you the night she died?" His eyes widened. "She was murdered in her own home, right above us. If you had been here, *you would have known.*"

He shoved me at the bedroom, and my feet skidded across the hardwood floors, almost landing me on my butt. "I was away on a business trip to Hong Kong," he growled, his jaw set.

My face dropped, and I groaned. Really? If he had been gone, then the only other person who could have killed her was Hisashi. I didn't believe it. He loved her!

What if everything I believed about love was false? Hisashi had loved her and killed her. I was close to tears, my thoughts reeling from Hisashi to Takahara closing in on me to Yasahiro. What had happened with Yasahiro and Amanda? What if he had loved her, and he cheated on her? He'd never said he loved me. Who did I trust?

Could I trust anybody? My brain shut down, and my mouth dried out. Nothing made sense!

An evil grin crossed Takahara's face, and I sensed I was in a lot of trouble. I was debating love and betrayal in my head while a hungry and obviously desperate man had me cornered in a bedroom. I glanced around the room, hoping to find a weapon of some sort — anything would do, a lamp or even a heavy book. But my gaze skipped over the bare room and landed on the nightstand.

Etsuko's phone! Her phone that had been missing since she was killed! It was sitting *right there*, and there was no mistaking it was hers with the bright pink owl case and charm dangling from the side. My breathing deepened, and my ears rushed with heat. He had lied. Of course, he'd lied!

Takahara followed my line of sight, and his face contorted in anger before he lunged across the bed at me. I opened my mouth and screamed, the kind of scream I'd only ever heard come of out me in the burning barn. I was sure people could hear it for kilometers.

Dodging to the side, I slammed into the doors of the closet, knocking one of its tracks enough for the door to come tumbling down on me. Takahara crashed against the wall, groaning before jumping up and scrambling after me. I made it to the hallway before his hand clasped onto the waistband of my jeans, pulling my feet out from under me. My butt hit the hardwood floor with a thump, and a shock of pain radiated up my tailbone. The door to the apartment exploded open with a deafening crack, slamming into the wall with bits of wood flying in every direction.

"Halt!" Goro ran in and vaulted over the cardboard boxes in his way. Takahara let me go, pushing me over, and sprinting into the bedroom. I turned my head in time to watch him slide open the window and crawl out, jumping to the ground.

"Kayo!" Goro bellowed, so loud I had to cover my ears with my hands. I struggled to my feet and followed him to the window. We both leaned out and looked down. Takahara was writhing on the snow covered ground, clutching his leg while Kayo and another police officer stood over him. Two other officers ran up the block, one shouting into a phone for backup and an ambulance.

I breathed a huge sigh of relief and threw my arms around Goro, laughing and thanking him over and over.

"Mei, are you okay?" he asked, looking into my red, tear-stained face. "Did he hurt you?" He patted me down, checking to make sure I was uninjured.

"I'll be okay." I sniffed up and pointed to the bedside table. "Look. It's Etsuko's phone. I saw it here and that's when Takahara tried to attack me."

I sat down on the bed, my legs shaking so badly I couldn't stand. Goro took two large steps to the table, as sirens blared in the distance. He pulled a glove from his pocket, put it on, and picked up the phone. "It's still locked," he said, sighing. "Maybe he was trying the PIN number over and over. We're lucky he hadn't figured out how to wipe the memory yet."

Kayo came running into the apartment.

"Is everyone okay?" She glanced at us both and nodded her head as we nodded ours. "Takahara broke his leg in the fall. Not very bright to jump from a second-story window."

"He doubtless thought he was invincible," Goro muttered. "Do you have an evidence bag?" Kayo produced one from her pocket, and Goro dropped the phone in. "This is Etsuko's missing phone. We'll have to inventory everything in here, and then the prosecutor can handle contacting the owners of all that stuff." He waved to the boxes out in the living space.

"What happened?" Kayo asked, and I leaned forward to put my face in my hands, trying to compose myself.

"Mei cornered and confronted him, he tried to attack her, and I broke in just in time." Goro sat next to me on the bed. "This one is made of bravery." He patted my knee before putting his arm around my shoulder. "Good job, Mei. We got him."

I guessed I was a lot braver than I gave myself credit for.

CHAPTER
THIRTY

I t was Christmas Day, and the bitter cold weather of December had finally edged away, some snow had melted, and water was flowing at the farmhouse. Mom was at home a few days per week, but I was not. I'd decided I wasn't going home until the house could warm itself. Instead, I was wrapped in a blanket with Yasahiro on his couch. This was our favorite place to be, beside the bed. I loved to sit between his legs, press my back against his chest, and talk for hours. Today, though, we were waiting for Hisashi to drop by. After Takahara had been arrested, he confessed his crimes and now sat in jail where he should be. I wasn't usually a vengeful person, but I hoped he would stay there for the rest of his life.

"After Hisashi stops by for a visit, I want to talk about your Christmas present," Yasahiro said, leaning forward and kissing me on my neck. Warmth spread across my chest until I realized what he'd said.

"Christmas present? I didn't realize we were going to exchange Christmas presents." My stomach sank in despair. I was still barely scraping by, making only a couple hundred yen per week, and eating Yasahiro's food. I didn't expect to be financially solvent until summer when Mom and I were harvesting vegetables consistently every week. Until then, I was broke.

"Were not exchanging Christmas presents. I'm *giving you* a Christmas present. There's a difference." He squeezed me in his arms, and I couldn't turn around to discern how serious he was. Maybe the gift was something small, something he had purchased in Paris, and I didn't have to worry about feeling indebted to him? He took a deep breath and squeezed me again, sighing out a long exhale as I rested my head on his chest. "I missed you while I was gone, and this last week has been so hectic between the restaurant, your clients, and your statements to the police. I was thinking we'd take off three days next week and head out to an onsen for the weekend. How about it? We'll go for the new year and ring it in together."

"I'd love to! Oh, I haven't had a vacation or time off in almost two years." I stared wistfully out the window and dreamed of soaking in the hot water, laughing while eating good food and drinking saké, sleeping together in a bed that wasn't our own. A romantic getaway! "Unfortunately, I don't count being unemployed as a vacation."

He laughed, and I savored the sound of his voice. "No. Sometimes being unemployed is harder work than being employed what with the constant resume sending, interviews, ..." He didn't need to go on. I hadn't been invited to any interviews from the hundreds of resumes I had sent. I had promised myself I would start over in January, and I was dreading starting up again. There was nothing worse than rejection on a daily basis.

The doorbell rang, and our snuggling time was over. Yasahiro jumped up from his couch and ran to the door to buzz Hisashi in. I stood up, folded our blanket, and put it away in the basket at the end of the couch. Hisashi entered on a gust of cold air, and I was surprised by how changed he was. I hadn't seen him since Etsuko's death. He had been in police custody, and once Takahara had been arrested, Hisashi was released and returned home to Chiba.

His face was thin, and his clothes hung off of him. His skin, mottled with a tint of unhealthy gray, was papery and dry, and he just seemed sad. Even his hair seemed sad, all shaggy and unkempt. It was as if the life had been sucked out of him by Etsuko's death and his false imprisonment.

"Hey," he said softly, clearing his throat like he hadn't talked in a year. He waved to me, and I bowed while he clasped hands with Yasahiro.

"Thanks for coming by," Yasahiro said, directing him to the dining table. "This wasn't something we could do over the phone."

"That's okay. But I feel strange about coming back here, and I doubt I'll ever come here again. I quit my job on Monday." He sank into a chair at the table. "And I think I'm going to move south, to Nagoya. I don't know. I'm packed and ready to go, but for some reason, I just can't move on."

"I understand, more than you know." Yasahiro's voice was solemn and sympathetic, and once again, I wondered what happened between him and Amanda. He had a past I was unaware of, and it had made him a complex and wonderful person. I really wondered...

"Can I get you some coffee?" I turned to the kitchen, but Yasahiro caught my arm. He was gentle with me lately, knowing the painful bruises on my arm and shoulder from my fight with Takahara were still tender.

"Let me serve coffee. You go get the box."

Hisashi's eyebrows drew together, but I headed into the bedroom without explanation. Getting on my hands and knees, I reached under the bed and drew out Etsuko's cashbox. Goro told me only one person brought up the fact that Etsuko had no cash on hand in her office, and he was immediately silenced by the chief. They'd theorized she took the money and stashed it someplace because she was sure she was in danger. They considered the money a loss and moved on to other parts of the investigation.

I held the box between my hands and set it on the table in front of Hisashi.

"I have something for you," I said, sitting down across from him. "When Goro and I were searching Etsuko's office, we found this cashbox. After looking at a few invoices, we were sure this was her legitimate money. This was money she made from selling bento boxes, and I felt it was wrong to be seized by the police. It was my idea to take the money and hold it in trust for you."

He stared at the gray, metal box, so I reached out and pushed it to him. He hesitantly fiddled with the front clasp before opening the box.

"I counted it twice, and that's 313,400 yen. Enough for you to get a head start someplace else. You can use it for a deposit on a new apartment or something."

"No," he said, pushing the box to me. "I can't take this money."

"Of course you can." I pushed the box back to him. "She worked hard to earn this money. She wanted to start a family with you someday." His eyes began to water, but I kept going. "She would've wanted you to have this money. It was important to her."

Yasahiro sat next to me, setting a coffee cup down in front of Hisashi. "You know how much she loved you," Yasahiro said softly.

"If she loved me so much, why did she get involved with Takahara? I've been asking myself this question over and over. Why did she do this when she could've just asked me for help? The bento box company was one thing. She loved it. But the money laundering?" He hissed, drawing air through his teeth and closing his eyes. He sounded like a wounded animal, his voice distorted by the intense emotions he had locked up inside.

"Try not to be too hard on her. From what I can tell, she got mixed up in this without realizing she was laundering money. She thought he was an investor. By the time she figured out his scheme, it was too late." I got up from the table and retrieved a box of tissues from the bathroom. He took one, dabbing at his eyes.

"Regardless, I can't take this money. It's over. Her life is over, and that part of my life with her is over. I want a clean slate now. I want to live someplace where I'm not constantly reminded of her — to move on." His voice quavered and cracked, his head dipping. "And I feel so guilty for saying that, for wanting that. But I can't take the money."

I placed my hand over my heart to stop the ache.

"Okay," I whispered. "I understand. Is there anything you want me to do with the money? I can donate it or gift it to someone in particular..."

He sucked in a deep breath to compose himself, taking a noisy sip of his coffee. "Are you still working with Mrs. Murata? The woman who lives across the hall from where Etsuko lived?"

"Yes." I perked up, hoping he'd tell me to give the money to her. "I see her four times a week."

"Goro was telling me about your business ideas, and he said you were thinking about opening a tea house in town, as a place for the elderly to meet up, like Mrs. Murata."

Yasahiro took my hand under the table and squeezed. He'd been listening to me talk about this idea for the last week, quietly absorbing my chatter, even though I always concluded I couldn't pull it off. I had a business degree and knew what was involved in starting a business but getting the money and investors were another story.

"I've been thinking about it. Well, I've been talking about it a lot." I laughed, trying to inject a little humor into the situation. "I don't know what I'm going to do, but I'm going to do something."

Hisashi closed the cashbox and pushed it to me. "Here. Etsuko loved spending time with Mrs. Murata. She always said

Murata reminded her of her grandmother. I think if she were here, she would have loved your idea and she would want to invest."

I opened my mouth to object, but he raised his hand and silenced me. "Trust me. This money should stay in Chikata. Etsuko never wanted to leave this town, and I had hoped to have raised our children here someday. It's the right thing to do."

He stood up giving me no chance to argue any further. "I need to get going. Thank you for having me over, especially on Christmas Day." He glanced down at the cashbox again but turned for the door.

I sat in stunned silence, unable to stand up and see him off.

While Yasahiro walked Hisashi down the stairs, I shook off the shock and went to the windows over the street. From here I could see Etsuko's family's izakaya down the block, the dry cleaner open and busy across the street, and the cobbler right next door. Not many people took off Christmas Day since it wasn't a national holiday here. The Emperor's birthday was only a few days ago, and many people had taken that day off instead. On the sidewalk, Yasahiro and Hisashi spoke to each other, shook hands, bowed, and Hisashi walked off in the direction away from the izakaya.

"It's warmer outside," Yasahiro said, returning to the apartment, "but it's still pretty cold out there." He glanced between me at the window and the cashbox sitting on the dining table. He walked over and placed his hand on it. "Mei, this is an unexpected gift. I had no idea he would do that."

"Me neither. I don't feel like I deserve it, though. That money should stay with her family."

"I knew you'd say that, but you put a lot of work and devotion into catching Etsuko's murderer. You helped put Takahara in jail. That's worth a lot all on its own." He joined me and squeezed my hand. "Put on your shoes and come downstairs with me."

I raised my eyebrows at him and he laughed.

"I'm not saying anything until you come with me." He raised his eyebrows back at me, and for some reason (probably hormones), I couldn't resist him.

I slipped on my shoes and followed him down the stairs. He hadn't told me to put on a coat, and he wasn't wearing one himself, so I wasn't surprised when he opened the door to the vacant retail space.

"Oh good!" I clutched at his sweater. "I've been dying to see inside of here. Mr. Hasé, from next door, said this place used to be owned by a brush maker, and he was bought out by a famous brush maker in the North. I had never been here as a kid."

He ushered me in and flipped on the lights. The space wasn't big, given the footprint of his apartment above. Glass cases lined the front window, and along the other three sides were many wooden shelves. A small cash register spot sat opposite the door.

"This was only the retail area. I was told that they kept hundreds of brushes in stock at all times, and people shopped for them in here." Yasahiro waved his hands in a circular motion. "But there's a workshop in back. Come." He pulled me to a sliding door that led to the back.

Now I understood how the space was divided up. The back half of the building was covered in old tatami mats and low tables. The woodworking tools were gone, but I imagined crafts-people sitting at these tables, making brushes. There was a bath-room off to the right, but a big window to the left let in natural light to a small kitchen.

"They probably worked here, made lunch for everyone at the little kitchen, and smoked cigarettes out in the back alley." Yasahiro laughed, shaking his head. "I bet this was a lively place with lots of inside jokes and friendly banter. I can even imagine people meeting and falling in love here."

I smiled, dragging my fingers through the dust on the long tables. He was a romantic, always thinking the best of a place or situation. When I daydreamed, I wasn't always so easy on myself. When Yasahiro daydreamed, he went to the moon and back.

"So, what do you think of the space?" he asked, sitting on a stool across the room from me.

"I think it's fantastic. I'm surprised you didn't make it into a restaurant. You should, you know? This is a prime location, right in the center of the business district, as small as that is. I know this isn't near the station, but I'm sure you could make something of it."

"Well, I'm glad I didn't because I have the perfect tenant in mind."

"Did someone contact you while you were in Paris?" He had seemed distracted while he was there but I'd assumed it was due to all the classes he taught. "I'm sure you'll make a lot of money off this place." I wondered what it would be like for him to live above a new business that wasn't his own. I hoped he liked the new renter otherwise this could have been a real problem. But that was just me thinking negatively...

"Making money is not my first priority in this instance. Creating someplace that's good for the community and good for you is my top priority." His eyes met mine across the room, and he was intense, staring straight into my soul, knowing more than what he was telling me. My mind swirled in a torrent of thoughts, trying to put together what he was saying and what he wasn't saying.

"What are you talking about?" But deep inside, I could feel the excitement growing. I thought... No, I believed...

"Merry Christmas, Mei. I want *you* to have the space. I want you to turn this into whatever you need it to be. Make it a home away from home for people who are lonely. Make it a place full of love." His jaw quivered, and I crossed the room in three long steps to get to him as quickly as possible. I stood so close to him, his emotions flooded over me. "Whatever you make of it, it was meant to be."

I slid my hands into both of his and looked around once more. This all could be mine. Oh god, this was all mine. How would I handle this big of a commitment? Could I handle it?

"Are you sure? I don't even think I can pay rent."

"No rent. And we'll work together to renovate it. I have some ideas, too. I've always wanted another place in town to sell bento boxes to the workers of this area."

I gasped and cover my mouth. "Yes! That's brilliant! An outpost of some sort? And bentos! It would be a tribute to Etsuko as well."

He smiled and pulled me in for a hug. "Perfect. We'll get started in the new year. Have I mentioned lately how happy I am to have met you? I'm so lucky."

We both turned away from each other to face the space and stare at it. Maybe now, my luck had finally turned to good.

"We're both lucky."

So many possibilities ahead for us, and we'd face them together.

THANK YOU!

Thank you so much for reading *The Daydreamer Detective Braves The Winter*. I hope you enjoyed the second book of this series! This is certainly not the end for Mei and her adventures, so please stay tuned!

If you want the next book in the series... *Ozoni and Onsens* is next! It's a little novella that takes place between *Braves The Winter* and *Opens A Tea Shop*.

Please leave a review of *The Daydreamer Detective Braves The Winter* wherever you purchased it. I welcome all reviews positive or negative. Reviews are so important to both authors and readers.

Want news of upcoming books, events, or free stuff? Subscribe to Steph's mailing list at https://www.stephgennaro.com/subscribe/

If you want more books like this one, you can check for

more books on my website at http://www.stephgennaro.com/books/

A NOTE ABOUT CHANGES TO THIS BOOK

In case you missed it in the Foreword...

In Japanese, the most common way of showing respect to another person's social standing is with the use of honorific suffixes that are appended on the end of either first or last names. The most common, -san, means either Mr., Ms., or Mrs.

In earlier versions of this book, and in the whole series, I did use these honorific suffixes. But for 2019 and onward, I have switched to the English way in order to make this series more accessible to English speakers. I hope you enjoy this version!

The town in this novel, Chikata, is completely fictional, though the area I put it in is not. Saitama prefecture is located to the west of Tokyo, and many of the eastern areas are considered to be suburbs of the city. Chikata is located farther out west, nearer to the prefectures of Nagano and Gunma.

ACKNOWLEDGMENTS

BIGGEST THANKS GOES to my critique partner, Tracy Krimmer. She continues to be my sounding board and best writing buddy. I heart her.

To Amy Evans. She gave me great ideas and helped me brainstorm even better ones for further books in this series. I can't wait to show you how Mei grows!

To Cori Wilbur. She reads everything I write. I'm so grateful for her!

Thank you to my entire ARC team! You all know who you are. They get the books before anyone else, read them, and then jump at the chance to review. Reviews are so important, and this team helps me get the lead on such a daunting task. I love them!

Big thanks to Lola Verroen of Lola's Blog Tours who helped me promote this book and get some new eyes on my work.

Again, thank you to Germaine Fletcher who continues to be a fan, good friend, excellent first reader, and eagle-eyed proofreader.

I continue to be grateful for my family especially my mother and father, Claire and Ray Bush, my sibling, B, and his family, my Pajonas side of the family, Vic and Karen, all of my husband's brothers and sisters. Thanks to my girls, C and D, again for letting mommy work in the afternoons and evenings after homework was done! My husband, Keith, still thinks I'm nuts but that's okay. I still love him.

Once again, thank you Japan for continuing to be an

inspiring place that makes me happy to have met your people, traveled your lands, and eaten your awesome food. You're the best.

ABOUT THE AUTHOR

Steph Gennaro is a long-time Japanophile, and she's been studying Japanese culture and language for over 20 years. She loves dreaming of far-off places, going for walks with her dog, Lulu Ninja Assassin, hanging out with her family, and reading outside in the summertime. There is no better season than summer. She's a Capricorn, mother, knitter, and web developer, and pasta is her favorite meal. Steph Gennaro is her pen name for cozy mysteries, but she also writes science fiction romance and many other genres.

Find her online at...
www.stephgennaro.com

f   facebook.com/StephGennaroAuthor
BB bookbub.com/authors/steph-gennaro

www.ingramcontent.com/pod-product-compliance
Lightning Source LLC
Chambersburg PA
CBHW020309200626
46814CB00006BA/2162